Safe Harbor

She broke his heart. He took his revenge. Then it all went wrong.

Auggie doesn't believe in happily ever after.

The one time he thought he might give love a chance, Haven squashed his hopes and chose another man.

Now she's on the run from a deadly murderer and needs the same protection from him that she rejected so easily before.

He'll have to put his ego aside to keep her safe, and no matter how strong the pull of attraction is between them, he'll have to deny it.

He'd be a fool to fall in love with the girl who causes him nothing but heartbreak.

—

Growing up in the projects, Haven never had a chance to soar.

Always running and hiding, she kept a low profile to blend in.

But Auggie challenges her to face the fears holding her back and embrace the world outside of her comfort zone. He could be the hero she's always waited for, if only she's brave enough to reach for him.

Safe Harbor is a standalone military romance and the third book in the Knight Security series.

Warning: This book is full of fast action and page-melting heat. Not appropriate for readers under eighteen.

You'll never know how strong your heart is until you learn to forgive the one who broke it.

Chapter 1 If Not For Sex

Auggie

"I won't be coming to visit you here anymore, Tatiana."

She sat on a barstool next to her kitchen and swirled her glass of wine. "Shall we meet somewhere else?"

We usually met here at her apartment in Atlanta. A neutral location that didn't reveal any information about me.

"Not for sex."

Her eyes slowly lifted and caught my gaze. "Why would we meet if not for sex?" She was trying to play it casual, but she had to be surprised at my change in tone. I'd been pursuing her heavily up until I left for Italy a few weeks ago. She was my main contact with the Bratva. The brigadier's daughter had access to the top leadership in the organization, and she'd come through for me with flying colors.

"I'd like to remain friends."

She took a large sip of wine and swallowed it loudly. "We were never friends, Dimitri."

I hated being Dimitri, the identity I'd created as my cover for this op. But nothing about infiltrating the Bratva and assassinating their leader was easy or enjoyable.

"I know you're pretending not to care. We had what we had while it lasted, but it's time for it to end." It was actually too soon to end it with her. It would be much smarter to keep her for an alibi, but I couldn't uphold the charade a second longer.

"What happened? Did you meet someone in Italy?"

"No." I thought of Haven and her sweet blue eyes. I did meet someone in Italy, and I hated to admit it, but she'd worked her way under my skin, and now I had to end it with Tatiana even if it wasn't the most strategic move on my part. "Yes. I met someone in Italy." I surprised myself with my answer. I didn't know where it came from, but it felt like I was telling her the truth despite the fact I'd been lying to her from the beginning.

"She must be very special if you're willing to jeopardize your position with Konstantin."

"Why do you say that? Why would this affect anything with Konstantin?"

"Don't be daft. I know you were using me to get to him. It was obvious."

For a second I felt like she'd seen through my entire cover. She knew I wanted to kill Konstantin and was using her to get close to him. But how could she know that? I'd been careful and hadn't slipped up once. As far as she was concerned, I was Dimitri, a wannabe Bratva soldier. "How so?"

"I know you wanted access to his inner circle. You have that now. You can stop pretending you're interested in me." She had a slight Russian accent despite being born in America. It had always bothered me, and tonight it just made her seem like a huge phony. Playing her role in a deadly crime syndicate. I couldn't trust her at all before. Now that I'd broken her heart, she'd become my enemy.

"I was not pretending." I was absolutely pretending at first, but Tatiana wasn't a bad person. She'd been born into the Bratva, and her family had forced her to stay. My heart wasn't fully dormant. I'd grown to care for her in a conspiratorial way. I'd chosen her as my mark because she was attractive, friendly, and approachable. It wasn't a burden to sleep with her these past few months. The sex was reciprocal and uncomplicated. She'd embraced her submissive nature as easily as I had my dominance. We didn't have to adjust for each other, and she didn't require a lot of talking or aftercare.

"Why do you say such things? I would genuinely like to remain friends."

"Only because it would benefit you in Konstantin's eyes."

"Not true. Konstantin doesn't give a shit about matters of the heart. He cares only about money and power. That's it. If we stop fucking, nothing will change."

"Perhaps." I ignored the veiled threat in her tone. I doubted she could wield the kind of power she was implying. Yes, I'd used her to reach his inner circle, but I could also maintain it without her as an ally. I was betting my life on it.

"I have to go now." I turned my back on her and headed to the door.

"Who is she? This woman?"

I stopped and looked back at her. The pain was beginning to show in the wrinkles around her eyes, the upturn of her chin, and the corners of her mouth twisting down. "It doesn't matter to you."

"I'm curious what kind of woman could break through your frozen heart. Clearly I didn't have what it takes."

"Tachi, please don't blame yourself. " I used my nickname for her for two reasons. One, I was trying to salvage any remnants of goodwill she might carry for me, and secondly, I felt a pang of guilt for using her like I had. "I've simply met someone else. That's all."

"Someone that you like better?"

"Not better. Just different." Much different.

The girl I had in mind had essentially rejected me twice whereas Tatiana had always been open and eager for any scraps of attention Dimitri could muster. It was how most women reacted to me.

Not this one. After I'd rescued her from human traffickers in Rome, Haven had dropped me like old news and called some cretin named Cyrus to pick her up.

The guy was a tool. Looked like a gangster and treated Haven like an errant child. The next time I saw her, she was at a party with a bunch of bikers who were looking for trouble. We gave her a chance to leave him then, and she chose to stay in his clutches.

The woman was crazy. That was all I could deduce. She'd chosen a biker and a gangster over me, a man who could protect her and offer her everything. She'd turned up her nose and walked away. *Twice.*

I turned my attention back to Tatiana. "I said I'd like us to remain friends, if possible. Let's be civil about this. I'm sorry if you're hurt."

"I'm not hurt. I have three other men who meet my physical needs."

She had to be lying. I'd kept her quite satisfied, and she'd never mentioned needing or wanting more than what I'd given her.

Fine. I didn't care what she used as a self-defense mechanism to save face through this breakup. Either way, it ended now. I would no longer be using Tatiana to get to Konstantin. She'd given me enough access to reach him and plan the shot that would kill him. I didn't need her anymore. Konstantin would be dead by tomorrow, and his reign of terror would die with him.

She rose from her chair and stalked toward me. The desperation in her eyes filled me with pity for her but not love. Not that I knew much about love, but I was certain we didn't have it. I stopped her forward progress with a stern glare. "You'll find someone who's right for you. I'm sorry it's not me. Please don't let this break you. You're too good for that."

"This will not break me. I grew up in the Bratva. I'm stronger than I look." She pulled her shoulders back and did a poor job of masking the hurt in her eyes. "Goodbye, Dimitri. I wish you the best."

"Same to you. It will all work out somehow."

She nodded and turned her gaze toward her feet. I sensed she was close to tears. I knew I should probably comfort her, but I was the one causing her pain. I couldn't help her with this. She had girlfriends she was close with. They'd have to help her now. I turned and left Tatiana's apartment for the last time.

***

I sat in my Land Cruiser in her driveway and looked back at Tatiana's door. What was it about Haven that had me sabotaging a plan I'd set in motion years ago? Konstantin and his crew were vile criminals. They trafficked drugs and murdered people. His family was behind the death of my own.

They took everything from me. Now I took from them. It was what motivated me to get up every day, to keep going, to keep fighting through the dark life of the underworld.

What would I do after I killed Konstantin?

The zeal for revenge had faded and had been replaced by a new obsession. Find Haven and make her pay for what she'd done. It was petty and childish, but the other option could get me killed. Continuing my vendetta against the Bratva was a death sentence.

Messing with Haven was the much less dangerous option. Not my normal path either, but it could provide an interesting diversion while I laid low after the hit.

Where was she living now? The biker I'd last seen Haven with was named Duke. Shouldn't be too hard to locate him and find out if Haven was playing him like she'd played me.

Haven looked sweet and innocent with her honey blonde hair and ice blue eyes, but she had a ruthless side under there. She'd turn the knife in your back and do it with a smile on her luscious pink lips. I was a fool for tracking her down, and yet I couldn't stop myself if I wanted to. I had to see her again.

Chapter 2 Red Cups

Haven

The abandoned plastic cups on the pool table formed the shape of a figure eight. The party goers had long left, but the infinity symbol made of red plastic was a reminder that they'd be back eventually. There was always another party at the Devil's Advocates Motorcycle Club in Central Atlanta, and I was always there to clean it up.

I checked the room first before I pulled my camera from the pocket of my hoodie. Duke and some girl were passed out on the couch, but otherwise, I was alone. I kneeled and took pictures of the cups from the side. In the tiny preview window, they rose like monoliths from the table. The shots from this cheap camera always came out grainy and blurry, but at least I'd created some memory of the moment. Enough to inspire me.

Later, I'd make up a tale about the characters who drank from the cups and left them. Most people probably thought a party in a poor neighborhood like this was ugly and unappealing, but they were missing out. The projects had some of the most colorful people and places anywhere in Atlanta. Duke, for example, had red, blue, and green tattoos up his arm that were actually works of art. He didn't know it, but I'd created an intricate plot about him and how he chose his tattoos. The character I'd based on him was an unlikely hero. He looked like a loser on the outside, but inside, he was secretly saving people who desperately needed it.

"Bring me a beer, babe."

Or maybe he was just a loser. "We're outta beer, Duke."

He had woken up and caught me loitering around the pool table instead of cleaning it like I should've been doing. I quickly slipped the camera in the front pocket of my sweatpants hoping he didn't see it. I couldn't afford to lose the only camera I had.

"Check the keg outside."

"Keg's all foam."

"Then get me a fucking whiskey," he snapped as he pressed his palm to his head.

"How about an aspirin and some water?" I asked timidly.

He scrunched his eyes but didn't open them. "Woman, get me some fucking alcohol in the next thirty seconds, or I'll throw your ass out on the street."

Oh shoot. No. I didn't want that. I hustled over to the bar and found a bottle of tequila that wasn't completely empty. I poured him a shot and hurried to bring it to where he lay on the couch.

He squinted at me with one eye like the sun was shining directly on him even though all the windows were boarded up with black wood. He downed the shot and made a growly breathy sound as it went down. "That wasn't fucking whiskey."

"All I could find."

He handed me the empty shot glass, completely oblivious to the girl who was passed out face-down between his spread legs. "What were you doing over there?"

"Over where?"

"Right there at the pool table. Were you zonin' out again?"

"No," I lied quietly.

"Why were you on your knees?" He grinned like he en-joyed catching me in a lie and forcing me to lie again.

"I was just picking up some smoke butts from the floor."

He glared at me through squinted eyes before his grin widened to expose the crooked yellow teeth below. "If you like being on your knees, you can suck my cock anytime." He plopped his head back down on the couch and closed his eyes again, but his lips were still turned up in a smile. I'd bet the girl between his legs would be happy to (and probably did) suck his dick last night.

I scanned over her dirty tank top, dingy bra strap, and torn denim mini with her bare ass hanging out the bottom. It could be worse for me. I could be her. I had things bad, but at least I didn't have to sleep with Duke. He'd said none of the guys here would force me to have sex with them or give blow jobs. It was all consensual, and I'd told him as part of our deal that I wouldn't want to do that with any of the brothers. I'd just clean the place and in return, they gave me a room to crash.

I smiled at Duke. "Want another shot?"

"Sure." He rested his arm on his forehead and the girl be-tween his legs stirred and turned sideways.

As I walked back to the bar, I heard his voice in my head.

Bring me a beer.

Exactly the words he'd used at that humiliating party.

The party where Auggie saw me and I saw him for the first time since I'd split on him.

I wanted to crawl under the floorboards and die.

A couple of the bikers got rowdy at the food table and it escalated fast. Auggie escorted Duke and his brothers out of there, and it didn't turn into a rumble.

God, he looked so hot and in control.

So put together and brave.

Auggie was the most gorgeous man I'd ever met.

Way, way out of my league. I had no right to even be looking at him, but it was hard to look away.

Tall, toned muscles, short light-brown hair, shorn on the sides but longer on top, dark stubble covering the steep draw of his jaw. The man looked like he could be James Bond or Jason Bourne or whatever badass superhero he wanted to be.

Thor. Auggie would make a great Thor.

One of the many things I regretted from my short time with Auggie was that I didn't get any pictures of him. Just one shot could've kept my mind busy for hours imagining his secret life.

I forced myself to stop thinking about him and poured Duke another tequila shot.

When I got back to the couch, he was passed out again. "Duke?"

He didn't answer, so I left it on the table.

It took me two hours to clean the clubhouse after last night's get together. Used condoms, cigarette burns in the carpet, wine stains on the walls, barf next to the toilet. I didn't take pictures of any of that reality. No one wanted to see it or write about it.

I pushed my hair back from my head and dropped my paper towels into the supply box behind the bar before plopping down in one of the barstools to catch my breath.

Sweat dripped between my breasts, and my face felt oily. Even a long hot shower would not rinse this filth off me. Cleaning this place sucked, but I had to keep reminding myself why I was doing this.

Train would never come here.

I was safe. I could take a breather and let my frazzled nerves relax for a second. I rested my head on my arms on the bar for a short break before I would have to head outside and see what mess had been left out there.

Thoughts of Auggie returned to my mind. I was about to fall into a dream full of moss-green eyes and action heroes when the front door to the clubhouse creaked open and a swath of light passed through my lids. I was too exhausted to look up. Probably just another biker ready to start tonight's party early. More mess for me to clean up.

"Wake up, Duke. We got an appointment," a gruff voice said.

Uh oh. Duke did not like being talked to like that by anyone.

I expected to hear Duke's cussed reply, but instead I heard him cough and a rustle on the couch.

I looked up, and a big guy was standing with his back to me. Worn jeans that hung off his hips at the top of very long legs that stretched out from under a leather jacket. I couldn't see anything else from this angle, but the man had caught my attention. Definitely not one of the brothers, and non-brothers weren't allowed inside the clubhouse.

A stranger. A threat. Was he one of Train's guys here for me?

Was he a cop? My warning radar was sounding off the charts. I slipped from my stool and scrambled to hide behind the bar.

"Get gone, bitch," Duke said to the girl in his lap.

The girl tugged down her skirt and stumbled off Duke's body.

"You're on time," Duke said to his mystery visitor.

"You expected me to be late?"

"Of course."

"Well, I'm not." The deep, powerful voice sent a trickle of ice down my spine.

"Have a seat. You want a drink? Got tequila. Outta beer."

"None for me."

Phew. I was off the hook. My eyes were on the hallway, and I planned to run to my room before the guy saw me. I didn't know who he was, but I didn't want to be seen by anyone.

"You want some pussy? Crystal, get back here." That was her name. Crystal. I'd met her briefly and forgotten.

"Nah. I'll take her." I couldn't see who he was referring to, but I was the only girl in the room. I didn't think he'd seen me, but apparently he did.

"She don't put out," Duke replied. "She's just a house mouse."

Oh, boy. He was referring to me. A house mouse was a girl who cleaned in exchange for protection.

"She your ol' lady?"

"What? No. I ain't got no ol' lady. Are you fuckin' whack? Too much bunny for my dick to tie my balls to a chain like that." Duke always had such a lovely way with words.

"She anyone's?"

Why was this guy asking so many questions about me?

"No, man. You wanna talk about the bitch who cleans the place, or you wanna make a deal?" Duke thought his questions seemed excessively nosy too. This man was totally suspicious and scary.

"I wanna make a deal, but we got bunny ears over there."

"Haven. Get the fuck out."

Sure. I climbed up and started to leave. I couldn't wait to get away.

"On second thought. I'll have tequila," the stranger said.

My heart dropped to my feet.

"Tequila!" Duke shouted at me. Shoot. No. Shit. I didn't want to go near this unknown man who was here to make deals and wanted me because he thought I was pussy that puts out.

I poured two more shots with shaking hands. The bottle was almost empty. I walked slowly and carefully with my eyes on the glasses. I didn't want to spill the last bit of alcohol in the house.

When I got close, I saw his profile. Strong nose, deep set moss-green eyes.

Holy shit.

No.

It was Auggie.

His hair was longer, beard thicker, but it was definitely him.

I dropped both glasses, and the tequila splashed onto the floor.

The men stared at me in shock.

"What the fuck?" Duke asked.

"I'm sorry. I just uh, tripped. We're uh, out of booze. I'll run to the store and get more."

"No, you won't," Duke said. "I'll send a prospect to get it."

But I was already at the door with my purse in my hand. It had no money in it, but I needed an excuse to bolt.

"I'll get lots of booze for you," I called as I rushed out the door.

The sunlight blinded me, and I wobbled on the gravel. I didn't have a car, so I hoofed it out of the compound, around the corner, and down the sidewalk.

Holy crap.

Auggie showed up at the compound. He looked different.

His hair was more shaggy on the sides and much taller and longer on the top, still swept straight back but with added thickness and shine. He had light stubble before, but now he was sporting a full dark goatee with scraggly bits around the edges. He looked a lot rougher and much more angry.

What did he want? Why was he there?

It would forever remain a mystery to me because I was never going back to the compound. I didn't know where I was running, just that I had to get the heck away from Auggie.

Chapter 3 Burst Mode

Five hours later, I crept into the clubhouse through the back entrance. Bile rose in my throat when I heard the sound of a party out in the common area. I slammed my bedroom door behind me and locked it, trying to block out the noise and the thoughts.

Even if Auggie was here, I had to come back. The truth was that I had no place else to go.

I'd thought about going back to Cyrus, but Train had found me there a few weeks ago. He'd sent a box of dead black roses and a letter warning me to steer clear of Cyrus's turf or he'd go after Cyrus's kids. I loved those kids, so I'd packed up the few belongings I had and begged Duke to take me in.

The compound was the safest place I could think of right now. Train wasn't afraid of anybody, but he respected biker territory. Someone banged into the wall in the hallway and thumped on my door. I climbed onto my bed with my notebook and curled up in the corner.

My guess was that Auggie had left already. He didn't seem like the kind of guy who would hang out at a club party. Then again, he also didn't seem like the type to make deals with Duke, so what did I know?

As the evening dragged on and the crowd grew louder, my incessant curiosity kept knocking on the little door in my head that I hid behind. What if Auggie had stayed and was right outside? I focused on my notebook and tried to think of anyone but him. No matter how hard I tried, I could not stop the nagging thought that if Auggie was out there, I wanted a picture of him.

He showed up earlier looking completely different than the mental picture I'd been harboring. The longer hair and rough beard were, oh my gosh, so freaking hot, but made him look more like a criminal. In Italy, he'd given off powerful good-guy-in-control vibes.

And those eyes really looked different. They were stunning before, but with all the dark hair, they glowed like beacons. I needed a picture of this new look. I didn't know which one I liked better. Both were fantastic, but this rugged version of him was even more attractive than the clean-cut look he'd sported in Italy.

Why did he change his appearance so much? Was he an undercover cop? He did ask a lot of questions earlier. If he was, was it my place to warn Duke?

If I told Duke my theory, he'd retaliate against Auggie, and it could easily turn violent. I didn't want to cause trouble when I didn't even know if it was true. That was something my mother would do but not me. However, if Auggie arrested Duke and he went to prison, I'd lose my hideout and protection.

I spent all night worrying about this and getting nowhere.

If I saw him, if I had a photo, then I could decide what to do.

I would look into his eyes and know if he was a cop. His eyes wouldn't hide the truth. I needed to see him.

In a fleeting moment of bravery, or possibly insanity, I swiped up my pocket camera and left my room. The music beat off the walls of the hallway as I tried to act casual when really my heart was pounding against my ribcage. Auggie probably wasn't even here, and I'd spent hours agonizing over whether to leave my room or not.

I hid in the doorway and peeked out. A few members were shooting pool with Duke. A group of people stood around the bar smoking cigarettes. One couple was dancing.

No Auggie.

I sighed in relief. I wanted a picture, but I also didn't want to go through the stress of seeing him again.

I turned back down the hallway and headed for my room.

A giggle stopped me short.

The door to my right hung open, a couple inside, a man sitting on the end of a bed. A girl on her knees between his legs. His head was leaned back, throat exposed. I knew that Adam's apple. The most gorgeous one I'd ever seen. I knew that black and red tattoo on his wrist. The wrist that now gripped her hair and clenched it.

She moaned and bobbed her he.

I stood in the doorway, paralyzed. My heart seized and cracked to pieces.

His shirt was lifted up, his jeans open, and the fly spread apart.

All I could see was tan skin and muscle. The cut rise of his hip, the glimpse of a six-pack above her head. A small trail of hair up his abdomen that extended above his belly button into his shirt. I couldn't see everything because her head blocked my view, but there was no question what was happening.

Auggie was getting sucked off by Crystal.

I thought I'd known pain before then, but I was wrong. This was pain.

Excruciating, humiliating pain.

He wasn't mine. I had no claim to him anyway. I was the one who'd left him more than once, but it still burned and raged like a forest fire through dry kindling.

He lifted his head. I should've run, but my feet stayed planted. My brain was memorizing the scene before me, so I could remember this pain over and over for the rest of my life. Maybe then I'd learn my lesson. Never seek out trouble. Always hide in your room.

He made eye contact with me. His moss-green gaze locked on mine. He didn't flinch or seem embarrassed. His face was lax, eyelids half-closed. Gruesomely beautiful.

His hand massaged her head, and his upper lip pulled back as he jammed her face down hard into his groin. She moaned, dug into his thighs with her long nails, and doubled down on her sucking action, her head bobbing twice as fast, deeper, more vigorously. The slobbery sound made me gag.

Oh God. Oh no. This could not be happening, and yet there it was in front of me.

Now I knew he wasn't a cop. I didn't see any clues in his eyes, and he definitely didn't need to get a blowjob from Crystal in order to arrest Duke.

Auggie was just an asshole. Plain and simple.

Good. Good. I should thank him for dissolving my notion that true heroes existed. Men were all scum. Out to get their cocks sucked, and they didn't care who did it.

No one would ever care about me. I would forever be just another woman like Crystal to be used and tossed away.

Or maybe it was more than a coincidence. Maybe he knew I was here and came for revenge? He wanted to hurt me like I'd hurt him. Congratulations, Auggie. You succeeded.

My fingers squeezed my camera so hard that it turned on and the lens popped out. The mechanical sound felt loud, but I knew it wasn't compared to the music and the noises Crystal was making.

Without a thought, on automatic pilot, I raised my camera and pressed the button. I held it down hard, and because it was in burst mode, it took a succession of fast, continuous photos like you would take at a sporting event.

It took lots of pictures.

I'd be able to make a stop-motion movie of her head bobbing if I wanted to.

With his other hand, Auggie took a shot of tequila and stared me down. He posed for my camera like a porn star proud of his prowess.

I released a harsh breath and finally stopped shooting pictures of the gut-wrenching sight. If this was what he wanted, I couldn't stop him, but I didn't have to watch and let him see the hurt on my face.

I lifted my finger from the shutter and lowered my hand.

The corners of his mouth turned up in smug satisfaction, and he slowly dropped his head back again, showing me that ridiculously large Adam's apple on his scruffy neck.

"Oh yeah." He dropped the empty shot glass onto the bed.

Auggie didn't care what I thought of him.

He knew exactly what he was doing. He was a criminal and a thug like all the others. He wasn't an Avenger, he was the villain.

I never knew who the players were in my world. They all seemed like bad guys to me. This hurt. It would take me a long time to get over my disillusionment, but I would survive like I always did.

He'd never even kissed me. He was free to be with anyone he wanted. A good, long cry and some ice cream was called for here.

Before any tears started to fall, I turned and ran to my room. In a blurry panic, I packed a bag, not even looking at what I was throwing in.

Leaving and getting away from him was the most important thing in my life. Even if Train caught me and killed me, I didn't care. I couldn't stay here and watch him hook up with Crystal.

With no cash and only twenty bucks in my account, my choices were limited. Maybe I'd take my chances with Cyrus or camp out somewhere. Anywhere but here.

Me and my broken heart burst through the back door.

"Haven!"

Was Auggie chasing after me to apologize? No. Duke had followed me out. My feet kept running through the parking lot, and I put more juice into it until Duke gave up his chase.

The tears fell as I fled the compound for the second time today.

This time I was definitely not coming back.

I finally had a picture of Auggie, probably had a hundred of them.

And they were the ugliest, most disgusting pictures I'd ever taken in my life.

Chapter 4 Skittish

Auggie

Just after midnight, Haven finally came out of her room. I ducked through the first open door in the hallway and watched her walk past. Her brows were pushed down like she was executing a scheme she'd been working on all night.

Maybe she was itching to work me over again. Looking all beautiful like she did with her long, lustrous blonde hair, all she had to do was talk with her hint of a Southern accent, and I'd be putty in her hands. She'd love the chance. She'd laugh as she crushed me again without a second thought.

While I was distracted by Haven, I felt Crystal follow me into the room. She'd been doing it for hours despite the fact I'd completely ignored her. Now that I was alone, she was making her move.

"Hey there, handsome." She smiled like a Cheshire cat that had cornered a mouse.

I didn't have time or patience for another woman right now, and I didn't want Haven to see me in here alone with her. Why? Why did I care if Haven saw me with Crystal? Not like she was anything to me or I was anything to her. In fact, if she saw me with Crystal, it might be sweet. Revenge served up cold-hearted was my specialty.

"Come here, Crystal." I sat down on the bed and spread my legs.

Within seconds, she was right up between them with an eager smile on her painted lips. "You want somethin'?"

I did. I wanted to hurt Haven like she'd hurt me. I wanted to make her cry. It would be wrong to use Crystal like that, and yet, fate had handed me an opportunity I couldn't pass up.

"Get on your knees."

Crystal's eyes lit, and she glanced back at the open door. "Don't you want some privacy?"

"You gonna do it or not?"

She dropped to her knees and braced her weight with her arms on my thighs. I opened the top button of my fly and leaned back. She reached for it, and I blocked her wrist. "Don't touch. Just keep your head right there and do whatever I say."

Her lips quirked up. "Alright, sugar."

She thought we were playing some kind of game where I would feed her my cock if she won. The truth was I had no intention of actually letting her suck it. I just needed it to look like she was blowing me. I gripped her hair, and she bobbed down trying to reach my fly. When I held her off of it, she giggled and moaned. It would look real if Haven walked by again.

I didn't have to wait long. She walked by, stopped, and came back to stand in the doorway. Crystal kept trying to get closer to my crotch. Haven's eyes widened, and she froze solid. I threw my head back and played it up with a moan. Crystal was totally into it, wiggling and making noises to entice me to let her have it.

For one short second, I thought I might've pulled it off. The shock on Haven's face was as sweet as I'd hoped. Her features went blank like she couldn't comprehend what she was seeing. Her brows pulled down, and her mouth twisted with a flash of anger that quickly morphed into the face girls make before an ugly cry.

This was what I expected. What I did not expect was the darkness that passed through her eyes. She held up her camera, and her lips quivered. I had to give her credit that she didn't cry, but she was definitely in pain. She took pictures of it all, and I knew right then I'd fucked up.

I'd thought revenge would feel good. It didn't. It felt like shit. Haven didn't want me. She'd left me twice for other dudes. My ego was bruised, but she didn't deserve this.

She wasn't playing me. The girl had no game. I saw it in her face. She was terrified. I didn't get a good look at her earlier, but now I saw it. There were ghosts in her eyes. Something was haunting her.

She ran away, and I pushed Crystal's head aside. "Get off."

"Hey!"

I stood up and turned my back on her as I buttoned my fly. "Get up and get out."

"What was that? You're just teasing me?"

"I changed my mind. Get out."

She made a bunch of huffing and puffing sounds trying to get me to engage with her, but I had nothing else to say to her.

"You're a crazy fuck. You know that?"

I didn't even look at her as I ran my hands through my hair. Why in the fuck did I do that? That had to be one of the dumbest moves I'd ever made. I wanted to hurt her and I did. Now, I felt like shit.

"Whatever." She stomped out of the room.

I took a deep breath and decided to go look for Haven, so I could apologize. I wasn't sure what I could say to make it better, but I had to check on her.

I ran into Duke in the hallway. He was hunched forward and shaking his head.

"You seen Haven?" I asked him.

He stopped and looked at the back door as he swayed on his feet. This late into the night he was probably pretty shit faced. "She just ran out of the parking lot in a tizzy." He scratched his head. "Why're you asking?"

She left the compound? I had to act unconcerned in front of Duke, but my senses were on overdrive trying to figure out what was going on with her. "No, nothin'. She just seemed upset, that's all."

He lumbered back out to the party, and I followed him to the bar. He slammed two beers on the wood, and I took one. I wanted to ask him about Haven, but didn't want to seem too interested. Luckily, he started talking. "That girl is drama central. She's a scared little bird always flittin' around. I was trying to help her, man, but she's too skittish."

That was a good way to describe the look I saw on her face. "Why's she skittish?"

"Hell if I know. She's got a lot of history around here. Maybe some of it's getting to her head. Maybe she's on drugs. It's a shame too 'cause she's a beautiful girl." He popped the cap off of his beer and seemed surprised when the foam overflowed and oozed over his hand. The idiot had just slammed it on the counter then opened it. What else did he expect?

"You know where she mighta gone?" I kept my voice even, but I was getting nervous about all I was seeing and hearing. Ghosts in her eyes, Duke saying she had a lot of history around here. The girl was in some serious trouble.

"Maybe back to Cyrus. Not sure if he's the one who's got a line on her. He's pretty high up in the LGs."

I knew who Cyrus was. He'd picked her up at the hospital and claimed to be her fiancé even though she had no engagement ring, and I'd found her at a party where trafficked girls were being forced to perform sex acts for money. "LGs?"

"Lamar Garden Gang. Small gang on the South Side."

I thought the guy who'd picked her up from the hospital looked like a gang member but wasn't sure. Now I knew. Maybe he had her running scared. "How do you know her?"

"She walked in here one day asking for a job and looking like a lost lamb. I'd heard of her but didn't know her. I took her in because she's cute, and Cyrus won't come on my turf, so she'd have a break from him if he was harassing her. But, hell, she could be running from her own shadow. She didn't tell me shit about herself."

Haven didn't tell me anything either when I'd had a chance to talk to her. She'd stayed locked up tight and bailed at the first opportunity. I had to talk to Cyrus to find out the real situation.

"I need you to set up a meet between me and Cyrus."

His head flinched back. "Why the hell you wanna do that?"

"I got a feeling there's something more going on with Haven. She's not just skittish. I'd like to have a sit down with Cyrus about that."

He chuckled. "A sit down with Cyrus? Listen. Right now the only thing I know of you is you're promising me a crazy good deal, and you got an unhealthy interest in the girl who takes care of this place."

He was right to be suspicious. In his world, you only trusted your brothers, and I was an outsider.

"If Cyrus gets wind I was sheltering Haven, it's gonna stir up a bunch of blowback for me and my guys, and right now we are copacetic with the LGs. They stay outta my territory. I stay outta theirs. I'm not putting myself out there to get you the meet till I know who the hell you are and what you're after."

"I understand you don't trust me. I'll rectify that when I deliver on the deal tomorrow night, but I'm telling you now, that girl needs someone to look after her. If you drop the ball and she gets hurt, it's on you."

He rubbed his chin with his index finger and thumb as he assessed me. He'd claimed he was trying to help her. Now it was time to prove it. "Alright. If tomorrow's transfer goes down without a hitch, and I don't find the fucking SWAT team at my door, I'll get you a meet with Cyrus."

I gave him a tip of my head. "Appreciate it." I left my unopened beer on the counter and headed toward the door. "If you hear from her in the meantime, hit me up right away."

"Gotcha."

***

I left the compound and drove straight to Stella's. She was our office manager and all around information gatherer. She had helped me find Duke in the first place.

It was one in the morning, but luckily she answered the door. She was wearing a silky pink sleep outfit with black letters swirled all over it. "Hey, sweetcheeks. Howzit hanging?"

Stella was one of the few people unimpressed with my military background. Most people caught wind that I was a team guy and took a step back. If they happened to find out about my former life as a Russian Alpha team member, they'd basically shit their pants. Not Stella. She'd laugh and get up in your face like you were her baby brother.

"You know anyone at Lamar Gardens?" I asked her.

She opened the door and motioned for me to enter. I kept my feet planted on her porch. This wouldn't take long, and I didn't feel like entering her place was the right thing to do. "Lamar Gardens? Not my neighborhood. Why?"

"Duke said that guy Cyrus who picked up Haven from the hospital is an LG."

She pursed her lips and frowned at me as she leaned on the door. "Haven again? So you went and talked to Duke, and now you're chasing down Cyrus? You're sure spending a lot of time on her."

She didn't know half of it. Not only had I talked to Duke, I was working an arms deal with him.

"Shouldn't you be packing? The rest of the team is prepping to deploy to..."

I held up my hand to stop her from blabbing classified intel with her door wide open. "Stella. I know where they're going. I'm going with them. I'm checking out this Cyrus character first. Can you help me?" We had a big op planned in Syria. Several million for an assassination of a high-ranking military official. It should've been my top priority tonight, but I couldn't get Haven's horrified face out of my head. God, I'd fucked up so bad. I needed to fix this before I left.

"I'll work with Jade to get you the deets on Cyrus."

"I need a last name, address, and full criminal background on Cyrus from Lamar Gardens."

"Got it. Let me see what I can do. Get back to you tomorrow." She looked at her watch. "I guess that's today now."

"Thanks."

I heard her lock up as I jogged down her stairs.

Stella's question stuck with me. I did have more important things to do. I'd committed to joining the team headed out to Syria in a few days, and I'd just murdered the head of the Bratva. I should've been laying low and packing my gear.

But I'd been an ass to Haven and making it right just rose to the top of my priority list.

***

I spent the next hour scouring the immediate vicinity of the compound for Haven. Worst-case scenarios kept forming in my head. She ran off alone, unprotected, and upset. I didn't spot any signs of her, so I headed back to the Bravo safe house to catch some shuteye.

In the morning, Stella sent me a rap sheet for Cyrus that was so expansive my phone struggled to open the file.

Car-jacking, assault, bribery, laundering money through a strip club, prostitution charges through the same club, unlawful possession of firearms. He'd served six months and was released. He'd gotten off on all the other charges somehow.

She sent some links to news articles about the gang violence in the neighborhood, but I didn't read them. Atlanta had hundreds of small gangs, and the story was always the same. Brutal violence in the name of revenge. Something I knew a lot about, but Haven would have no clue how to protect herself from.

My uneasiness grew with each passing minute. With no idea where to search for her, and Cyrus my only contact, it wasn't looking good. I needed more time to make sure she was safe.

I texted Vander, the owner of Knight Security.

Me: I have to pull out of the op.

There was no way I was leaving for Syria in a few days with Haven missing and so many questions unanswered.

Vander: Something up?

Me: I got it covered.

Vander: You need resources?

It was extremely generous of Vander to offer me resources after I'd just told him I was bailing on a critical op for the team. Millions were on the line, and Vander and his brothers had announced this was the last high value, high profile target they would pursue in Southeast Asia. The mission had a crazy high exposure risk, but the payoff would set the company up financially for life. Even though he was stretched thin and on edge, he still had more to give me.

Me: Appreciated. Not right now.

Vander: You need us, if we're not on a plane, we're here for you.

My bitter, war-weary heart warmed at the veracity in his words. These men, if I needed them, would drop even the most important mission to stand by my side.

Me: Gotcha. Thank you.

Chapter 5 Cyrus

Duke had a full staff of men guarding the meeting spot for our trade. It wasn't necessary. I wanted the deal to go smoothly, so I'd have street cred with him, and he'd put his neck out for Haven.

I came to the warehouse alone and turned over a trunk full of the rifles and handguns he'd wanted. A collection of brands and models that were exclusively available to military personnel. He gave me the cash, and I repeated my request for a meet with Cyrus. Truth be told, I didn't need to go through Duke. I wasn't afraid to roll into Lamar Gardens and ask about her, but it would help to have a local contact him first.

After another day of searching Atlanta for Haven, Duke came through for me, and I found myself seated across from Cyrus in the office of his strip club.

He looked the same as I remembered. A tall, buff black dude with too much bling, a tight silk shirt, and arrows shaved into his hair. The look didn't do anything for me, but I couldn't pull it off, so who was I to judge?

He stared me down and pressed his lips together. "You don't know someone from around here, you know you ain't safe here. You hear what I'm saying?" Cyrus started off trying to intimidate me, but I could see right through him. Gang-bangers like him were all talk. I had at least a foot of height on him and fifty pounds. He didn't have the balls to test me.

"Duke vouched for me."

"Duke ain't from Lamar Gardens neither."

I leaned forward with my elbows on my knees and looked him square in the eye. "I get that you need to identify me as an outsider." He also needed to come at me on the defense because I'd called him out for screwing up with Haven once before. When he showed up at the hospital and claimed her as his *baby* and his fiancée, I'd made it clear she'd been through some serious shit and he'd failed to protect her. He'd looked like a fool then, and I was about to do it again. "Haven's missing and seeing as you're planning on marrying her, I thought you might be interested in hearing about that."

He leaned back and his mouth dropped open. "I know she's missing. What the fuck does Duke know about that?"

So Cyrus didn't know that Haven was staying at Duke's. That meant Haven didn't want him to know. It was possible that she was running from Cyrus, but I didn't get that vibe from her when she left with him from the hospital. She'd chosen to call him to pick her up, and she'd kissed him on the lips.

"Is she hiding from you?" I asked him.

"Nah, man. She don't have any money, and I let her stay here for free. She's gonna be the momma to my kids." Cyrus was singing the same song he sang when I first met him. He makes all kinds of claims to Haven, but doesn't give a shit about her.

I leaned back and eyed him casually. "You know where she is?"

"I told you before and you're seeing now for yourself, keeping tabs on the girl is like herding cats. She's there one day, gone the next."

Cyrus had written her off as flighty, but I was sure something else was going on here. Why was she so skittish? "Where did she spend her time when she was here?"

"She volunteered at the community center. My kids would hang out with her there. They haven't seen her in a while."

It bothered me to hear that she spent time with his kids. Was she really planning to marry this guy, but she also ran from him on a regular basis?

"Anyplace else?"

"She liked the cantina on the corner. I already checked for her there."

He wanted me to give him credit for looking out his front window for her. Bravo, Cyrus. You're a fucking sleuth.

What else did I know about her? The camera. She took pictures. "Did she leave her phone here?"

"I don't know, man. You think I keep track of her shit?"

"Did she have a desk? Maybe a dressing room?"

"Haven don't strip," he said defensively.

So far Duke had told me she didn't have sex with the bikers, and now Cyrus was saying she didn't strip. She just hung out with these guys, why? Because of their charm and style? Probably not.

All the signs were pointing to the idea that she was hiding from someone.

"Do you know anyone else she hangs out with?"

He scrunched his nose like he smelled something bad. "You don't know nothing about Lamar Gardens. Do you?"

"No. Educate me."

"There wasn't always gangs around here. It was always poor, but no gangs. Then my dad bought this place and Haven's mom started stripping here, and before you knew it, the LGs was up. A few counter gangs formed. Small stuff, but still serious shit. Something went down with her mom and a brother from a rival gang started a war. A lot of people died, and the LGs took over the turf. We've been owning these streets since then, man. I took over for my dad when he was murdered."

This was all interesting but didn't answer my question. "Who else has she been with?"

"No one, homeboy. No one wanted to sleep with the daughter of the woman who started the war. You know why no one will bang the hottest piece of ass in the hood? Because her momma made sure of it. We don't know if she's our sister, our cousin. No. One. Knows." He tilted his head with each word.

"Say what?"

"Before she died, the momma made a big deal of saying any one of our dads could be her father. Any of us could be her brother. Shit. That's what started the war. Different guys claiming her or denying her. My dad, Eugene, God rest his soul, claimed her. He wouldn't let no one touch her. Wouldn't let her start stripping. Her momma went all around town stirring up shit. Haven don't look much like any of us, seeing as she has light skin, blue eyes, and blonde hair, but ain't nobody gonna risk the chance of starting another war by sleeping with your own sister. That shit is whack and exactly the kind of thing that happens here." He sat back in his seat and gave me a look like I told ya so, but the truth was his story was shit.

"You're marrying her, and she could be your sister?"

"She'll be a good momma to my kids. I'm not fucking her and not making any kids with her. Had my shit snipped."

"You don't love her?" I asked him.

"I love her like a sister because she could be mine, but my baby momma was killed in a shooting a few years back. Those kids love Haven, and I'm gonna make her their momma."

He loved her like a sister so he was gonna marry her but spent a good five minutes explaining why he couldn't fuck her because she might be his sister. I blew it off because gangs like these had all kinds of rules and lore that didn't make sense. I wasn't gonna change that. Again, Cyrus had colorful stories, but he'd gone off track. "Did she have a calendar, keep notes? Did she use any of your computers?"

"Computers? Yeah, she used that one there for her pictures." He pointed his thumb over his shoulder to a monitor in the corner. "It's nothing but weird shit. The girl is obsessed with trash and dirt. Lots of candy wrappers and bugs. Won't tell you where she is."

"Can I see them?"

"You want to see pictures of candy wrappers?"

"Yes."

He shook his head. "I can't let you see my books, man."

"I won't look at your numbers. I'm only interested in her pictures."

"I can't do that."

"Cyrus." I stood and towered over him. I could see him literally shaking in his sneakers. "I believe Haven is in danger and needs help. No one has seen her in three days, and she's running scared. You've done shit to protect her so far, so the least you can do is get the fuck out of my way, so I can try to find her."

"I checked the cantina," he offered defensively.

"Good job. Now, can I see the pictures?"

He spun in his chair and entered the passcode into the login screen of the PC. He started clicking around. "I don't know where she keeps them. I'm shit at tech stuff."

I stepped around the desk and leaned over, forcing him to move back. A quick search of the library for jpeg files turned up thousands of pictures. He was right. Many of them looked like trash or dirt. I clicked on one to zoom in on it. A red ladybug with black spots on a patch of sand. A close up of granite rocks. Fishing string tangled around a hook. A pink bobber buried in the mud. A picnic bench. An art sculpture that looked like it marked the entry to a public space. "Where is this?"

"Fuck if I know."

That meant it was probably outside of Lamar Gardens since he knew the neighborhood, and there weren't any natural areas around here.

Running a quick reverse image search turned up a fairly good match. "That looks like Blalock Reservoir on the West Side."

"You think she's there?"

I scrolled through the rest of the pictures. Of all the locations, the most common and more recent ones looked like they were taken at that park by the reservoir. "It's a start." I pulled out my phone and snapped a picture of the screen. "Download these to a flash drive for me."

"What the fuck?"

I didn't have a flash drive on me, and it would take too long to share them with Jade from here. "Nevermind. Don't delete these. If I don't find her, I'll be back."

I was already half-way out the door when I heard his reply. "You're just leavin' like that? I'm coming with you."

Too late. My car door was already shut and locked. He'd have to follow me if he wanted to come. Heaven forbid he'd have to look up the location of the lake himself.

I felt his eyes on me as my tires kicked up dirt from the strip club lot. Eat my dust, Cyrus.

***

The main entry to the park was locked since it was after sunset, but the gate wasn't functional, just a suggestion to keep cars out. My Land Cruiser easily skirted around the stone pillars at the edges of the road, and I was heading deep into the center of the park.

I lost Cyrus's lights behind me because he couldn't figure out how to bypass the gate. What an absolute tool this guy was. He was lucky he only had to survive in the projects. In Russia, he would be dead on the street.

My phone pointed me in the direction of the reservoir, and a spike of adrenaline chilled my bones when I caught sight of the lake through the trees. An eerie fog hung over the water's surface, and nothing lit the area except the moon.

This was a place where a girl could easily disappear.

A great place to dump a body.

The entrance road ended in a parking lot, and I whipped into a spot. I mounted a night scope on my rifle and chambered it with a .308 Winchester, my preferred setup for night shooting through wooded areas. I grabbed my flashlight and set out down the trail on foot before Cyrus had even cleared the entrance gate.

My hunting instincts kicked in. At night, listening became ultra important. Bugs, bats, wind bouncing off the lake, a rodent scrambling across the footpath.

Fifteen minutes in and still no sign of people.

Maybe this was a bad idea. Just because she had pictures of this location and hadn't been seen in three days didn't mean she was in here. I didn't even know for sure if she was in danger. She could be staying at a friend's house. But her face at the club. The memory tormented me. I'd caused it, yet it was so much more than just me.

The sheer terror, the ghosts in her eyes. Something was haunting this girl. From the looks of it, Cyrus wasn't interested in her enough to cause such panic. Another entity was at play here, but the girl was too locked up to tell anyone.

As soon as I found her, that would change.

I'd have to find a way to force her to trust me. It would be an uphill battle after all I'd done, but she had a secret that was hurting her. She needed help, and the only men in her life were Cyrus and Duke who were both clueless.

The main walking path was clear, but some broken twigs off to the left caught my attention. A small trail had been forged there that went deep into the woods.

I followed it to an area where it opened up.

A torn up tent. A soiled sleeping bag. A camera in the dirt.

Her fucking camera.

I turned it on. The last pictures were blurry like she was running.

One picture of an angry as fuck man coming straight for her.

Shit. Fuck.

My heart pounded, and the sinking feeling in my bones became so intense, I struggled to concentrate.

Too late. I was too late.

Where was she?

Now we were looking for her body.

God. Why did I wait so long?

My fucking ego could've killed this girl.

As I cleared a ridge, I heard a scuffle and the moonlight hit what looked like a man carrying something white at the shore of the reservoir. "Hey!" The man took off running. I got two shots off and missed then lowered my rifle. I didn't know for sure who was running from me. I would've chased him, but I had a feeling the white object was a body.

I slid down through the brush on my heels, using one hand for balance, the other to hold the flashlight and block the twigs from hitting my face.

"Haven!"

Jesus, fuck.

I found her face down in the dirt and turned her to her back. She was wearing only a skirt and a bra. She had blood smeared on her face. I dropped the rifle, removed my outer shirt, and used it to wipe her eyes, nose, and mouth. "Haven?"

She moaned.

Thank fuck.

She wasn't dead.

I wrapped my shirt around her torso the best I could manage, tying the sleeves together at her neck. She groaned again when I crouched in front of her and pulled her arms over my shoulders, her front resting on my back. We had to hike up the hill to get back to the car, and this seemed like it would be the best way to carry her based on her obvious injuries.

With my rifle hanging in front, I started up the slope.

A few yards in she spoke. "Am I dead?"

God, it was good to hear her voice. It was weak, but she was alive. "You're not dead."

"I thought I died."

"You didn't die, and you're not going to die. Try to hold on."

I had one hand gripping her forearm and one on her leg. She threw her other arm over, and her legs tightened around my hips. All good signs.

I loaded her in the front seat of my car and called London, our team doctor.

Luckily, he was at headquarters and available. "Her face is bleeding. Not sure what else is wrong. She's conscious and spoke to me."

"Alright. I'm ready."

"Be there in ten."

I rammed through the park gates instead of going around Cyrus, who was blocking the way I had come in. It would damage my vehicle, but I didn't care. I needed to get her help ASAP.

"Why didn't he kill me?" Haven asked.

"Who?"

She pressed her lips flat and flinched in pain. Her eyes were puffy like she'd been hit. God. I wanted to kill someone. "Who did this to you, Haven?" Give me a name so I knew who would die.

"I just don't get why he didn't kill me."

"Maybe he thought he did."

He'd left her unconscious at the bottom of a ravine. He wouldn't have known if she survived or not.

"Oh."

I didn't question her further, but when the time came, she would be answering questions.

For now, she was alive and safe.

The relief that coursed through me was like nothing I'd ever felt. I'd had many missions and rescued a lot of hostages, but this one cut me to the core. It sliced into a portion of my humanity I'd long thought dead. I didn't feel emotions like this or get invested when it was work. This wasn't work. This was personal.

Chapter 6 Cowards

Haven

I didn't die and Auggie found me.

I couldn't believe it.

I thought for sure I was going to die at the reservoir that I loved so much. But he found me. When I woke up to his hand wiping the mud from my face, I could breathe again. I never thought anyone would find me there, but he did.

The engine of Auggie's car revved beneath me, and the outside lights flew by in a blur. The shock of not being dead quickly morphed into pain. So much pain. My face, head, back, and arms. I'd fought off Train as hard as I could, but he was much stronger than me.

I turned my head to Auggie in the driver's seat and attempted to focus on him. "How did you find me?"

He clenched the wheel and glared at the cars in our way. "Cyrus had some of your pictures on his computer. I saw the reservoir and went out there looking for you."

"You did? Why?"

"Because you were missing."

He spoke matter of factly like it should make logical sense to me, but it didn't. He'd figured out I was missing and asked Cyrus where I might be? Then he found my pictures and took the initiative to go look for me in the dark?

"I thought you hated me."

A wave of guilt layered through all the aches in my body. I'd been so ungrateful to him for all he'd done before this. I'd run from him more than once. He'd let Crystal give him a blowjob and laughed when I took pictures. He hated me. Yet, he'd saved my life?

"I don't hate you, Haven."

With the anger in his voice, I didn't believe him. He sounded like he was lying or just saying it to placate me.

I moaned and closed my eyes. The throbbing in my head forced me to stop thinking about what was happening. I pressed my palm to my forehead and moaned.

"We're almost there. I'm getting you some help."

"Okay."

We entered a below-ground structure under a tall building and parked near an elevator. We were surrounded by shiny black cars. Most of them SUVs, but I also spotted a few sports cars and trucks too. Other areas of the garage had normal cars, but we'd clearly parked in a designated area. Everything ached as he helped me out of the car.

"I can carry you." He crouched down like he was ready to pick me up. I didn't really want Auggie to carry me. This whole thing was humiliating enough, and I hated to drag him into it. He'd actually involved himself, so that wasn't my fault, but I still felt terrible about it.

"No. I can walk."

He didn't move far away. He kept one hand around my back and supported my weight as I hobbled toward the elevator.

After he entered the code, the doors opened, and he looked back to watch a car pull into the structure. Auggie's back stiffened, and he ushered me inside the elevator as Cyrus parked in a different area of the garage and jogged up to us. What the heck was he doing here?

"Haven. Are you okay?" He was out of breath by the time he reached us. He pressed his palm to the elevator doors to hold them open.

Auggie pivoted so he was between me and Cyrus. "I got this."

"Is she hurt? Where are you taking her?" Cyrus was frantically looking from me to Auggie as he tried to figure out the situation.

"I have someone upstairs who can administer medical care," Auggie replied formally.

"You have someone in this building? Like you got a doctor in your pocket?"

The doors clanged like they wanted to close. "Release the door and go home, Cyrus." Auggie gave orders in such a commanding tone, I was worried for Cyrus. Auggie was not messing around.

"Fuck that." He stepped inside, and the doors closed behind him.

The negative energy poured off of Auggie as the elevator dinged and moved upward. I started to regret my decision to walk instead of letting him carry me. My legs felt weak. My body shook even though I wasn't cold. I could've died. Train had found me at the reservoir and tried to kill me. The realization rattled my bones, and I closed my eyes to ward it off.

By the time we'd reached our destination, Auggie had bent and swooped an arm behind my legs to carry me. I briefly registered that he had no trouble lifting me, and he was a lot bigger than I remembered.

Cyrus scoffed but followed us through dimly lit office corridors that led to a room that seemed like it was empty, but inside a man waited for us. He motioned for Auggie to place me on a padded exam table that was covered with a long paper like you would see at a doctor's office.

I groaned as each of my bones felt like it was falling to settle on the pad below me. Auggie stood at the top of the table and swiped the dirt off my forehead.

"Where does it hurt?" the doctor asked me. He had a pleasant British accent, and he seemed very concerned for me.

"I'm fine."

"You have to tell me where your injuries are, so I can help you."

"My eye." Everything was hurting, but I didn't want to tell him that. My eye was obviously swollen, so I wasn't revealing anything new.

"Can you take a deep breath?"

I was able to do so with only a little pain in my ribs as he listened to my chest. Auggie pressed a cold softpack above my eye. I flinched, and he backed off but slowly lowered it to my swollen lid.

The doctor wrapped a cuff around my arm. I closed my eyes and let him do his job. Auggie dropped the cold pack for a moment. He left and returned with a wet towel, which he brushed across my forehead and hair. It helped me to focus on the cool, wet fabric on my skin.

"Duke is waiting outside the parking structure," Cyrus said.

"Tell him to get lost," Auggie snapped back. "No. On second thought, wait right here."

Auggie's hand left my head, and I felt his energy leave the room. I was alone with the doctor and Cyrus.

"How's she doing?" he asked the doctor.

I turned my head to the side, so I could see Cyrus through squinted eyes.

"So far, okay. Some cuts, and she'll have bruises, but I don't see any serious injuries from my initial exam. We might want to run some x-rays to make sure nothing is broken."

"You're gonna be okay, Haven. Just relax. You're shaking like crazy."

Relax. How could I relax? I thought I was going to die.

Auggie walked into the room and scowled as Duke followed behind him. When he saw me, he gasped and reached for my hand. "Holy shit. Who did this to you?"

"You did this, genius." Auggie pushed Duke back by the shoulder, and he never made contact with my hand. "She took off running that night, and you didn't follow her? You were the last person to see her before this happened. This is on you." Auggie pointed a sharp finger at him and punctuated the word *you*.

"Fuck you," Duke spit back. "Didn't see you take off in a sprint either."

Oh no. They were going to fight. I could barely see their faces from this angle, but they sounded angry, and I could feel the tension building in the room.

"I didn't know she was skittish. I didn't know she was in danger. You knew." Auggie's voice grew deeper and louder.

"Everyone is skittish around me and no, I told you I didn't know shit about her situation."

Auggie growled and looked to the ceiling. I sighed in relief he wasn't going to escalate it.

"What is this place?" Duke asked.

"This is my work office," Auggie replied impatiently.

If that was true, I had a lot of questions. This didn't look like a police station. Maybe this was some kind of secret FBI hangout where they kept doctors on hand for emergencies?

"Who's this guy?" Duke tilted his head toward the man who'd been examining me.

"He's a doctor," Auggie answered shortly.

"I'm Doctor London Sawyer."

Duke stared at the physician but didn't ask any more questions. I wanted to know what kind of business it was and why there was a doctor here, but now wasn't a good time as I struggled through the pain. "My head is throbbing."

"Let me get you something for that." The doctor, who I now knew was Dr. Sawyer, left the exam table and walked toward a cabinet on the wall.

"Whoever did this to her is dead. Tell me who, Haven. I swear to God I'll kill him." Duke puffed up his chest and stepped around Auggie to get closer to me.

"I'll pop that sucker in the mouth for doing this to you," Cyrus chimed in with bravado. "Doesn't matter who he is, he's got an expiration date now."

Dr. Sawyer returned, and the head of the table started to rise. A wave of dizziness made everything blurry for a second. He handed me a glass of water and a large white tablet. "Some acetaminophen. I can give you something stronger for the pain if you need it."

"Thank you. This is fine." I swallowed the pill and looked around at all that I could see now that I was vertical.

Auggie was pacing the room, which was quite a feat as the space was getting crowded. When he came close to us, he whipped my camera out of his pocket and turned it on.

"My camera." I thought I'd never see it again. I'd dropped it when I was running from Train.

"You're not gonna tell us who did this. Are you?" Cyrus asked me. He'd tried several times to get the information out of me, but I refused to drag him into the mess that was my life.

"I don't think I should. It could put you and your kids in danger." Cyrus didn't know about the dead roses I'd received with the threat to his kids. I'd panicked when I'd seen them and tossed them in a dumpster in the alley. I'd left his place right away and ran to Duke's.

"I ain't afraid of no one." Cyrus was getting angry, and while he was a formidable gangster in Lamar Gardens, I had a feeling Train had long since passed him up on the path to violent crime.

"Not even this guy?" Auggie held up my phone and showed them the display.

Cyrus's eyes paled and Duke squinted to look closer. Cyrus stepped back. "Whoa."

"Who is he?" Auggie asked Cyrus.

"Someone you don't wanna mess with."

I remembered I'd managed a few shots of Train before he'd caught me. Auggie must've been showing them those pictures.

"I need a name." Auggie gritted his teeth, sounding impatient and on the verge of blowing up.

Cyrus looked down and scuffed his feet on the floor.

Auggie shared a glance and an eyebrow raise with the doctor. They were figuring it out. Cyrus was afraid of Train like everyone else.

"You know what? I gotta get back to my kids. It's late." He shuffled toward the door, leaving Duke standing frozen in shock, still staring at the camera screen that Auggie was holding. Cyrus looked at me and stopped. "I'm glad you're okay, Haven. I'll tell the kids not to worry about you." And then he was out the door.

Auggie grunted and placed the camera back in his pocket as he turned to Duke. "What about you, Duke? You suddenly gotta be somewhere else and can't mention this guy's name?"

Duke was better at hiding his fear, but he knew exactly who Train was and how speaking of him was a death sentence. "Never seen that guy before." He flat-out lied.

Seriously? The man who I thought was a big bad biker prez lied through his teeth and denied knowing Train when he was there during the war? He was younger and not yet club president, but he was a member. He witnessed the carnage that Train rained down on Lamar Gardens first hand. He lost many brothers to Train's trigger finger and willingness to act on a mere rumor.

It was bloody and unfair. A very dark time, not only for me because I lost my mom, but for all of us who grew up in the projects.

"I know you're lying," Auggie said wisely. Duke was a terrible liar.

He shoved his hands in his pockets and shrugged his shoulders. "I don't know who that is."

"Sure." Auggie paced the room again, the anger pouring off him.

Duke walked up to me like he was walking up to a casket to say his final goodbyes. Great. I'd lost another hiding place where I was safe. This was exactly why I'd never told Duke that I was hiding from Train. "If you need anything, you call. Hear me?"

"Okay." Another lie. He wanted nothing to do with Train, and he'd be running scared behind Cyrus to get the heck out of dodge before Train found out they were involved with me. He looked tough with his leather cut that said Devil's Advocates on the back and his patches loaded all down the front, but when it came down to it, he shook in his boots at the sight of Train.

Duke left and Auggie shared a disbelieving look with the doctor. "What a bunch of fucking pussies." The way he said pussies had an edge to it. The *S* was sharp. He had a slight accent, but I didn't recognize it.

Dr. Sawyer smirked. "Cowards. You know the type. Run the other way when shit gets real."

"They're a liability. I didn't want those jackasses around any—" Auggie turned his attention to me and cut his words off like he'd forgotten I was listening.

I closed my eyes. This was it. He was going to badger me and bombard me with questions until I told him who it was in the picture. If I squeezed my eyes tight enough, he couldn't get to me.

That was how I'd gotten through a lot of difficult situations these past few years. I squeezed my eyes and pretended it wasn't happening, and a lot of the time, when I opened my eyes, it was gone. This also worked with spiders crawling in the shower. I ignored them and they disappeared. Poof.

"Haven?" Auggie's voice sounded gentle, but it hit me like steel darts. Another attack. I didn't know Auggie all that well, except that he was gorgeous and kind of a jerk, but he seemed very committed and determined. Not at all like the type of guy that would give up before he acquired the information he needed. He was coming to get me, and I felt so weak. My face hurt. The pain muddled my thoughts.

"Hey." His fingers wrapped around my hands, which I hadn't even realized I'd put over my face to hide meanwhile smearing dirt into the blood on my cheeks. He gently pulled my hands away and wiped my face with the cool towel. "Relax. You're safe now. Don't worry about anything. Just focus on recovering."

He was trying to calm me down so I'd talk. It was another lie. I couldn't trust him any more than I could trust Duke or Cyrus. If he was a cop and Train found out I'd talked to him, he'd make sure to come back and finish the job he'd started tonight. He would find me. He always found me.

Dr. Sawyer brought over a sheet and draped it over my chest. He raised it and peeled back Auggie's shirt that was wrapped loosely around my shoulders.

He strategically moved the sheet around so he could inspect various regions of my torso without exposing my breasts. This struck me as unusually gentle and caring. Although I assumed it was what doctors did, I appreciated him allowing me to maintain some modesty in my situation.

"Check out this wound on her face, London." Auggie dabbed the cloth under my cheekbone. I thought it was interesting that Auggie called him London instead of Doctor Sawyer. It showed they were friends, not just work acquaintances.

Dr. Sawyer cleaned my wound with an antiseptic wipe and examined it closely. "Small abrasion. Likely a scrape from her fall or a blunt force."

Auggie growled. "Did he punch you in the face?"

I winced and turned away.

Dr. Sawyer used his palms to angle my head back toward him. "I'll just clean it up and bandage it to heal on its own."

Auggie was back to pacing the room, his fists clenched.

The doctor took care of my face and returned to examining my body. "Her knees are pretty banged up."

Auggie grunted and walked to the window. This time he didn't make the trek back. He crossed his arms and stared out.

Dr. Sawyer wiped my scraped knees and applied an ointment before wrapping bandages around them. I was wearing a denim skirt, which he gently lifted to inspect my thighs. He didn't attempt to look inside my underwear, and I was grateful for that. "I know it's hard to discuss, but I need to know if he..."

"He didn't," I managed to get out. Train had never sexually assaulted me. He was all about emotional control, not as much physical, although he had hit me before. This wasn't the first time, but it was definitely the worst.

The doctor nodded and stepped back like he was done checking me over.

"She's been through a lot tonight." Auggie turned from the window and looked at me again. His brows were furrowed deep, and his eyes looked tired. I had no idea what time it was. "Are you done with her?"

Dr. Sawyer nodded slowly as he walked around to the other side of the table and finished his circle around me. "Yes. Watch her for signs of concussion, trouble breathing. Make sure she stays hydrated and gets some rest. Her body needs to recover from the trauma. We'll need to discuss the option to send her to the hospital for some x-rays." Dr. Sawyer started cleaning the room, putting stuff away. The exam was over. I didn't die, and all I needed was an ice pack and some bandages. I was so lucky to be alive at all. Thanks to Auggie.

"Do you want to stay with Stella?" Auggie asked me quietly.

"Uh." His question surprised me. It was the first time he'd acknowledged he even knew who I was since I'd seen him last. I'd betrayed Stella by leaving without notice or even a thank you after she'd been so kind to me and offered me a place to stay. I was a complete stranger, and she'd taken me in like a beloved sister. Then I'd bailed on her before she'd woken up. "No." I answered his question. I didn't want to stay with Stella. I couldn't face her again after what I'd done, and I didn't want to lead Train to her or her friends.

"Do you have a place to go?" he asked.

Was he trying to get rid of me? No. I didn't have any-where to go. Cyrus and Duke had just walked out on me and left me here. That's why I was at the reservoir in the first place.

I'm lost, Auggie. I'm lost and alone. I'm confused and hurt and scared that Train will find me again and kill me this time. So no, I don't have anywhere to go.

I didn't say any of that out loud. Instead, I closed my eyes and fought back the tears. It hurt too much to admit the truth to him, worse than any punch or scrape. Having no safe place was my greatest fear.

An awkward silence fell over the room, and I had a sense they were struggling with what to do with me. They'd res-cued me, treated my wounds, and now they needed to get rid of me.

The silence was broken by a loud commotion coming down the hallway. It sounded like a stampede, and I held my breath, hoping like hell it wasn't Train or one of his men coming to get me. I propped myself on my elbows to get a better view of all that was going on.

Men. Lots of big tall men and a few gorgeous women marched into the small examination room. They looked at Auggie first then at me. I recognized Steel and Brandy. The rest I vaguely recognized from the previous times I'd seen Auggie's friends.

Scowling faces stared at me, looked at my wounds, and scowled deeper. Creased brows all around. Two of them turned away like they couldn't look.

Well shoot. Maybe he was FBI or something and these were FBI agents. This was it. Train would know now that I'd spoken to the FBI. The fear coiled in my stomach and exploded in a wave of nausea.

On top of the fear was the embarrassment and guilt. I'd treated these people so badly, and they had no idea why. At least Stella wasn't here. I felt the worst about hurting her.

Loudest of all, Stella made a grand entrance through the door. All I could see was her head and long sweeping braids hanging down on her shoulders. "Where is she?"

Oh no, no, no. Stella was here for revenge, just like Auggie came to the club to get back at me. I dropped back to the table and covered my face.

Dear floor, please swallow me whole right now. I am not here. I'm not here. I'm linoleum tile. Yep, that's me. Not lying here on a table, nope. I am under the floor hiding. They can't see me.

I peeked and they were all still there. They conversed in a loud din of grumbles. Their large bodies blocked the only exit. I didn't die, but I was trapped by a mob of extremely angry people.

Chapter 7 Convoy

I didn't know what time it was, but it had to be late. Train had found me around eleven o'clock at night. It could be past midnight by now. This large group showed up for Auggie in the middle of the night?

"Did London call you?"

I overheard Auggie talking to one of the men. He had the same dark features as Steel, but carried more bulk, and his face was a lot scarier because he had a big scar across the left side.

"No. We saw the activity on the security feed and got nosy. Saw it was Haven and came right up."

The man with the scar knew my name was Haven. I think I remembered him from the hospital, but that night was such a blur.

A pretty woman with short brown hair approached me. "Hi. I'm Jade. Are you okay?"

"I'm fine."

"Let me know if you need anything."

"Okay."

That was weird. If they were the FBI, why was she being nice to me? She stood next to Auggie for a few moments as he talked to the guy with the scar then Auggie handed her my camera. Auggie took it back as if remembering something then played with the control dial. His large fingers pressed the tiny buttons quickly.

Oh gosh. The pictures of him and Crystal were still on there. He frowned then hit the center dial repeatedly. He was deleting the pictures before he turned it over to Jade. She took it and quickly left the room.

Darn. I needed that camera. It was the only one I had, and I couldn't afford another. Oh well, it was evidence now. I'd probably never get it back.

Auggie glanced at me and lowered his eyes as he turned away. What? He felt guilty? Sorry, Charlie. You got a blowjob from a biker babe and left the door open, and you shouldn't have done that then posed for the pictures if you didn't want anyone to see.

At least they were gone now. Neither one of us had to see them again. I wouldn't be making a stop-motion movie out of them or writing any stories about them. They had been deleted. If only I could delete it from my memory.

The chatting in the room died down and everyone looked at Auggie expectantly.

He cleared his throat. "Haven was one of Rico's victims in Italy. Steel and I brought her back on the plane with Brandy."

Oh no. He was going through the whole story. My cheeks burned. Everyone would know I'd betrayed these kind people. I closed my eyes again, but my trick didn't work. I couldn't pretend this wasn't happening because Auggie's authoritative voice was filling the room while the others listened with arms crossed over their chests. "She was staying with a biker named Duke from Devil's Advocates, and I happened to be there for unrelated reasons. She seemed skittish and took off and that got my radar up."

He cleared his throat again and reached for a bottle of water. Was that all he was telling them? That was a seriously watered down version of events, and it didn't include the most embarrassing part that I had run from them when they offered me help after the party. It certainly didn't include the blowjob and photo session from hell that sent me running in the first place. I understood why he wouldn't want to share that.

The tightness in my lungs and the heat in my cheeks died down. The worst of the story was over, and he didn't make me look as bad as he could have.

"She had another contact named Cyrus from the LGs. He didn't know what might've spooked her, but he gave me some pictures that led me to Blalock Reservoir. I found her there," he motioned to me and his voice grew deeper and more growly, "in this condition."

The guys listening fidgeted and grumbled back. The anger rolling off them hit me like a hot wind, and a burst of sadness swelled in my heart. They cared about me and my condition? I thought they were here to arrest me, but this was making me feel like they held genuine concern for my well-being. Imagine that. No one had ever given a crap about me before, and these strangers were having a serious meeting in the middle of the night about "my condition."

Auggie continued. "I clocked an unknown male heading east and got off two missed shots. Pulled back because I didn't know where she was and hadn't confirmed the target."

Wow. He'd shot at someone? I hadn't even heard it. What if he'd killed Train? I would've been relieved. It was horrible to wish for someone's death, but I wouldn't shed a tear if Auggie had killed Train. Of course, then Train's men would be hellbent on revenge, and Auggie would be their main target.

The guy with the scar nodded. "Want to call in the feds?"

Auggie shook his head. "Not yet. I want to handle this on my own."

"You're not on your own anymore," Steel said. "We're in."

"I didn't call you in," Auggie countered.

"And yet here we are. You need a team at the lake, one scouting for the perp, and one on her." I wasn't sure exactly what was being said, but Steel's voice was stern, and Auggie didn't argue further.

"We'll send a team to the reservoir," the guy with the scar announced.

Auggie nodded. "He's probably long gone but look for a tent and sleeping bag off the south entrance parking area by the lake. I'll give you the coordinates."

Jade returned and stood in the doorway. "Auggie?"

"What?"

The room grew quiet, and Jade spoke to everyone.

"There was a GPS unit installed in the camera."

No one responded. They all stood and stared at Jade for a long second.

"What does that mean?" I asked. I knew what GPS was, but why would my old camera have that feature?

"Someone could be tracking you." Jade answered my question.

Train had given me that camera as a gift. Was this why? He'd installed a tracking device on it? I hadn't considered it before, but it sounded like something Train might do.

"We need to move her," Auggie said urgently, reacting quickly to the news that I was still digesting.

"Take her to the Bravo site," the man with the scar replied.

"Is Delta stocked and fortified?" Auggie returned.

"Of course," Stella answered defensively.

"I'll use the Delta site. More remote and secure. We use my Land Cruiser as a decoy from the underground and route a convoy from the dock exits."

It sounded like they were talking in a foreign language.

"A little overkill for a street thug. Don't you think?" one of the guys asked.

Auggie propped his hands on his hips and turned to face me. "This wasn't the first time he followed you. Was it?"

I shook my head no.

"He finds you all the time. Doesn't he?"

I nodded slowly, still in shock at how quickly this had escalated.

"That right there." He pointed to me. Everyone in the room looked at me. My hands shook, my face frozen. "That's why I need a fucking convoy to get her to the Delta site safely."

The guy with the scar cleared his throat to get their attention. "Talon in the Land Cruiser as decoy, Jade tailing him. Magnum in the lead, Steel, Auggie, and me travel with the target, London in the rear. Helix and Misha take Stella and Brandy to get her some supplies then meet up with Talon to hand them off."

Stella made a face and raised a hand.

"Stella?" The man talking seemed impatient with her interrupting his string of commands. "I'd like to go to the Delta safe house to get her settled."

Safe house? They had safe houses, and they were taking me to one?

"Me too," Brandy said.

The man rolled his eyes. "Fine. Talon will escort you to the Delta site, and you can get your girl settled."

Stella nodded. "Thank you very much."

I assumed he meant me by "your girl?"

This was all so surreal. Did these people all forgive me without an apology? And now they were putting themselves out there again knowing I might do it again? Cyrus had taken off running, but that didn't deter this crowd at all. Maybe they didn't fully understand.

"Uh." My voice sounded so weak in a room full of such big personalities. "You guys should know about the danger."

They all stared at me with blank faces.

Auggie stepped closer to me and looked down into my eyes. "You ready to give us the name of this asshole?" he asked quietly.

"No."

His gaze shifted over my head. "Then we're aware of the danger. It's not a problem."

No one else in the room seemed concerned about what I'd said, and they started to file out the door without asking any questions.

Then it hit me. "He knows I'm here?" Oh God, no. The camera was here. He'd see it on the GPS.

Auggie placed a warm hand on my upper arm. "You're safe."

"He knows I'm here? With you?" Now he would go after them. He'd kill them.

He lowered his head to my level. "Listen. I don't give a fuck if he knows where I am. You are safe with me. Understand?"

I nodded, but Train was ruthless and evil. Auggie didn't know that, so he couldn't promise me anything.

"Aug, get kitted up and rendezvous here in ten." The guy with the scar gave him the order and left the room.

Auggie nodded and stood up straight again. "I gotta go get some stuff ready. You stay here with Brandy and Stella." He spun and darted out of the room, leaving me in the dust of the flurry that had just occurred.

I held the sheet to my chest and avoided eye contact with Brandy. I'd betrayed her too, and she was smiling at me like we were besties.

"Here, girl. Take my jacket." Stella pulled her arms out of a lush suede jacket and wrapped it over my shoulders. She and Brandy worked together to cover my breasts while I slipped my arms into the smooth silk lining. It was big enough that I could close it in the front. Stella helped me zip it up, and my shoulders settled in the comfy jacket. It felt good to be covered, especially if all those men were going to be coming back.

Stella had literally given me the shirt off her back.

"You're very nice," I said and looked down. "You're being kind to me."

"Of course." She laughed and embraced me in a gentle hug. "You are in need, my friend, and we are here to provide for you. You probably aren't used to that up till now, but that's going to change. It takes a while, but you'll accept it."

She was acting like what happened before didn't happen.

"But I left. I didn't tell you."

"Oh, that was my fault. Stella in all her glory can be a little intimidating, and you were in a bad place. I understand why you ran from my big ol' mouth."

"That wasn't it. No. Please don't think that."

"I'm attempting to tone it down this time so you don't spook again."

This was her version of toning it down? My gosh, this woman was so colorful and amazing. I wished I had my camera so I could take pictures of her. She had smooth brown skin that shined white in the light like she moisturized the heck out of it. The thick braids wrapping from one side of her head to the other looked like an intricate tapestry, also well moisturized and strong. The soft wrinkles around the corners of her eyes told me she wasn't young and innocent, and any creams she'd been using to fight off the wrinkles were starting to lose the battle. She'd lived this life and she'd done it large. The stories I could make up about her would probably pale in comparison to reality. If I ever got a chance to sit down and talk with her, I'd ask her to tell me all about it.

"I need to go shopping for you. My stuff will all be too big. What are you, a size seven? A five? Girl, you are tiny."

I was normally a size ten, but the stress of the last few months had taken its toll. I wasn't eating well at all and had withered to skin and bones. I didn't even know what size I was now. "Please don't buy me any clothes."

"What're you gonna wear? My jacket and that bra forever? Won't be comfy to sleep in. Ooh, you need something to drive old Auggie over there a little insane." She angled a thumb over her shoulder at the open door to the now mostly empty exam room.

"What? Oh no. I don't... with him. I'm not. We're not." I felt a hot blush on my neck. I couldn't believe she'd said that out loud. I mean, Auggie was gorgeous, and we'd collided paths a few times, but we hadn't kissed. We hadn't even admitted we liked each other. In fact, I was pretty sure he hated me for what I'd done, and I kinda hated him for what he'd done, but now he'd saved me again and brought me to a doctor and told me he didn't hate me. I blew out a long breath. "I'm confused."

She rubbed my back. "You're gonna be alone with a hot commando in a safe house. You need seductive sleepwear just in case." She winked and the side of her lip curled up.

I had to laugh at how ridiculous it sounded that I would seduce Auggie. I had bandages all over, I'd been beaten and bruised, and most importantly, Auggie hated me.

"Wait. Commando? What the heck?"

"You don't know?" Brandy asked me.

"Know what?"

"Auggie didn't tell you? Just like Steel didn't tell me. These boys and their top secret shit create a lot of problems."

"Top secret?"

Stella lowered her chin and leveled her eyes on me. "This is classified intel, but girl, they are SEALs. Navy SEALs."

Stella waved her hands as she talked and didn't lower her voice even though she was admittedly spilling something she shouldn't. "Like SEAL Team Six hot commandos best of the best, baddest of the badass commandos."

My mouth dropped open and a silent "what" came out.

"Yas. It's true. Sailing huge fighter ships all around the world. Pow, pow, pow. Mortal combat in the sand. Ziplining from helicopters into the ocean. You name it, they do it."

"Wow."

Stella took that as a request from me to keep talking. "They have seen it all." She raised her eyebrows and looked at her red fingernails like she was considering what color to paint them next. I had a feeling she'd pick another shade of red. "They resigned from the Navy to form a private security company and took only the cream of the crop with them so they could kick ass with their own special brand of justice without all the government red tape holding them back."

Brandy was nodding along with her tongue poked in her cheek. "Shocking, isn't it?"

"Yes."

"Steel didn't tell me either. I thought he was a doctor." Her voice sounded bitter, but she was also grinning underneath it.

"I thought Auggie was a cop or an FBI agent," I admitted.

"You were closer than me. Nope. They're private military contractors." She made air quotes with her hands and sneered a little.

The puzzle pieces started to fill in. The way he tracked me down in the woods and carried me with ease up a steep hill. Shooting a rifle in the dark. The way he thought Cyrus and Duke were cowards. Of course they were compared to him. The way the guy with the scar called out commands and they organized so quickly. All the jargon about convoys and stuff. Yes, those were all militaristic type things.

Holy wow.

I'd been rescued by a real-life superhero.

"How do you know them?" I asked Stella.

"I'm the office manager. Brandy is my assistant. We keep them in line."

I had a feeling Stella was overstating the importance of her role at the company. They didn't look like they let anyone tell them what to do. "That doesn't sound easy."

"It's not, but I'm good at it so they keep me around. Brandy's fucking the boss so she has job security."

"Stella," Brandy warned.

"Exsqueeze me. Brandy is having relations with the boss, so she has job security."

Brandy giggled and rolled her eyes.

Chapter 8 Ocean's Eleven

A few minutes later, Auggie returned to the exam room transformed. His T-shirt and jeans had been replaced with a sleek, tight, long-sleeved sweater, midnight black cargo pants, and a canvas pack strapped to his chest like I'd seen cops wear before. A dark cap and a face mask covered his forehead, mouth, and nose, but I recognized his beautiful moss-green eyes.

He held a leather jacket in his hands that I assumed he would put on to cover the gun holster over his shoulders and the two pistols tucked into his sides.

I thought Auggie was wow before. Now, he was just plain breathtaking. Broad shoulders, thin waist. All muscle. Not an ounce of fat on him. He really did make Cyrus and Duke look like amateurs playing in the sandbox. He reminded me of Ocean's Eleven bandits planning a heist.

"Looking good, hot stuff." Stella smacked him on the butt, and I gasped.

Auggie glanced back at her and then turned his attention back to me. We shared a look. I didn't know what it meant, but he had to see the way I was devouring him. The corners of his eyes crinkled like he was smiling, but I couldn't tell with the mask hiding most of his face. I would've loved to see him smile. Had I ever even seen it? He was always frowning around me.

"We're gonna go get her some clothes, and we'll see you in a jiffy." Stella patted Auggie on the shoulder and swung her hips as she left.

Brandy followed behind her with a lot more grace and less flourish.

One by one, the other members of his team returned to the room dressed in equally black, sleek, concealing outfits. There were two women with them. One of them was Jade, the other I didn't know her name, but she was mysterious and voluptuous. She looked like a Bond girl who was totally comfortable in a room full of commandos, as Stella had called them.

They were adjusting things in their ears, slipping on masks, and checking their guns like they did this every morning after breakfast. After a brief meeting, where they restated their assignments, most of them left except Auggie, Steel, and the guy with the scar.

Auggie kept his eyes on his watch as Steel turned toward me. "This is my brother, Vander Knight." Steel, who was also decked out like a spy, pointed to the guy with the scar who held out a gloved hand for me to shake. It was huge and strong when it took mine in his, but he didn't squeeze it hard.

"Time," Auggie said curtly.

He helped me off the exam table and guided me out the door with one hand on each of my shoulders. At the end of the corridor, Vander moved in front of us, and Steel stood behind us. They did all this silently, no one giving directions.

The three of us climbed down several flights of stairs then exited a side door that led to another larger elevator that looked like it was for loading cargo. It opened to a huge warehouse full of metal storage containers.

Another wave of nausea hit me and I struggled to stay conscious. I could easily pass out under all this pressure.

"Almost there," Auggie whispered in my ear.

That gave me the strength I needed to keep walking. We stayed in formation and walked to a black SUV parked in the middle of the warehouse.

Auggie and I got in the back, Steel took the wheel, and Vander folded into the passenger seat. Their eyes were constantly moving, scanning everything.

When the car started up, the interior lights went out, and Steel pulled out of the parking space, another black car pulled out in front of us, and they all looked in the mirrors as a third car rolled in place behind us.

Auggie removed his hands from my shoulders. "You can relax now."

Ha. Easy for him to say. That trip to the car totally stressed me out. We followed the lead car, criss-crossing through the backstreets of the city.

"Aren't we going in circles?" I'd seen the iconic eagle statue on the college campus go by several times.

"Easiest way to spot a tail or lose it," Vander replied.

"Oh."

After another ten minutes of going nowhere, we finally headed onto the expressway and out of downtown Atlanta. All three men remained quiet, and there was no contact from the men in the other cars. They continued to scan the mirrors and windows, but I assumed everything was going fine based on their relaxed postures and lack of words exchanged.

It surprised me how they could coordinate all of this without talking. I felt like blurting out all that I was thinking and everything I saw, but I picked up on the vibe from them that was not what was expected. If Stella were here, she'd probably be breaking the silence with her colorful words, but since it was just me, I kept quiet like I usually did.

We arrived at what I assumed was the Delta site. It looked like a normal free-standing house to me. Big yard, no close neighbors, lots of trees around the edges.

Three cars pulled into the driveway and parked side by side. We were in the middle car. They repeated the shielding me procedure as I entered through a back door. They left wordlessly through the front door.

Finally, once the door was locked and all the windows checked, Auggie took off his mask and hat and set them on a shelf by the door.

"That was interesting."

He stood sideways by the window and looked out with one eye as he peeled the blinds back with a finger.

"We weren't followed."

"No. I would think not. Is it okay if I look around?"

"Sure." He continued to watch out of the window.

The place had one bedroom, a locked door, a kitchen and a dining area. I didn't find anything elaborate that would identify it as a safe house, but maybe that was the point.

I found a clock that said 2:34. Since it was dark outside, that meant it was almost three in the morning. The sun would start coming up soon. I stared at the locked door at the end of the hallway for a long time wondering what might be in there. Guns? Maybe a high-tech computer room with

cameras and buttons that activated killer lasers? It all felt surreal like I would wake up from this dream at any moment
and snap back into reality.

I didn't hear anyone knock, but Auggie moved to the
front door and opened it. Stella and Brandy walked in, both
of them grinning. Stella wheeled a small red suitcase over
to the coffee table in the living room. "The stores are closed
right now so these are mostly things from Brandy's closet,
but we will go shopping in the morning and then bring you
more stuff."

"I don't need more. This is fine." I met them at the couch
and watched Stella open the suitcase. She started pulling out
clothes and tossing them around on the table. "Do not take
away the fun part. What's your favorite color?"

Did I even have a favorite color? I chose gray most of the
time to blend in. "Mossy green," I found myself saying.

"Really?" She paused and looked up at me. "Like algae?"

"Yes."

"Like bad sour cream?" Brandy asked.

"Like a sprout from the soil, like a new twig on an old
tree, like a lily pad floating on a pond." Like Auggie's eyes.

"Bless your heart. Are you one of those?" Stella gave me a
sympathetic smile.

"Those what?"

"A Boho incense frog candle girl?"

"What?" I laughed because I had no idea what she was
referring to. "I just appreciate the colors of nature."

"That's good because I loathe paisley, but I get what you
mean. I like it when my lipstick is the perfect rose red."

"Well, yeah." That wasn't exactly what I meant, but Stella was trying to follow along in her own way. "I mean I guess makeup is inspired by nature."

"You guys gotta go now. She needs to rest." Auggie came into the room and spoke rudely to Stella and Brandy.

They didn't seem to mind and stood quickly as they prepared to go. "It's late. We'll pick up here tomorrow, which is today." Stella hugged my shoulders and kissed my cheek in the sweetest way. Like a sister.

"Thank you so much." It was a completely insufficient way to express my gratitude for all they'd done for me, but I was too tired to come up with more to say.

They left, and Auggie watched them drive away.

He turned back toward the room and gathered up the clothes in the suitcase. He carried it to the bathroom and set it on the counter. "Shower," he ordered and left the room.

I was too tired to argue and showered in a daze.

I didn't put on the nightie Stella had added to the suitcase. I just picked a comfy baby blue hoodie and matching leggings.

The exhaustion of the day hit me hard, and I wandered toward the bed without saying anything to Auggie. I crawled up to the pillow. That was it. I couldn't move if I wanted to. I didn't even know where Auggie was going to sleep or if he ever would. All I knew was that my head had found a pillow, and I felt safe for the first time in a very long time.

***

"Mmm." Warm fingers on my temple woke me from my snoozing. I recognized Auggie's touch from earlier. "Hey."

"Hey."

I turned to the side and found him crouching next to the bed with his head just above mine. "Everything okay?" He'd done such a good job of keeping watch, but he had to be tired by now.

"Yep. You can sleep easy tonight. You're safe now." The finger at my temple trailed through the hair behind my ear.

"Where are you gonna sleep?" I asked him.

"On the couch."

"Oh." Silly me. For a second, I'd thought he might join me in this bed. Of course he wouldn't. This was a safe house and he was keeping me safe. That was it.

He hadn't asked me about Train again, but the guilt of keeping information from him was eating at me. It was considerate of him to give me time to process the reality of what had happened to me, but it was wrong for me to keep it from him any longer. He and his friends had already become deeply involved, and Train was probably making plans to kill them, so he had a right to know what he was up against.

"If I tell you his name, will it help you sleep easy?" I asked him.

He stilled and stared at me for a second. "Yes," he whispered.

"His name is Train."

He squeezed my neck and dropped his head so his forehead was touching mine. His warm, soft breath brushed my cheek. My body instantly responded to his closeness. He was like a huge magnet, and I was a ball of metal. My lips tingled with the urge to kiss him.

"Thank you," he whispered.

Gravity pushed my head closer to his like a force field that I couldn't break if I tried. I tilted my neck back and our lips nearly touched. He didn't pull away, and I couldn't wait for him any longer. It felt natural, like I had to do it or I'd regret it forever.

So I kissed him.

I pressed my mouth to his and caught his upper lip between mine. He turned to stone, the warm breath disappeared, his hand left my neck, and I was left kissing a freaking statue like an idiot.

Gah! Why did I do that? It was so stupid.

He hadn't given me any signs he liked me. He'd laughed at me while he got a blowjob and had been nothing but angry since he'd showed up at the Devil's Advocates compound. But he'd also given me a smile from under his mask, he'd passionately declared that he needed a convoy to protect me, he'd wiped my head and kept his hands on my arms when I walked, and tonight he'd basically hugged me and run his fingers through my hair.

I'd been through a lot of trauma, and I didn't know what to think. Was he just being nice to me because he felt sorry for me, or was something more going on here? It sure felt like something more before I'd kissed him, but now that he was stone man, I was doubting everything.

He stood up slowly and backed away. "Just Train? Any other names?" He cleared his throat and pretended like I didn't just humiliate myself by kissing him. I'd almost forgotten all about Train, but when I heard his name on Auggie's lips, the image of his fists coming at me chilled my bones. It took me a moment to remember Train's given name. It had been so long since anyone referred to him by it.

"His real name is Marcus Ocampo, and he's dangerous. There was a rumor that some guy was informing the cops, and they found him chopped up in the trunk of his car."

I could only see the shadow of Auggie's giant form, but his fists clenched, and I felt the tension rolling off him.

"Ocampo? Are you certain?"

"Yes. He grew up in Lamar Gardens too."

"Were you in Italy with him?"

I'd opened a can of worms by mentioning Train. I knew I shouldn't have done it. Keeping silent was the only way to minimize the damage, but now that it was out there, I owed it to Auggie to share the truth. "No. He sent me there with Rico."

He sighed and walked to the corner of the room and then came back again. Pacing. It seemed like Auggie did this when he was processing information. "And that's when I found you and got you out?" he asked.

"Yes."

"Alright. That's enough for tonight. Get some sleep. Don't worry about Train. He can't get to you here."

"It's hard to believe. I'm so conditioned to worrying."

"I know. That's why we're here. I want you to sleep easy. I don't want to see that terror in your eyes anymore."

Wow. I didn't realize he'd observed so much. Running from Train had taken its toll on my psyche, and it was showing in my face. Auggie noticed it and made all this happen so that I could sleep easy.

"I will for the first time in a long time because of you." I was still afraid of Train, and I wouldn't be able to truly relax until he was behind bars, but for tonight, I believed that he couldn't have figured out Auggie's Ocean's Eleven moves and had no idea where I was.

"Good." He tipped his chin and walked out of the room.

Now, I felt even more confused about the almost kiss we'd shared. Auggie had softened up just now and talked with me openly, but it was only about Train, not about us or kissing.

I shouldn't let my mind conjure up these ideas of us to-gether. Stella had made it worse by insisting something was going to happen between us. From the way he'd turned to stone, I knew I'd crossed a line I shouldn't have. Auggie was just the kind of guy who helped women in trouble. He'd do the same thing for any other woman he came across. It didn't mean I was special to him and he wanted to kiss me.

That was it. I wouldn't try to kiss him or get close to him again. If anything was going to happen between us, it would have to be him who made the move.

Chapter 9 Rosebud

The clock said 10:09 when I woke up to sunlight breaking through the curtains. My head spun as I shuffled to the bathroom, but most of the pounding headache had subsided. My face did not look great. The swelling on my eye had turned from red to blue and yellow. No wonder he didn't want to kiss me last night. I looked like the walking dead.

My muscles felt bruised all over, but at least it wasn't as painful as yesterday. I washed my face gently and dried it. I didn't have any makeup, and there was nothing I could do to hide it, so I just headed out to look for Auggie.

I found him standing at the kitchen counter. He'd changed into gray sweatpants that narrowed at the ankle. His tight maroon cotton tee stretched around his biceps that were flexed as he spread something with a knife. Maybe I hadn't seen him in short sleeves before or maybe I hadn't noticed, but his black and red arm tattoo wrapped from his wrist all the way up to his elbow. The neck of his shirt hung low, and I could see the legs of a spider crawling near his collar bone.

I liked seeing him in casual clothes with his shoulders relaxed. It felt like we were living together. Mmm. Waking up to this sight every day would not be a bad life.

On further inspection, it appeared he was preparing peanut butter and jelly sandwiches. That actually sounded really good because I was starving.

"Hey."

He glanced at me and winced when he saw my face. His shoulders drew up as he went back to making sandwiches. "You feeling okay?" he asked me.

"It feels a lot better. Thanks."

"Good." He stopped and made eye contact with me, and my tummy did an involuntary little flip. "I have a meeting with the team. Stella and Brandy are gonna be here in a minute to keep you company. Talon and Magnum will be guarding you."

Wow. He'd made a lot of plans while I was sleeping. "Okay."

He turned back to spreading the peanut butter on the bread. "If you need someone to talk to, you can trust Stella and Brandy."

Oh. I didn't expect him to say that. "Okay. Thank you. I like them."

He nodded but didn't say anything else. There was less anger pouring off of him than last night, but he was still an impenetrable iceberg in frigid waters.

Stella and Brandy arrived and handed me loads of shopping bags stuffed with clothes and other goodies.

We sat down on the couch and placed the bags on the coffee table. "This is more stuff than I've ever owned in my life."

"Go ahead, look." Stella grinned and peeked into the bags.

I went through each one, pulling out beautiful articles of clothing that I didn't deserve. Lots of moss green and embroidered leaves, but also pastel yellow, pink, and lavender. All soft colors.

Then I pulled out a bright red lacy camisole. Not something I would normally wear, but it was beautiful.

"That's from me." Stella raised her hand. "You can't wear a moss neglige. Eww."

We all laughed, but I also felt like crying. Their kindness continually overwhelmed me.

From the bottom of one of the bags, I pulled out a box with a picture of a red plastic object. "What's this?" I turned the box around but couldn't find a description.

Brandy giggled and looked away.

Stella grabbed it and held it sideways to show me the picture. "It's a vibe. It spins *and* vibrates." She opened the lid and pulled it out, holding it up in the air like a diamond. It was shaped like a rosebud with a little open circle at the tip.

"Stella." Brandy covered it with her hand. "My gosh."

The laugh that came from deep in my gut burst out of me loudly. One thing about me they didn't know. I loved to masturbate, and I definitely needed to after the unrequited heat I felt with Auggie last night. I tucked it in the pocket of my hoodie as I winked at them. "Thank you. I love it."

Stella gave Brandy an *I told you so* look, and we all grinned like idiots for a little while.

My lips quivered trying to hold it in when Auggie handed me a plate with a sandwich sliced neatly down the center. He glared at Stella as he placed a glass of water on the table in the middle of all the bags. "I'm going to check the perimeter." Auggie was all business all the time, and we were being silly, but I needed to laugh too. It felt great. How long had it been since I'd had a good chuckle with girlfriends? Forever?

My only friends had been the strippers at the club and their kids when they hung out. We did have some good times, but after I lost my best girlfriend in a drive-by shooting, I didn't get close to anyone again. I felt like everyone around me ended up dead, but Stella and Brandy were forcing their way through the barriers I'd hid behind for too long.

"Okay. Bye." I wiggled my fingers at him and shared a conspiratorial look with my new friends.

He stepped outside, and we all let out another round of quiet giggles as we watched his figure pass by the window. I took a bite of the sandwich. The peanut butter and jelly blended perfectly and the bread was fresh and sweet.

"So, give us the dirt." Stella rubbed her hands together quickly. "Did you do the wango tango?"

"What? No." I tried to talk with my mouth full. I'm sure it wasn't attractive.

She shrugged and held up her bent arms, palms up. "Third base?"

I took a sip of the water and swallowed the food. "Nope. He didn't even pitch a ball."

"He didn't?" Brandy frowned. "I thought for sure he'd make a move."

"Actually." I hesitated and set my sandwich back on the plate. I wasn't sure what I should tell them, but Auggie had told me I could trust them. "He came close and our lips had a near miss."

Stella leaned back and laughed. "Awesome."

"Nope. Not so great. He froze up and left me like I was a leper. Didn't see him again until this morning."

"Did you talk?" Brandy asked me.

"Not really. He's not much of a talker. It's like there's this brick wall around him. He's hyper focused on keeping me safe but nothing else."

Brandy nodded.

Stella scrunched her lips and nose together. "I think it's more than that. He reminds me of Helix. It's hard as hell to get him to talk. Especially when he gets home from a mission. We've known each other forever and have barely scratched the surface."

I didn't know which one of the guys was Helix, but I could relate to her description. "Yes. It's like that."

"It's like trying to open a can after you've pulled the tab off and can't put it back on," Stella said.

"It's like the lid of a pickle jar that won't twist off no matter how many times you tap it on the kitchen tile," Brandy said and evoked a laugh from all of us.

"It's like trying to pull a turtle's head out of his shell." I added my analogy which drew more laughter.

"More like pulling his head out of his ass." Stella grumbled and then held up a finger. "I have an idea. If you can't rip the lid of a can, you take a can opener and force that puppy off with sheer determination and crank power."

"I don't know if I have any crank power," I admitted.

"If you could go anywhere, where would you choose?" She stared at me like everything depended on my answer.

I had never even thought of going anywhere. I'd lived my life in the projects, and the furthest I'd ever gone was a walk to the junior college or out to the reservoir.

"I really can't go anywhere."

"But if you could, what would you choose?" She wasn't going to give up until I gave her an answer, so I thought hard about it. I loved the lake and the treasures I found along the shore.

"The beach. I love seashells and rocks."

"That is not why I go to the beach. I go for cabana boys and margaritas, but to each his own. A lot depends on what happens at that meeting today, but based on what they decide, I'll implement my own plan."

"We probably shouldn't mess with Auggie. He's hard core," I warned her.

Stella brushed me off with a wave of her hand. "All these guys are puppy dogs underneath it all."

I seriously doubted that, but she knew them better than me.

"Steel is not really a puppy dog." Brandy shook her head. "He's pretty much a beast underneath, but I'm able to tame it. Sometimes. Most of the time I have to step back and let him blow things up."

Stella nodded. "This is also wise but not my thing. I don't let 'em get away with the whole bull-in-a-china-shop routine. They are human beings, and they have normal human needs and wants. They just deny it longer than most, but deep inside they crave love and belonging."

"And sex," Brandy added. "Lots of hot sex."

Auggie entered the room with a serious scowl, and we pressed our lips together to stifle the giggles. I took a bite of the sandwich to hide my smile.

"I'm leaving now. The unit is secure, Talon and Mag are in position. You don't leave no matter what. You don't answer the door. Let them handle anything that comes up."

I gave him a salute. "Aye, Aye, Captain." I still had food in my mouth, so it came out extra geeky.

He rolled his eyes, but I could swear I saw his lips quirk up.

Chapter 10 Stupid Boy

As soon as Auggie left, Stella grabbed a separate canvas bag from the floor and sauntered off to the kitchen. "Mimosa time," she pulled three glasses and a bottle of champagne out of the bag like Mary Poppins. Her questioning gaze surveyed the kitchen then stopped on me. "Does this place have orange juice?"

"I don't know." I laughed. This was not my place. All I'd done here was sleep for a few hours.

After looking in the fridge, she made a goofy face, tongue out, eyes bugged, as she held the door open. "Looks like we're just having champagne then."

I loved Stella. She emitted an infectious radiance that made all the negative stuff seem insignificant.

"Wait a minute. Auggie said you stock this place? There were fresh bananas?"

She pursed her lips. "I pay the people who stock the safe houses. I don't micromanage, but clearly I need to make sure they bring orange juice for mimosas in the future."

She proceeded to pull food out of her bag and set it up artfully on a wooden board. "This is my world famous charcuterie."

"What's that?" I asked her.

"You're about to find out."

I joined her in the kitchen. "Can I help?"

She looked at me doubtfully. "Sure. You can open this wheel of brie and cut off the rind. Now some folks say you can eat that white crap, but I say hell to the no on that. No to the mold. You with me?"

I had no idea what she was talking about, and I'd never even heard of brie. "Oh. Um. I was thinking more like washing grapes or something."

Brandy joined us in the kitchen and took the wrapped wheel from Stella. "I'll prep the brie. Haven, you relax because you're injured and recovering."

"I'm feeling much better today."

"Still. Have a seat and relax." She pointed to a barstool by the counter.

I figured Stella and Brandy could handle the fancy board preparation, and I took a seat. Stella poured me a glass of champagne. I didn't drink it though. Alcohol was the last thing my body needed to heal, and it looked sort of caustic with the bubbles fizzing in there.

"I'm cooking up a plan to get you two alone together so you can shuck the shell off that clam." Stella picked up our conversation from the living room assuming we'd all follow along.

"Is Auggie the clam?" I asked.

"Yes. He's locked up tight like a hard-as-nails cockle." She pointed at me with the knife she was wielding on a long, thin loaf of bread.

I chuckled. "Assuming a cockle is a clam and Auggie is the cockle, your plan, whatever it is, is not a good idea."

"It is."

I fiddled with the stem of my glass. "He doesn't like me. He's just doing all of this to protect me."

She shook her head. "I know these men. They do not take up causes that don't pay. He canceled a trip overseas that would've earned him triple time. Thousands of dollars to stay here with you. He digs you."

"Ugh." I threw my head back and sighed. "I dig him too."

"Yas, girl. Mmm-hmm."

"But not in the way you're describing. I dig him like a school girl digs Thor. Not in any real-world application. He might as well be a superhero up on the screen. That's how much of a chance I have with him. He is so far out of my league, this conversation is embarrassing."

Brandy stayed quiet as she worked on unwrapping the cheese. Stella listened and opened her mouth like she wanted to interrupt and then closed it again like she was holding back. When I stopped talking, she jumped in. "I don't believe that. You underestimate yourself. I do it too. We all do."

She may have been right, but it was complicated with Auggie. I decided to tell them the one thing that was bothering me the most. "I caught him getting a blowjob from a biker babe."

Brandy paused and gasped. "You what?"

"At a party at the Devil's Advocate's compound. I heard her laughing, the door was open, he saw me and posed for pictures."

Stella moved slowly as she placed the board of food in front of me. "That sucks, girl. I'm so sorry that happened, but something doesn't add up. Auggie is trained in the art of deception. If he got caught that means he wanted to be seen. He did it to make you jealous."

"Or get back at me." I'd had that thought too when I'd first seen him with Crystal but found it hard to believe he'd really done it for that reason.

"Yes. Stupid boy." She poured herself a glass of champagne and came to sit next to me.

"I was pretty awful to him." He'd risked his life and everything to rescue me from human traffickers and give me a private plane ride to the States, and I'd walked out on him the second we'd hit the ground. He didn't know I was terrified of Train, but that was why I called Cyrus to pick me up. I didn't want Auggie involved in my mess of a life.

"He was looking for you. He came to me and asked how to find Duke, and I set him up." Stella eyed me sideways as she took a sip from her champagne flute.

"Really?"

"Yep. He sought you out and found you then pulled that act with the biker babe."

Brandy placed the round white cheese on the board and sat next to me on my other side. "That's just wrong in so many ways. No matter what you did, he shouldn't use another woman to make you jealous. Not to mention going out of his way to find you and then use her to get back at you. I don't like it at all."

Stella dove into the brie with a round knife and managed to scoop out a dollop of the goo and spread it on a slice of bread. "I believe Auggie lacks social skills. He's been in the military culture too long plus growing up in Russia..."

My eyes snapped to Stella's. "Whoa, whoa. Wait. He's Russian?"

"Yes. He hides it well, but the accent comes out when he drinks vodka."

"I saw him drink tequila, and he didn't speak with an accent. Of course, he didn't say much while Crystal was sucking his dick."

She frowned. "Like I said, stupid move on his part. He shouldn't have done it. He probably regrets it. I don't know. I do know that tequila and vodka are not the same poison to him."

"Ahh. I see."

"That's about all I can tell you about him. You'll have to find out the rest when you're alone with him. Men always start talking after sex."

Oh my. I had to cough to clear my clogged throat. "I'm really not sure I can do that. You're a grown woman with breasts. I'm a girl from the projects whose sexual awakening was cut short by a kidnapper, and my boobs are half their normal size right now because I've been on the run."

I heard a gasp. "You were kidnapped?" Brandy asked.

Oops. I'd kinda let that slip. Oh well, Auggie said I could trust them. "Yeah. A guy named Train grabbed me off the street, held me in a house with some other girls, then sent me to Italy where Auggie found me."

Brandy wrapped her arm over my shoulders and gave me a squeeze. "I saw you at Rico's sex party in Rome. I wanted to save everyone, but I just couldn't. And I was sick. I hated to leave you behind."

"It's okay. It worked out. Auggie came in and asked me to leave with him, and we snuck out the back."

I'd forgotten that in a way she'd left me behind in Rome. I didn't hold a grudge, so maybe I understood better why she and Stella weren't still angry at me.

Stella handed me a plate with crackers, meat, grapes, and cheese. "Start eating, girl. Get those boobs back. Auggie wants you. I'm sure of it. He won't care about all this stuff you're worried about."

I'd already had a few bites of the sandwich, but I took a cracker with cheese from the board. "How do you know that? He's not giving me any signs." She seemed so certain of this, but I had no reason to believe Auggie was interested in anything but protecting me from Train.

"He's a man of action. Not words. He's putting himself out there for you big time. He got his ego bruised when you brushed him off. He didn't handle it well, but he also didn't know you were on the run. He'll forgive you, and you'll forgive him just like we forgave each other for the screw ups in the past. You'll get through this."

"I've never even been with a real man. Only dildos." Stella froze, and Brandy sputtered champagne on the kitchen counter. "My mom spread rumors about me plus Cyrus' dad, Eugene, sorta adopted me as a daughter and made sure none of the neighborhood boys touched me. After he died, I decided my big move would be to go to the junior college. I met a guy there that was so geeky, he didn't know what to do. We made out a little bit, but I'd call it a big failure. I was working up the nerve to try something crazy. Have a one-night stand for my first time, just to get it over with, then I got kidnapped, and I've been on the run ever since."

Brandy put her hand on my knee. "Oh my gosh, Haven. You've been through so much."

"You tell him this. He'll love it all. Well, not the kidnapping part, but the virgin part, yes. He'll love that. He'll know what to do. He might not be gentle about it, but he's been around. He knows how to handle a woman."

Everything she was saying was not making me feel better. If he was used to worldly women, I was definitely not his type. "I doubt he will be attracted to an inexperienced girl like me."

"He will see in you what I do. A gilded heart. No matter your roots. My background isn't Park Avenue either. I grew up on the South Side. I fake it till I make it a lot." She added a piece of bread stacked with brie and some kind of orange jelly to my plate.

"Well, you're good at it. I should learn from you."

"I am no role model. Trust me. My love life is a mess."

I took a bite of the bread, cheese, jelly mixture she'd offered. It was weird and creamy and salty and sweet, but somehow it all worked together and was yummy. "Are you seeing someone?"

Stella leaned forward and braced her elbows on the counter. "Promise not to tell?"

"Of course."

"Helix and I had a thing." She pressed her lips together and looked up at me through her lashes. "But we also have history which means we can't have a thing."

"What history?" I asked her.

"When my brother died, he stepped in. We're unofficial siblings. My mom thinks of us both as her kids." She lowered her chin and leveled her pretty brown eyes on me. "We can't fuck." She sounded extremely disappointed with this news.

"But you did?"

"Once." She held up one finger and grinned at the memory. "It was a mistake. Won't happen again."

I had trouble believing her. She clearly wanted him. If they loved each other, they should be together regardless of what their family thought of them. "Why don't I plan something for you and Helix where you'll be forced to be alone with him?"

"Nope. Not happening. Me and Helix are social distancing. Keeping his giant cock at least six feet away from my no-no zone."

"Giant?" Brandy asked.

Stella's eyes grew big and round. "Humongous. More like seven feet of distance is required when he's erect if you know what I mean."

We all cackled loudly, and Stella and Brady shared a high-five. Hanging out with these women was my new favorite pastime.

"Anyway." Stella looked at me. "I want a report on Auggie's equipment when you get back."

"Oh my." My cheeks flushed with heat. "I don't think I will ever be seeing Auggie's equipment. If I did, I wouldn't know what to do with it."

"Like I said, he'll know what to do." She nodded her head knowingly. I admired her confidence, but I seriously could not imagine anything like that actually happening.

"I'm with Haven on this one." Brandy spoke up, and we all turned to listen to her. "I don't think we should force it.

He was with another girl to make her jealous? What else will he do when he's angry? I didn't know Auggie was vindictive like that. He's too quiet. Too closed up. She could get hurt, and she needs someone she can depend on after all she's been through. I'm sorry, but I don't see Auggie being that guy."

Stella chewed her lip. "If he apologizes for the blowjob and continues to fight for you like he's doing, I'm sticking with Team Auggie. If he doesn't do those two things or pulls any more dick moves, I'm Team Rosebud. You recharge the batteries in that thing, you don't need a stupid boy to make you happy."

Chapter 11 Forced Downtime

We swallowed our laughter when the front door opened and Auggie walked into the kitchen. He carried a large backpack on his shoulder as he eyed us cautiously. "What were you talking about?" He placed the pack on the table. "Nevermind. I don't wanna know."

"I'll never tell," Stella said.

"Me either," Brandy teased.

Auggie shook his head and worked on unpacking. He gave us a lovely view of his tight ass as he bent over his bag. Narrow waist, thick thighs, broad shoulders with muscles bending and twisting under his tee. Stella poked her tongue in her cheek and mouthed, "Team Auggie."

As if he could sense her taunting, he turned and gave her the evil eye.

Stella cleared her throat. "So how was the meeting?" Her fake smile was totally adorable.

"Not great. The hunt for Train is on ice for a while till the feds get their shit together."

"The feds? Like the FBI?" My voice rose in pitch at the end.

"Yeah," he answered casually without looking at me.

"I didn't want them involved." I'd told him that last night. I didn't want to end up chopped up into pieces in the trunk of a car.

"Me either, but they've already got a bead on him. Marcus Ocampo has been on their most-wanted list for a long time, and they made it clear I'm expected to keep my distance from their op unless I'm invited to participate." His voice rang with bitter sarcasm.

"So you have a break?" Stella asked. "I heard you're not going on the big overseas mission."

He glanced at her with one brow raised. "Correct. I'm not going." His gaze finally slid to me after avoiding eye contact since he'd been in the house.

"I have an excellent idea. I know just the place where you guys can get some R and R."

"Don't start, Stella."

"You both need to get away from all this."

He propped his hands on his hips and scowled at her. "I need to find out all I can about Ocampo and his operation so I can take them down."

"The feds told you to back off for a little bit." Stella was very brave to keep sparing with a visibly hostile Auggie.

"I don't do what I'm told." The muscles in his neck were tight. Stella was poking the bear.

"Auggie," Stella still did not give up, "Haven has been through a traumatic experience. She's terrified. She needs to recuperate. And you look like shit yourself. You need some downtime."

His brow furrowed, and his voice grew even more frustrated. "I don't take downtime."

"I could have Vander force you."

I nearly gasped out loud. Stella was the bravest fool I'd ever met.

He took a deep breath and turned away from her. "Stella. Get the fuck out of here."

"Fine." She stood and winked at me. "I need to talk to Vander about something anyway."

Oh no. Stella was taking this over Auggie's head. The woman had no fear.

She packed up her stuff and hugged me on her way out. Brandy was very quiet the entire time, and I kept thinking about what she'd said. *I don't like it. I don't see Auggie being that guy.*

"Let us know if you need anything else." Brandy rubbed my upper arm.

"Thank you so much."

Stella leaned in for a hug and whispered in my ear, "If my plan works out, you won't be needing that rosebud for long." She pulled me into her chest and squeezed. It caused a little pain in my bruised areas, but it was okay. I enjoyed her hug through the pain.

Brandy hugged me more gently, and they left with lots of smiles and winks. Their visit brightened up a very dark situation. No matter what happened with Auggie, I'd never betray them again, and I'd always be grateful for the help they gave me when I was at my lowest.

After they left, I hesitated to bring it up with Auggie, but I was nervous about him talking to the authorities.

"So what exactly happened with the FBI?"

"Ocampo is the head of a worldwide human trafficking ring. Did you know this?" He removed a rifle from his pack and placed it on the table.

"Worldwide trafficking? No. I mean I knew he was dangerous and powerful but not that."

"They want to take him and his cohorts down in a big sting. They don't want me to kill him." He slammed a box of something heavy on the table. Bullets to go with all the guns he was unearthing from the pack?

"You'd kill him?" I took a few steps closer to him.

"Yes. In a heartbeat. But they said no. This makes me angry."

"I can see that."

Now that Stella had told me he was Russian, and he was finally talking to me, I was starting to hear the accent more. Subtle little differences in emphasis and phrasing.

He grunted and fussed with the contents of his pack. What he did not do was look at me.

Where was Stella getting these ideas that he cared about me? I wasn't seeing it. I was seeing a pissed off mercenary who was hungry for his next kill. It had very little to do with me.

"Is it true?" he asked me over his shoulder.

"What?"

"You're terrified? Even here? After I told you you're safe."

I sighed. "I believe I'm safe here. It's only been a day. I'm still nervous, and Train has been messing with my head for a long time. I can't just turn that off."

"Are you ready to tell me about it?"

"Yes, but not right now exactly." It wasn't hard to share with Stella and Brandy, but Auggie's nostrils were flared, and all his muscles were tight. Telling him the details of my kidnapping and subsequent stalking would only make it worse.

"Do you think you need a vacation?" He looked at my hands which were clenched tightly together.

"I don't know how that would help. He finds me wherever I go. I'll always be afraid." My voice wavered.

"What if he's dead? Will you still be afraid?"

"He doesn't work alone. He has an army of loyal subjects. If you kill him, I'd be worried about starting another war. He'll kill you and everyone you love. He'll go after Stella and Brandy. You see why we can't do this?" I sounded crazy but the memory of the attack was still fresh in my mind. I didn't want anything like that to happen to my new friends.

He put down what he was doing and walked over to me. He sat next to me on the couch. "Ocampo is not the first egomaniac crime lord I've gone up against. Me and my team eat guys like him for breakfast. With the feds behind us, we can't lose. You have to believe me. We do have to wait for the right time, but he will go down with his inner circle, and they will all rot in prison if they survive the raid."

"It's true," I said.

"What?"

"I'm terrified."

His big hand reached out behind my neck, and he brought me in for a hug as he pressed my cheek to his hard chest. "I know. I see it in your eyes. When this is over, he'll be gone. I'm looking forward to seeing your face when you're free of those ghosts."

Okay, maybe some of this did have to do with me, and perhaps Stella was right about a few things. "That would be awesome. I wouldn't know what to do with myself if I wasn't worrying about Train catching me all the time."

"You'll find something. What do you like to do?"

I was trying to think of an answer when he pulled back and checked his phone. He took a call and listened for a long time. His forehead slowly bent down into a serious crease. "No fucking way, Vander. No."

He listened again, and his teeth ground together, jaw tight. "It's not a good time for a vacation." He rolled his eyes. "Okay." He ended the call and looked at me. "Fucking Stella convinced Vander to give me forced downtime. We're leaving for Jamaica tomorrow."

"Wow. Jamaica?" I didn't even know where Jamaica was. All I knew about Jamaica was Bob Marley. This sounded like a dream. I'd never even left the projects.

"Stella doesn't do anything small. It's all larger than life, and we're her next victims. Some exclusive beach resort." His voice was extremely unenthusiastic about doing something amazing like going to another country and staying at a resort.

Uh oh. Traveling meant flying. "Do we have to take a plane?"

"Yes."

"I'm afraid of fly," I admitted.

"I remember."

So he'd noticed on the plane home from Italy that I was scared. I was trying to hide it but I guess I sucked at it.

"Maybe a trip is a good way to face your fears."

Okay, both Stella and Auggie were way too into persuading me to face my fears. I'd done that yesterday. I'd fought Train as hard as I could and lost. My breath hitched and tears sprung up, making my sight blurry. I'd be strong enough to face this someday, but not today while my eye hurt, my knees were sore, and my ability to face any of these fears felt like it was hiding under a shell.

"Hey," he said gently and brought my cheek back to his chest. I couldn't hold back. His warmth and strength pulled the tears from me, and I heaved it out. Why did my life have to be so unfair? Why did I have to hide from Train all the time when there were nice guys out there like Auggie? Why did I always feel so weak when I wanted to be strong? Because being brave was scary as hell. Auggie was good at it. Stella could do it, but me, nope. Being brave would just get us all killed like it did my mother and all my friends.

"You need some time to process what happened. Stella's idea isn't bad. When you're ready to talk about it, I'll be there."

Wow. That was shockingly nice, and he'd said similar things before.

"It's okay to be scared," he said like he'd read my mind.

"I shouldn't let him get to me, but he does. He does all the time, and whenever I think I've broken free, he shows up again and smashes me down and reminds me he could kill me and sell my organs."

His hand stiffened on my neck. "What?"

"When he catches me, he threatens to kill me and sell my organs. He hasn't done it yet. I'm just lucky to be alive, but it's coming. I know he'll come through on his threat as soon as he finds out I'm alive and I talked to the FBI."

"He's harvesting organs?"

"I don't know if he's really doing it. It could just be a threat, but he has no respect for human life. He's horrible, and he gets away with it every time." I hated the weakness in my voice. I hated that Train had this power over me.

"Not this time. Okay? Not this time. You need a break right now, so you can recover emotionally and physically, but you'll be safe. I'll guard you with my life. Then when we get back, he'll pay for all the misery he's created. I promise you."

I looked up at him and nodded. He stared at my lips, and I felt that pull toward him again. This time I knew better than to try and kiss him after the thorough rejection last time. Instead I wet my lips with my tongue and bit my bottom lip with my teeth. His hand tightened on my neck again, and his eyes grew dark. If he wanted to kiss me, now was his chance.

"You're really beautiful. You know that?"

I laughed. "No, I'm not." I was a mess.

"I hate seeing you like this." He touched my temple with the tip of his index finger. "The fear in your eyes, knowing he took his fists to you. It all drives me insane." His face moved even closer, and I caught a hint of his scent. He smelled clean and fresh like water. God, I wanted him to kiss me so badly, I nearly screamed.

"I made a deal with the feds. I don't kill him, and you don't testify. He won't know you're involved at all. You will not have to relive whatever happened to you in a courtroom, and you will not have to fear retribution from his gang of criminals."

"You did that for me?"

He nodded. "It wasn't easy. My skin itches with the need to hunt him down and make him suffer until he cries like a baby before I take his life with a knife to his throat."

"Um." Auggie's intensity scared me and flattered me. It showed he cared, but it was also a little scary how easily he spoke of murdering someone.

His hands left my face, and he stood up, taking a step back from the couch. "Maybe I need some downtime too."

"You do seem a little stressed." That was an understatement, but I didn't know that wasn't Auggie's constant state of being. I guessed I'd find out if we went on vacation together.

He nodded and mumbled something about prepping and making calls. Once again, he'd left me confused. It had really seemed like he'd wanted to kiss me. He'd said that he hated seeing me in pain, and he would kill Train because of it. Stella was so sure about him, but I still had my doubts. Auggie did what came naturally to him, protecting people and fighting evil. He obviously felt very strongly about it. I was lucky he was protecting me because I had a lot of confidence in him. As far as kissing though, if he'd wanted to kiss me, he'd had two chances and decided against it. Auggie was a true mystery.

I didn't have too much time to ponder it though because I was leaving for Jamaica in the morning, and I needed to talk to Stella about helping me pack.

Chapter 12 Overwater Bungalow

Turned out Jamaica was only a three hour flight from Atlanta. All these years I'd lived there, and I'd never known. Auggie was his usual silent self during the trip to the airport. He'd remained alert yet calm as we were again the center car in a convoy of commandos. His head had constantly scanned the windows. I didn't feel the confusion and panic I'd felt the first time they'd done this. Now I knew they were Navy SEALs turned private military contractors, and I was their security detail. I felt special. I felt safe. I was getting this treatment for free. I'm sure it would cost anyone else thousands of dollars for their time and expertise.

Stella and Brandy didn't come to the airport, but Steel, Vander, and Magnum gave me a warm sendoff with waves and knowing grins that had me wondering if there was an inside joke I was missing.

Now that I knew more about them, I saw more in their interactions. They didn't smile often, but they made a lot of eye contact, they had a synergy together, a vibe that was impossible to deny. If I had a camera, I'd take a picture of their firm handshakes, the meaningful smacks on the arm and back that they gave to Auggie, the strong nods from one square jaw to another. So much was said with their body language, it was almost deafening.

Maybe that's what Stella meant when she'd said Auggie was a man of action. I needed to start listening to the cues his body was sending me. If I did that, oh boy, maybe I knew why they were grinning because Auggie's body had been close to mine, gripping my shoulders, clenching his jaw when I talked about Train, offering hugs when I felt scared, and nearly kissing me twice. Even when I'd caught him with Crystal, he was telling me things, and I hadn't been listening.

I didn't have time to think about how scary this information was because a greater fear took its place as the plane taxied down the runway and lifted off. Like when we'd left Rome, we were the only passengers on a private jet. Auggie had briefly greeted the pilot then come to sit next to me in a lush leather chair with plenty of legroom. When the plane started to shake and rattle, I gripped the armrest so tight, my knuckles turned white.

Auggie turned his head slightly toward me and placed his big warm palm over mine. I could feel it. I got the message. He understood I was scared, and he was comforting me.

It worked too. Auggie had probably been on many flights in his life, some much less safe than this luxurious jet. I'd seen pictures of military men cramped inside huge cargo holds of giant planes. Their seats were their packs.

Once the plane leveled out, I decided to ask him about it. I was curious how much he was willing to share with me.

"Have you flown a lot?"

"Yes," he answered curtly but left the door open for a follow up.

"In the Navy?"

His head turned fully toward me, and he removed his hand from its place over mine. "Stella told you?"

"Yes."

He nodded. "Well then, yes, lots of planes, ships, and tanks in the Navy. Submarines in the Russian army."

Good. He was offering more information than what I'd asked.

"What's it like on a submarine?"

"Nothing like this. What else did Stella tell you?"

"She said that you were a man of action, not words so much."

"True."

"Do you like Stella?"

He chewed his lip as he thought about it. "Yes," he decided, "I like Stella."

I grinned because it was funny he had to think about it so long.

During the rest of the flight, I asked him more questions about planes, submarines, and ships. His words flowed easily when he talked about the details of the sleeping conditions, the food, the risks. He seemed to accept all the hardships as part of the job and didn't complain much. He even mentioned some of the places he'd been. Afghanistan, Iraq, Syria, Colombia, and several seas I'd never heard of. He didn't mention Russia again and I didn't ask, but I really wanted to hear about what it was like growing up in Russia. Even more so, I wanted to know how he'd ended up in the American Navy.

His eyes lit when he talked about the biggest, the fastest, the most-elite ships, weapons, and teams he'd been on. He became vague when I asked about awards and honors he'd received. I had a feeling he'd earned a lot of respect during his time in the Navy and was a decorated veteran. Oh my God. I would kill to see pictures of Auggie in his uniform. Shiny dress blues, shorn hair, his beautiful eyes under a sailor's cap.

"Were you scared?" I asked him.

"When?"

"When you were deployed in a tough situation knowing there were hidden enemies all around?"

He lifted the armrest and leaned in close. He looked into my eyes, and I held my breath. Wow. "I was scared. Many nights I thought I wouldn't survive to see the light of day. But I believed in myself, in my skills, my training, my drive, and most importantly, my team. The fear doesn't go away. You learn to overcome it, to be strong despite it, use it to motivate you to get even, to force justice to speed up, and to survive and make sure the people you love make it through too."

Holy moly. Auggie was intense. He lived in a world so different from mine. But then again, the people I loved were struggling to survive too, just in Lamar Gardens in Atlanta. Maybe I did understand him more than I'd thought possible.

I took a deep breath to break the trance he had me in and pretended to be very interested in the view out of the window. A land mass appeared amidst all the never ending blue water. "Is that it? Are we there?"

He leaned even closer to look out too, and the heat of his body washed over me like a caress. "Yes," he said low and deep.

How could he make the word *yes* so darn sexy?

My hands started to shake. The runway looked like a tiny strip squished between a lot of water and a lush green hillside. One miscalculation, and we'd crash land in the beautiful blue water.

"Have you ever been on vacation?" he asked me.

I laughed. "No. My mom didn't take vacations. She was always working or partying. We didn't have a lot of money to spare." That was a nice way of saying we were dirt poor and struggling to get through each day.

The plane started to descend, and my stomach lurched. He sat back in his chair and casually placed his hand over mine. "It's only fair I should tell you that Cyrus informed me about your mother." He sounded very formal when my mother was anything but formal. She was a hot mess.

I pulled my gaze from the treacherous approach and looked at him. "He did? What did he say?"

"He said she was a stripper at his father's club. She told everyone she didn't know who your father was so she had them all thinking they were related to you."

"Yes. It was crazy. I don't even look like any of them."

"He told me she started a turf war and that reputation also follows you."

"Yes." I looked down. This was so embarrassing. "They think I'll start a war too, but I'm nothing like her. She was gossipy and loved the drama. I never get involved in stuff like that."

"I can tell you that whatever your mother did doesn't reflect on you. You are your own person. Don't carry it around anymore."

"Thank you. That's a nice thing to say."

Auggie squeezed my hand. "We just landed in Montego Bay."

Out my window, I saw the runway below the wing, and the brightly colored buildings of the airport moving closer. "I didn't even notice. You distracted me."

He grinned. "It worked."

"It did."

Auggie thanked the pilot and helped me down the stairs. It didn't take long to get a rental car and before I knew it, we were driving along a gorgeous stretch of white beach.

"What is that out on the water?" From the road, a series of thatched-roof huts supported by round white pillars appeared to be floating over the turquoise blue water.

"That's where we're staying."

I gasped and stared at him to see if he was laughing. He looked serious. "No way."

"As I said, Stella lives large. Overwater bungalows."

The phrase sounded so odd, but that was exactly what I was looking at. Bungalows suspended above the water.

A handsome young Jamaican man in a white suit introduced himself as Rajerio. "I will be your butler."

I'd never had a butler in my life. I'd never even had a maid or any help at all. Rajerio carried my bags, and Auggie carried his own. We followed him down a long narrow wooden pier to the bungalow at the end.

My mouth nearly hung on the floor when I saw the inside of the bungalow. Glossy wood, luscious plants, everything was clean and top notch. The most stunning part was the views from every room. Water was everywhere. Most of the walls were windows that had been slid open. One set of stairs off the bedroom led to an infinity pool that was exactly the same color as the ocean. Another set of stairs off the living room disappeared into the water instead of a concrete sidewalk or grass like you would expect.

Rajerio placed my bags on a luggage rack in the bedroom and pointed to a fancy golden sash hanging from the ceiling. "Simply ring the bell if you need anything at all. You don't need to leave your villa if you do not wish. Everything will be provided for you."

"Thank you."

He bowed and turned to leave.

Auggie stopped him. "Rajerio."

He smiled at Auggie.

"Miss Woodward is a bit of a celebrity, and she's here on a getaway for seclusion. Do you understand me?"

Audrey Woodward was the name I'd used to fly here. Auggie lied easily about my celebrity status. I certainly didn't look like a celebrity in my sweatpants and hoodie, a bandage on my face, and hair up in a messy bun.

"Of course."

"If you see anyone suspicious that might be paparazzi or fans trying to catch a glimpse, you should intercept them immediately and then bring it to my attention."

"Certainly. I will keep an extra eye out for you."

"Excellent." Auggie slipped him a bill, and Rajerio left us alone in the room. That was a smart idea to enlist Rajerios help in watching out for us. He was probably very alert and familiar with the resort. He'd notice anything out of the ordinary fairly quickly.

I stood there taking in all the luxurious details as Auggie checked the bathroom like he was looking for a burglar.

One gorgeous bed draped in netting and huge palm leaves sat ominously in the center of the room. The last two nights, Auggie had slept on the couch at the safe house. Where would he sleep tonight?

"Can you swim?" Auggie asked me after he'd checked the closet, which seemed a little late because we were already here, and if I couldn't swim I'd be panicking.

"A little. I swam in the lake before. A few backyards with above-ground pools. Never in the ocean."

"There's a first time for everything."

What did he mean by that? His tone felt steeped in innuendo. Did Stella tell him my secret? If she did, I couldn't blame her. It was who she was. She spoke the truth to people. I admired that about her even if she revealed private stuff about me.

"Do you think there's any way Train could find me here?" I asked him.

"No." He finished his inspection and leaned back on his hip with his arms crossed. He was still wound up tight. We were both wearing our normal clothes, and I felt extremely out of place in the casual vacation resort.

"We should change. We look like city slickers," I told him.

"Fair enough. You take the bathroom."

I brought my bags of clothes from Stella into the bathroom. Digging through that bag was a fashion extravaganza. So many bathing suits of all different shapes and colors. Sarongs made of sheer silk and tulle. Oh my. One of the covers was basically made of chains. Three longer ones that were shoulder straps and three shorter ones that would wrap around the waist. It had a thin mesh fabric twisted through the links and torn strips that hung from the belt. I groaned.

It was so elaborate and sexy like a costume. It looked like a reinforced toga that a mystical tomb raider might wear while fighting off mummies and snakes. Next to it, there was a bikini made of aged leather with tattered edges that was clearly meant to be worn with the cover. It would look stunning on Stella with her dark skin, luscious curves, and confidence. I certainly didn't feel like wearing it now, but maybe after some drinks I could work up the courage.

I picked the one with the most coverage, which was still quite revealing. A black one-piece with a severe rise at the hip and a deep plunging neckline to the navel. The only thing that kept it from flying open was a brass ring between my breasts, which felt wonderful as the strong cold metal pressed against my skin. It also had a slim bronze belt at the waist that served no purpose except to highlight how the hips of the suit rose above it.

I pulled a white cotton babydoll eyelet dress over it and felt more covered. I'd save the toga dress and sexy bikinis for another time when I was feeling more fearless. I took my hair out of the bun I'd been wearing and let the curls fall over my shoulders. There. I was starting to look more like a girl on vacation, not a girl on the run from a psycho. I felt nervous about walking out there wearing this, but my friend Stella whispered in my ear, *You underestimate yourself. I do it too. We all do.*

Okay. I conceded that I looked good in the outfit. I had long legs, curvy hips, and decent-sized breasts. When I was carrying more weight, it was more pronounced, but I was still my mother's daughter in that sense.

I took a deep breath for confidence and emerged from the bathroom. He was standing at the edge of an open floor with his shoulder resting against a beam as he looked out over the ocean. The way the missing wall was aligned gave the illusion he could step right off into the water. He was wearing board shorts with white and blue panels in cool angular patterns that looked like waves or fins. They hung tight at his hips and loose at the knee. He also wore a cotton tee that said "Jogging for Frogmen" and had a drawing of a splattered frog plastered across the back of his broad shoulders. He looked like he was surveilling the horizon for incoming pirate ships.

He also looked freaking incredible, and I could only imagine how I would lose my cool if he ever took that tee off. My mouth watered, and I had to bite my lip to stop from moaning.

As if he sensed me ogling him, he turned slowly and looked me up and down. His eyes flared as he stared at my legs. He turned his gaze to the floor, crossed his arms, and shuffled his feet. It was the most emotional I'd ever seen him. He looked like a shy groom who had just seen his bride for the first time.

I had to be reading him wrong. Why would he feel that way about me? When I looked down to check myself out, I realized the eyelet lace of the cover I was wearing was see-through, and you could very clearly see the risque cut of the black bathing suit beneath. Jeez. Stella went all out on her shopping trip and made sure I had nothing baggy or concealing to hide behind.

"Are you trying to kill me?" he asked.

"What? No. This is what Stella packed for me."

"Stella is evil."

I walked up next to him, and we both peered out through the missing wall of the room. "Wow." The shiny clear blue water and sky went on forever. Only a small island broke up the horizon. Once again I felt like I was in a dream standing next to a leading man who I was wholly inadequate to pursue, and yet Stella's words kept tickling my ear. *He digs you*. And what did he mean by that, *Are you trying to kill me*?

"It's fantastic. Gotta give Stella that," he admitted.

Since he'd brought her up again, and my mind was sick of wondering, I decided to just ask him. "I don't think she's evil. She has good intentions. She just misreads things sometimes."

He nodded.

"For example, she thinks you're attracted to me." I accidentally snorted when I laughed and then blushed because I'd snorted.

I held my breath as I waited for his response.

He crossed his arms over his chest. "She's wrong."

Okay. Now I'd done it. Maybe I didn't want to know the truth. Maybe I wanted to keep my fantasy alive in my head, and I didn't need external confirmation from Auggie. I could conduct a full-on relationship in my imagination and just use him for visual inspiration.

He cleared his throat. "What I feel for you has surpassed attraction and is now borderline unhealthy obsession." He looked down and shuffled his feet again like the shy groom.

Did I hear him right? Did he just say what I thought he'd said? Sweet mother of holy moly. I thought I'd heard him say something about being obsessed with me. My cheeks burned like someone had doused them in lighter fluid and lit a match between my teeth. "Uh." I stumbled and mumbled through several almost thoughts, but I couldn't get a complete one out. "Mmm," was all I came up with.

"I'm going to swim out to that island." He pointed to the landmass that looked like it was several miles away.

My mouth dropped open. "That seems very far."

"I can easily swim it."

"Oh, well. I don't doubt that, but *I* can't." Oops. I snorted again. Auggie had me all tongue-tied and twisted. If he swam away, I'd be here alone. I was not ready to be alone. I believed Train couldn't find us here, but I would just feel better if he was close by.

He turned to look at me with his eyebrows pulled together. He seemed to get the message and snapped out of it. "Yes. Okay. You're right. Not a good idea. Get in the boat."

Boat? What boat? I didn't see any boat.

Chapter 13 Slippery When Wet

My heart was still fluttering as I followed him down the steps to an outrigger canoe that was shaped like a dragon. He held it with his foot and offered me a hand while I climbed in and wobbled to the wooden seat in the back.

He took the front with much more grace and ease than me and whipped out a paddle from somewhere I didn't see. A man on a mission, he pushed off from the dock and started paddling us out to sea. The wind and sun kissed my face and distracted me from the burn in my cheeks over Auggie's confession. I took a deep breath of the salty air and stared in awe at Auggie's muscles moving under his tee.

What I feel for you has surpassed attraction and is now borderline unhealthy obsession.

Unbelievable. Confusing. Exciting. I wanted to call Stella and squeal like Michael Jackson and then ask her to explain it to me, but then I realized Auggie was working hard to get us to this island, and I was just sitting there like dead weight.

"Do you want me to paddle too?" I asked him.

"No."

Okay then. I guess I was free to sit and freak out behind him and let the wind cool my skin.

Now that I was closer I could see that the Jogging for Frogmen event was a charity marathon in San Diego, California a few years back. "To honor Naval Special Warfare service members." The thought of Auggie running for charity was so sweet. A hardcore man like him took breaks from saving the world for events to help veterans. It was a little bit of humanity on a man who seemed out of touch with society and the real world.

I tapped him on the shoulder. "Are those bungalows safe?"

"What?"

I spoke louder so he could hear me. "What if a huge wave comes up?"

He thought about it for a second. "The water here seems mostly calm, but there could be a storm surge or a hurricane. I checked the weather, and it looked good for our trip. Those bungalows are elevated a good ten feet, but they are also probably designed to flood and drain."

I was impressed with his knowledge. "What about a tsunami?"

"You worry a lot."

"We're staying in a hut over the water. My first thought is tsunami."

He chuckled. "I'll find out about their warning system. Tsunamis usually follow seismic activity, and they will sound warnings to get to higher ground."

"Scary."

He looked back at me over his shoulder. "If there is a tsunami, I will keep you safe."

I patted him on his shoulder. "There is no one else I'd rather experience a tsunami with than you."

He chuckled, but I wasn't joking. If we needed to get to safety fast, he would know how to do it and make it happen. It sounded insignificant on the surface, but it actually meant a lot to me. A new and unusual feeling had filled me. I felt

safe. I believed Train wouldn't find me here, and I fully trusted him to take care of any emergency. I sighed and drank
that in. It felt good. I let out a long deep breath, and as it left
my lungs, I imagined shedding my fears out over the water.
This place was peaceful and beautiful. There was no room to
be scared. With that breath, I gave myself permission to relax
and enjoy the gifts that were being given to me.

So I sat back on my seat, watched Auggie's arms work the
oar, and smiled like a fool who was free for the first time in
her stupid life.

***

After twenty minutes of vigorous paddling, there was mirac-
ulously no sign of sweat on his skin. I'd be dripping like a pig
if I had to paddle us out that far. We rolled right up onto the
shore of the island, and he turned to offer me a hand.

"What is this place?"

"Let's go explore." I'd barely stepped out of the boat, and
he'd left me to march up a path through the palm trees. He
was barefoot, and I was wearing thin slip-on sandals. I had to
scuttle to catch up to him.

We hiked at a fast pace up the trail, and I was huffing and
puffing to keep up. I slipped on a wet stone and ended up on
my knees. I'd taken the bandages off, but I still had scabs on
my scrapes.

He stopped and looked back, and then down, at me. "Jesus. Sorry. I got ahead of myself. Get on." He held out his
hand.

"Get on what?" I asked as I took his hand. I loved the feel of his warm skin on mine.

"Get on my back." He crouched down as he tugged my hand over his shoulder. "Come on."

"Uh. No. I'll just hoof it."

"It's going to get more slippery as we get closer to the waterfall."

"How do you know there's a waterfall?"

"I can hear it. Can't you?"

I twisted my head like a dog listening to a record. "No."

He chuckled and yanked my hand. I fell onto his back, and he scooped me up. "Wrap your legs around me like you did before."

The last time I'd ridden on his back, he'd been rescuing me from a steep fall and I'd been half-conscious. This was totally different because he looked hot in board shorts and a white charity tee, and I was very aware of my skimpy swimwear and *oh my goodness, he'd said he was obsessed with me.* I had to brush it off and focus on the task at hand, or he'd think I'd gone catatonic.

I did as he said and wrapped my legs around him like a monkey. He caught onto my thighs and bounced me up higher on his back. This caused a lot of rubbing of our bodies in sensitive spots. The hard muscles near his shoulder blades scraped against my nipples, and my core bounced up and down his spine. I could feel every single vertebrae move with each step he took. He leaped onto a steep rock and the resulting bounce between my legs hit me hard. Lord help me. I was going to have an orgasm from a piggyback ride. I couldn't hold back the grunt that came out right in his ear. How totally freaking embarrassing.

"Does it hurt?" he asked me.

"Uh, no. I'm fine." It definitely didn't hurt. It was the best darn piggyback ride I'd ever had. Not that I'd had a ton of them, but still, this was the best.

After a few more minutes of brisk hiking, the air became very wet. Our hair and clothes were soaked. We reached a precipice, and the sight that came into view blew my mind. An incredibly tall waterfall cascaded down into a giant basin of still blue water. Tourists stood on the craggy rocks that surrounded the white trail of water as it hit the surface below.

Auggie set me on my feet. I barely had my footing before he tore off his tee and tossed it on the ground. He roared what sounded like "Hooyah" and jumped off the cliff with no preamble.

"Auggie!"

He landed with his hands over his head, and his pointed toes entered the water with only a small splash. I held my breath till he resurfaced and swam to the edge of the pool at the bottom.

It all happened so fast. It didn't take him more than five seconds to assess the situation, take off his shirt, and dive into the water. It was then I noticed the other tourists jumping into the water too which made what he'd done seem slightly less crazy but still totally spontaneous and unexpected.

After a few minutes, he came up behind me, dripping water and smiling big. "That was fun."

I was gobsmacked as I stared at him. Pebbled skin dripping wet, tattoos glinting off his chest and arms, abs for miles, the chiseled lines of his hip bones, the way the wet nylon fabric clung to something curvy inside his trunks. His mossy eyes glowed under the sparkling water as he swept his hair back with his hand, which revealed coarse dark hair under his armpits. Hot damn. Auggie was sensational from head to toe, and when he smiled, the hotness factor ramped up to suffocating.

"Your turn." His grin turned wickedly playful.

"What? No."

He grabbed the bottom of my dress and yanked it up, forcing me to lift my arms so he could remove it. He paused and I thought I heard him mutter, "Fucking hell," when he saw me in the swimsuit.

"Shoes off."

I kicked off my sandals fast because his order seemed more like a threat.

"Good girl." He wrapped an arm around my waist and ushered me in front of him. We took three steps down with his front against my back.

"Wait. I'm not jumping."

"No. We are." I could swear I felt his chest rocking with laughter.

"We're not. I really don't want to. I mean I don't need to. I mean, I want to but I'm scared."

"Here we go." He nudged my toes to the edge of the rock, and bile rose in my throat.

"Auggie."

"One, two..." He didn't say three. He just jumped off the dang cliff with me in his arms. We plummeted straight down, and I opened my mouth to scream.

He let go of me right before a gush of cool water shocked my whole body and surged down my throat. Panic spread through me like wildfire, but before it could blossom, his strong arm returned to my waist and dragged me up to the surface. I coughed and gasped as I wiped the water from my eyes. "That was awesome."

He laughed. "See?" He continued to smile as he snaked an arm up my back and gripped the base of my scalp. His other hand brushed down over my backside and caressed my thigh. God, it felt good to have his hands on my bare skin. Was he making his move? We were both panting heavily and exhilarated from the jump.

I thought he might kiss me, but he turned away as he swung me around onto his back and swam across the pool to a rock formation. "Hold your breath."

"What?"

"Hold your breath. We're going under."

This time I knew he wouldn't give me a second to adjust, so I quickly took a deep breath and pressed my lips tight. He dove under a rock like a porpoise, and we resurfaced in a shallow cave.

The turquoise water reflected off the overhead rocks in a mystical dancing pattern. "This is really cool." The sudden silence magnified everything that had been muted by the noise of the tourists and the waterfall. Suddenly we were in our own secluded bubble, our breaths echoing off the walls, tiny drops hitting the water loudly in the little cavern.

He was treading water with me on his back, and every point of connection between us felt like it was lubricated with satin. My thighs flowed around his hips, my ankles fell naturally between his legs that were effortlessly keeping us both above water.

His fingertips dug into my ass cheeks and tugged with a force that didn't acknowledge the weight of the water. It defied the water and dared it to try to prolong the time it would take to bring me face-to-face with him.

As he brought me around, my nipples rubbed against his chest. I whimpered and tightened my legs around his hips. The responding hunger in his eyes wasn't subtle. It was intimidating and palpable. His hands raced up and down my back, from my shoulders to my thighs, his fingertips were hungry, his arms progressively pushing the water between us out until our bodies clung together by pure suction. The surface of the water lapped at my breasts, which were round and plump because he'd smashed me against him hard.

He stared at them as he spoke to me, and I could feel his desire to bend down and lick them. "Resisting you was torture before. Now it's impossible."

"Why are you resisting?" I asked breathlessly.

He looked up at the bruise over my eye, and his face fell like a child who had accidentally let go of his prized balloon and watched it disappear into the atmosphere. "You're injured."

"Really? You're worried about my injuries when you just manhandled me up the trail and threw me off a cliff?"

"I'm sorry. Am I being too rough?" He loosened his grip on my thighs.

"No!" I cinched my legs around his waist. "Do it, Auggie. If you want it. Do it. Don't worry about me. I'm fine. Really, really fine. Like it feels so good, I can barely speak. If you want it, take it. Please. I need you to do that so badly and if you don't, I'm gon—"

His palm wrapped around the back of my head and crashed our lips together. He forced my mouth open with his tongue and slid inside. We both groaned as our tongues collided and tangled. His hands gripped my shoulders and thrust me down onto the tip of his hard cock that was waiting just below my bottom.

I was in Heaven. His hard body, forceful hands, hot wet mouth that tasted like the sea. I climbed up on him, trying to get closer, frustrated with the water that pushed us apart. He propelled me down again, and his hard cock poked between my butt cheeks. Oh God. I wanted that. I ached to feel all of it everywhere, not just the tip between my cheeks. We devoured each other for a long time, our lips obnoxiously moving in a filthy pattern that said we wanted to eat each other alive. The wall of the cave amplified our desperate moaning. We'd waited far too long for this kiss.

The privacy of the cave made me feel naughty. Oh so terribly rebellious to be making out when we knew a child or anyone could also dive under and pop up right next to us at any moment. I wiggled my hips and captured his cock between us, squashing it with my public bone until I could feel the hard core of it. Oh my daylights, it was huge.

My hips hitched against it of their own volition. I didn't even think of it. I was writhing on him out of instinct. My clit swelled in celebration when I scrubbed it like dirty clothes on a washboard. I was already close to coming from that erotic piggyback ride. I just needed a few strokes at the right angle, and I'd be screaming out my orgasm against the walls of this cave. The tourists outside would surely hear it, but I didn't give a shit.

"Haven." He tried to pull his lips away, but I dove in deeper, locked my ankles behind his back, and rode that thing like a bull rider at PBR. "Jesus."

His voice was so deep and raspy, his cock so incredibly hard between us, massaging me in all the right spots, and I was gone.

It ripped through me, and there was no stopping it. My mouth fell open, and I closed my eyes as I rubbed through the rush of pleasure. I lost my hold on his hips as I convulsed under the water. This wasn't like any vibrator orgasm. This was a full-body tremor that throbbed and pulsed through me like an electrical shock from a taser. If his hands weren't holding me by the ass, I would have drowned. I could not have kept myself afloat during that onslaught.

I'd closed my eyes and thrown my head back. I was panting, lying with my arms spread, the water in my hair. "Oh, my, freaking, God."

"Haven." Auggie's voice seemed far away. Auggie. Oh my gosh. I'd almost forgotten about him. I opened my eyes and attempted to lift my head. His hand helped me return upright and when I looked in his eyes, the shock on his face quickly reminded me what I'd done. I'd lost awareness and gotten myself off on his dick without permission or care for him.

"I'm sorry. I, uh, got a little carried away there." I'd totally used him for my own selfish gratification. At least the water hid the sticky mess I'd probably made between my legs.

He cleared his throat. "You're fine. It's all good. That was fucking beautiful."

"Oh God. No." I hid my head in his neck. "I'm so embarrassed."

"No, babe. That was pure beauty. Watching you let go like that. Fuck. I almost came from the sight of it. Never be embarrassed about taking what you need."

He was making it so much worse trying to make me feel better. "Ugh. Can we go? I don't want to get caught in here. I'm so sorry."

"Don't say it. That was a gift." He released my butt and pulled me through the water until I was on his back again. I groaned when my sensitive core hit his vertebrae.

I thought I felt his chest quiver in a laugh as he said, "Hold your breath again." I inhaled before we went under like dolphins. We surfaced outside the cave, and he held my hand as we walked out to the place where we'd left the boat.

"Did you like the waterfall?" He grinned and licked the salt water off the side of his lip which reminded me he was probably still hard and horny. I peeked down at his trunks and yep, there was definitely a stiff board in there.

I smacked his chest and wrapped myself around him in a hug. "Stop teasing me. You know I loved it." His hands landed gently on the small of my back then quickly disappeared.

"Wait here. I'll run up and get our clothes." He took off running before I could reply.

***

He made it back in record time, and his face was exhilarated from his run. On the return trip, he took the seat in the back, so I started to move toward the front one. He stood, pulled me down by the waist, and I found myself sitting smack dab between his legs, pinned to his hard cock.

Even better than watching Auggie from behind was feeling his arms and chest push off the sand and paddle behind me. His tee and my dress and sandals lay in a wet heap on the bottom of the canoe, so we were skin-to-skin again as we had been for the last few hours.

I was getting to know his contours. He had a few bumpy scars on his back and his chest and several on his arms. His hair was more coarse on his head and chest than on his limbs. Most of Auggie was sleek, hard, cut muscle, and I could tell he intentionally chiseled every inch of it to perfection.

We stayed quiet on the ride back. We listened to the paddle breaching the surface of the water and the birds kawing above. I found his silence a little disconcerting but assumed he was just enjoying the view. Back at the bungalow, he helped me onto the dock and stepped away from me.

"I'm gonna work out," he announced in a cold tone. All the smiles and warmth had left him like he'd snapped back into bodyguard mode.

"Didn't you just do that?"

He dipped his chin and leveled me with a serious gaze. "I'm gonna work out."

"Okay. I'm going to um, go lay down, because uh, that was exhausting."

"Fine." He turned and dove into the water. "I'll stay close by," he called up.

"Okay." I scuttled off to the bathroom and threw on a soft nightshirt and shorts that Stella had packed for me. I plopped down on the luxurious bed and covered my eyes. What had I done? I had no chill at all when it came to him. The first chance I had, I'd jumped him. He must've thought I was so inexperienced and naive. I had a feeling Stella had told him I was a virgin, and he wanted nothing to do with that. I was in deep over my head with a man like him who had traveled the world and trained with elite special forces.

But then again, Stella had said they were puppy dogs underneath it all, he'd said he was obsessed and that resisting was hard, and he'd kissed me in a way that left no doubt about his desire for me. It was time to clear the air with Auggie. He'd opened up a little, but there was still so much he wasn't telling me. I'd give him his space while he worked out whatever was bothering him, but tonight we would talk.

In a spontaneous eruption of possibly misguided courage, I rang Rajerio and ordered a traditional Jamaican meal for dinner with a side of ice-cold Russian vodka. I eyed the sexy toga dress and loincloth bikini Stella had packed for me. I'd have to be brave and strap that thing on. I'd be putting myself out there for Auggie. The rejection would sting if he turned me down, but it was worth the risk and the chance he might kiss me again like he'd done in the cave.

Chapter 14 Reservations

Auggie

I swam for hours. Hundreds of reps. Legs, arms, abs. Every exercise I could think of. Worked my muscles until the burn turned to fatigue. The workout would be great for my physical strength, but nothing could erase her from my mind.

The warm water shimmering on her flawless skin like a fresh coat of wax on a vintage car. The hot curve of her tongue against mine, the eager little whimpers each time I moved, and the greedy tilt of her hips that kept dragging us into the danger zone.

I'd made weak attempts to hold off the torrent between us. In the end, I'd given up and succumbed to her mesmerizing writhing on my cock. Never seen anything like it. I'd seen women come before, but this was so completely different in a pristine way. Her actions were unpolluted with the motivation to please. Untainted by self-consciousness or fear.

After all the anxiety I'd seen on her face, watching her experience the pure joy of her own orgasm brought me so much satisfaction. It was like I had spilled myself. And even though she'd taken it on her own, I took ownership of it. I'd given her that. I'd made her collapse and moan in pure ecstasy. I could easily get addicted to that rush of control and power.

When I couldn't push my body or my mind any further, I entered the bungalow and jacked off in the shower. Twice. I came out wearing a towel, and she was standing there in a hot as fuck leather bikini that did not hide her pebbled nipples.

"Shit." Any of the edge I'd taken off was back once I saw that.

She quickly threw a cover over it that was torn shreds of fabric that barely reached her thigh. It had thick silver chains that crossed her chest and hips, and nope, that did not help at all. She looked like goddamn Lara Croft standing in front of me.

"I ordered some dinner," she said shyly.

I grunted and dried my hair with the towel. "I'll meet you out on the deck in a minute."

"Okay."

As I was dressing, I heard Rajerio arrive with the food and watched him set it up on the deck. He lit tiki torches and the fire pit as reggae music flowed in from a party on the beach. The sun was setting, and Haven looked deadly as she sat innocently on the couch waiting for me. She tucked a pink hibiscus flower behind her ear and toyed with the ends of her golden hair that was hanging loose over her shoulders.

I took a deep breath and prepared myself for another grueling session of trying-to-resist-Haven. I threw on some black board shorts and a gray linen shirt, leaving it unbuttoned because it was still warm out tonight.

Haven's gaze traveled up my body as I walked out to her and the huge spread on the coffee table. Ahh, a frosty bottle of Stoli waited among the food trays. "Looks good."

"Yes, it does." She grinned.

I meant the food, but whatever, she was cute. I handed her the phone and camera I was carrying with me. "These are for you."

Her mouth dropped open, and a huge smile blessed her face. "Really?"

"I'll be honest that they both have tracking enabled for your safety." That was an understatement. They were extremely high-tech, and we'd be able to find her, listen to her, and see her even if the battery died or the device dropped to the bottom of the ocean, but I didn't share those details. "They're secure."

She didn't show any interest in the phone, but the camera had all her attention. "Thank you. I've never had a camera like this. I'll have to read up on all its features." She turned it on and looked through the menu. The first thing she did was snap a photo of me, mostly my bottom half.

"You can take pictures of me but don't post them online anywhere or share them with friends."

"I won't. They're for me." She smiled and took one of my face.

I opened the lid on the food and checked out the spread.

"Rajerio said salt fish, jerk chicken, coco bread, and coconut balls are the local delicacies." She giggled. At what? Balls? Coconut balls. I chuckled too. She was cute as hell. "Will that go with the vodka?" she asked.

It touched me that she'd ordered vodka for me. In Russia, it was standard to have it with a meal. "Of course." I sat down and poured a shot for myself. "You?"

"No thanks. I'll stick with my fruity rum drink." She sucked on the straw in a curvy glass and looked at me with those big blue eyes. She looked damned good as her cheeks hollowed out.

I groaned and downed a shot. It was actually perfectly chilled and tasteless as it should be but left a nice bloom in my chest on the way down.

We ate in silence for a while, and I liked that she didn't feel the pressure to fill it with chatter. I should've brought up the topics we needed to discuss, but I was enjoying her company and didn't want to cast a dark shadow on the dinner she'd planned for us.

We finished eating, and she took a long draw from her drink. "Can I ask you something?"

"Yes."

"Why does it feel like you're pulling away from me? Earlier, we were having so much fun and then I made that huge mistake, and now you're a clam again."

I understood why she was confused by my behavior, but it wasn't her fault. "It wasn't a huge mistake. I told you that. However, it can't happen again."

Her shoulders deflated, and so did my heart. I hated to hurt her, but in the end I'd be saving her. "I have reservations about entering into a physical relationship with you."

She peered up at me. "Is this about me being a virgin?"

Hold up. What did she say? I flinched and leaned back. "You're a... "

"Stella told you. Didn't she? I want to be mad at her, but she's so nice. How can I be mad at her for telling you the truth?"

"It's true?" She'd completely thrown me off. I'd known she was innocent, but I'd never assumed she was untouched. "How did this happen?"

She looked up at the stars that were just starting to show up. "I told you my mom made sure none of the neighborhood guys wanted to sleep with the girl who started a deadly war and might be their sister. Cyrus's dad enforced it around the club and I stuck to the club because I felt safe there. When he died, I finally left the neighborhood to take a class at the junior college, and I met a guy. God, he was so geeky. He had no idea what to do, and I really needed someone to take charge. Ya know?"

"Mmm-hmm." I had to clear the large frog that was sitting in my throat. Was she trying to kill me? Again? "Haven... uh... I didn't know... about any of this. However, I'm even more hesitant to touch you now."

She cast her eyes down like a wounded lamb, and I felt that knife through my gut. "I knew it. I'm not your type. You are so far out of my league. You're all worldly and sexy. What was I thinking? I've never even been out of Lamar Gardens except for that horrific trip to Italy and my failed attempt to attend college. You probably want girls like Crystal. Don't you? Girls who've been around and know how to give an amazing blowjob. Not a girl like me who can't even handle a few rubs from your swim trunks." She hit her forehead with her palm and heaved in a breath like she was about to cry.

She thought I was rejecting her, which was the opposite of what I was trying to say. With only a few words, I'd already fucked this whole thing up and hurt her, and yet I didn't know how to explain it without making it worse. "Don't beat yourself up over this. It's not you." Shit. Also not the right thing to say.

Her eyes flared. "Excuse me." She held her hand over her mouth as she stood up and ran away from me.

Fuck. I took another shot of vodka and accepted the truth. I had no idea how to handle a woman like Haven. Innocent hearted, kind, open, smart. The opposite of me. My normal mode of operation would not work with her. She'd locked herself in the bathroom. I wrapped gently on the door. "Haven?"

"Go away, Auggie. I need some time," she said through the door.

"You don't because you have it all wrong. Please come out of there."

"I don't think I do. I saw you with Crystal." Fucking shit. I'd forgotten about Crystal but of course she hadn't. Another fuck up on my part. "You loved it. Go find yourself a girl like her if you like it so much."

"No." I rested my forearm on the door and leaned in toward her. Totally broken that I didn't know what to say to fix this. I could at least tell her the truth about that night. "I was never with Crystal."

"You weren't?" She sniffled.

"No. It was all an act. She never touched me."

She stayed quiet for a long time. "Why would you do that?"

"To hurt you," I admitted through the door.

"It worked."

"I know. I'm so sorry." I should've told her so much earlier, but my stubbornness got in the way again. "I'm not proud of what I did. Please come out. We need to talk."

"My face is all red and snotty."

"I don't care. Come out now."

After a few seconds, she slowly opened the door and peered up at me. She looked beautiful, even in tears. I took her hand and dug deep within myself to be what she needed right then. A gentle hand and sensitivity were not things that came easily to me. "Come. Sit with me."

I brought her over to the bed, and we sat on the edge of it, side by side. Where to start? More apologizing would be good. She deserved that. "I'm so sorry I pulled that bullshit with Crystal. It was a rash decision. I had no idea what you were going through with Train. I thought you'd been working me, so I tried to play you." It was a weak apology at best.

"I wasn't working you."

Of course she wasn't. The girl didn't play games. She lived an honest life. "I know that now. Please forgive me." I took her hand and pressed my lips to her forehead.

She leaned into it like it comforted her. She sniffled and wiped her nose. "I did kinda play you by leaving with Cyrus."

"No."

"I was running from Train."

"I know that now too. Can you forgive me for being so stupid?"

"Yes. Do you forgive me for what I did?"

"Of course." I slid my lips to her temple. She didn't need to apologize to me. I was the one who'd fucked up. "Are you ready to tell me about him now?"

She sighed. "I knew who he was, but I didn't know him growing up. He probably knew who I was too because of my mom. He kidnapped me and took me to a house with a bunch of other women."

My hand involuntarily tightened on hers. "He kidnapped you?" The fucking asshole would die a slow and painful death if I ever got my hands on him.

"He said he'd kill me if I ran or told anyone. Luckily, he didn't rape me because I'd told him I was a virgin, but then he sent me to Italy to work for Rico, and I knew then he was trying to sell me for sex. I planned to escape that night you showed up. You asked me to go, and I said yes, but I couldn't drag you into it. You see that now?"

"I see why you thought that, but you were wrong. I was exactly the person you should've dragged into it."

The girl had been through hell, and I'd been the asshole who'd made it worse. I'd never forgive myself for directing the rage from my injured ego on her.

"I thought I was safe with Cyrus, but Train found me and threatened to kill Cyrus's kids, so I ran to Duke. That's when you saw me at the party, and I had to run again. I didn't want to hurt you or Stella, but I did."

"I hear you. It's okay. Stella has forgiven you too. I wish you would've told me earlier, but at least now I know and I can help you." Thank God I was in Jamaica far away from Train because at this point I didn't give a shit what the FBI wanted. He needed to die.

She lay down on the bed with her head on the pillow, and I fell in behind her. It was so natural to spoon her to my torso and comfort her. Too natural, too right. So unfair.

I searched deep inside for the right words to say to get through to her. "My reservations have nothing to do with Train or your sexual experience. It's something else completely."

"What is it?"

I didn't know. What was it? Why was I resisting this woman that I obviously cared for and desired more than anyone I'd ever met in my life? I had to be honest with myself and with her because Jamaica was not reality. The reality of my life was waiting for me back in the States. "The life I lead is not conducive to a relationship. I don't even have a permanent residence. I'm in constant flux and chaos. I never know if I'm coming back alive. I couldn't do that to you. If I'm going to be with you, I'd want you by my side every day. I hate the fear that Train puts in your eyes. If I were your man, I'd want to be there to comfort you morning and night, not ask you to be strong while I'm away. Not expect you to pick up the pieces if I die. Do you see?" I still hadn't found the words to get to the heart of the matter, but I was narrowing in on it.

"Sorta."

I thought of the night I'd killed Konstantin just a few days ago. A clear shot to the skull through a high-rise window a thousand yards out. An excellent shot learned from years of practice and perfecting my precision. A man died and I felt no remorse at all. It was my job. "Even now I'm deep into a moonlighting op that kept me underground for months. You don't just walk away from those clean. If you betray people, and they discover who you really are, they will seek vengeance. It's an ugly world."

"I grew up in the projects. I know all about that," she reminded me.

The projects and gang life were rough too. She was so innocent and sweet, I'd sometimes forget her background. "It's remarkable that you grew up in that violence, and it hasn't tainted you. You've stayed true to who you are despite being in very difficult circumstances."

She laughed and leaned back onto my shoulder. I pulled my hips back because if she was touching my cock, I'd barely be able to maintain this conversation that I was already struggling with. "Don't make me sound noble. It was mostly out of fear and trying to remain invisible."

"You still did it. You deserve better than the life I could offer you. You finally have a chance to get out of the projects. You should live in a quiet neighborhood with a reliable man who comes home to you every night." I could see that for her. A safe house with big evergreen trees out front. A man who came home and cherished her like she deserved. It drove a fire in my gut to think of her with someone else, but it couldn't be me. Not with the life I had right now.

"I tried that too. I signed up for a matchmaking site and went on a date with this businessman type guy. He wore a suit on our date. Can you believe it? It was the most boring thing ever. He had no idea how to dominate me." She turned to face me, and I rolled onto my back, keeping my arm under her side but creating distance between her hot body and my cock.

I closed my eyes and tried to squeeze out the sharp pang of desire hearing her talk had triggered in me. Definitely trying to kill me. "You want to be dominated?"

"Yeah. I mean I think so based on what I've read in books and ya know..."

"I don't know."

"Porn," she said sheepishly, and I laughed out loud.

"Oh, Haven. You are golden and you make me smile."

"I know that's not reality, but there has to be more than just sex toys and masturbating. I've got years of pent-up energy ready to be explored while I'm in my sexual prime, and what happened between us earlier? That was unlike anything I'd ever felt on my own. I believe there's so much more out there waiting for me if I ever get the chance."

I sighed and mashed my palms into my eyes. "I am dead."

"What? Why?"

"You have killed me with your honesty. I don't know what to say."

"So you're saying we can't be in a relationship because your work is too dangerous?"

"Essentially."

"What if we just have sex?" she asked innocently.

My fists clenched, and my half-hard dick twitched. I was ready to take her right now. I could flip on top of her and have that ridiculously sexy bathing suit off of her in minutes. She'd be a deflowered puddle of goo, and I'd relish every second of it like the selfish asshole I am.

I rose from the bed to create some distance from her. "We can't do that." I ran my hands through my hair and tugged on it to attempt some kind of distraction from the temptation lying behind me.

"Why not?"

I turned back to her. "I have done that before. I've had sex without emotion. It comes easy to me normally. But you are different. So different. Not only because you're a virgin but because I already care for you. If I am ever lucky enough to sink inside you, I would never be able to walk away and not be in love."

Her eyes flared. "Why am I different?"

"I don't know. I just know that I could not have sex with you without without falling dangerously in love." There. I'd said it. The truth of the matter was on the table.

She blushed and turned her head to the side. "Oh." A satisfied grin grew on her face, and she raised her knee, teasing me with the supple curve of her leg, the tan on her skin, the peek at her ass. Now she knew the truth. I was helplessly at her mercy, and she was coming to realize her power over me. "And that would be bad because?"

"There is so much you don't know about me. If you did, you wouldn't ask that question. You wouldn't put yourself out there for that kind of misery."

She sat up on the bed, and her soulful eyes pleaded with me. "I don't think loving you would be misery. I think it would be the greatest experience of my life, and I would cherish it forever. Even if it didn't work out and your job tore us apart like you claim it would." She inched closer to me, walking on her knees, which was incredibly sexy. "Please, Auggie. Say you'll let me get to know you. Tell me more about growing up in Russia, tell me about the first time you had sex, tell me what you ache for, what you're afraid of. I want to know it all. Let me in, and I'll let you in my heart too." She bought her palm up over her breast. "After that, if

you still think we're not right together then at least we gave
it a chance." Her shoulders slumped and she sat back on her
heels. "At least we gave it a chance."

She looked so incredibly sexy and vulnerable. It would
be so easy to take her, and I wanted it more than I'd ever
wanted anything. But I'd seen it too many times. This life did
not lead to happy marriages. It led to a lot of divorce and
cheating and pain. Honest people who thought they'd loved
each other who eventually ended up hurting each other because it was inevitable. The life of a mercenary took up every
waking second of your being. I wouldn't be able to give her
even a fraction of the time and attention she deserved.

"I'm sorry I can't give that to you, Haven. I'm sorry I can't
give you what you need."

She flopped back on the bed and covered her eyes. I'd
hurt her again. I wished I could take it away and promise her
things, but it would be a lie. I'd isolated myself by creating
this life, and now that I'd found someone I actually wanted,
I didn't have a way out. I'd dug myself into a trench with no
exit, and she was the one paying the price for it.

She turned to her side and faced away from me. "Stay
with me anyway? Stay with me in the bed. Give me at least
that."

I couldn't deny her that simple thing. It would be pure
torture to lie next to her and not take her, but I was strong in
my conviction. Haven deserved a man who could be all that
she needed. I'd killed a man in cold blood less than a week
ago. If I was found out, I'd be dead within a week as well. I
didn't burden her with all that.

I climbed in bed behind her, wrapped an arm around her waist, and let the scent of the sunshine in her hair wash over me. And I knew then it was futile to resist. Haven was the forbidden fruit that would lead to my demise.

"Aug?" she asked sleepily.

I cinched her tighter around the waist. "Yeah, babe?"

"Your accent is really sexy."

"I have no accent." I'd made sure of it.

"You do when you drink vodka."

I chuckled. This was true. She'd found me out.

Chapter 15 Love Hurts

Haven

"Let's go test out your new camera."

Auggie had woken earlier than me and finished his workout by the time I'd crawled out of bed and dressed for the day.

He'd unfortunately kept his word last night, and we'd ended up just sleeping in the bed. A few times, he'd drawn my hips closer to him, but then he'd seem to remember himself and angle away.

It seemed like he was exerting a lot of effort, even in his sleep, to keep from poking me with his penis. I wanted to be poked. Hard. Lots of times. I'd even vividly imagined him losing control and poking my backside hoping it would spur him on, but nope. Auggie had ironclad self-control, and he'd sounded very firm in his belief that we could not have a healthy relationship because of the life he led.

He even had me convinced for a little while. Was I strong enough to be the girlfriend of a man like him? How did Brandy and Misha handle the stress of being married to over-the-top commandos? Stella had told me how hard it was to connect with Helix after he'd been on a mission. Did I want a life like that? I wouldn't choose it if I had a choice, and Auggie was very politely giving me that choice.

I'd resolved to myself that I couldn't answer that question in one night, and I'd have to ponder it for the rest of the trip. Perhaps the rest of my life. The truth was that it didn't matter. Even if I'd decided that I was woman enough to love a man like him, he'd proclaimed that he wouldn't give me that opportunity.

When he popped his head in the bedroom and asked me to go with him to test out my camera, I was surprised to see him reach out as I was expecting the cold shoulder from him for the rest of the trip. I threw on some cutoff denim shorts, a cropped white tank top, and a cute pink and blue tie-dye bikini with triangle top and bottom pieces and long strings for the ties. If Stella loathed paisley, she had no issues with tie-dye.

When I came out into the kitchen, he was sitting hunched over his phone, completely ignoring the lovely tray of fruit and juice in front of him.

"Something wrong?" I sat down next to him at the counter.

"Just checking on the team." He tucked the phone into the back pocket of his board shorts, which were the white and blue ones again from yesterday.

"They're on the mission without you?"

"Yes." His brow hung low over his eyes which weren't focused on me at all. He seemed to be staring beyond me to something I couldn't see.

"Are you feeling like you're missing out?" I spotted a pineapple wedge that looked exceptionally juicy and snaked it off the tray.

"Not missing out but just not there for them. What if they need my expertise? What if someone is hurt because they lacked my skill set?"

"Thank you for coming here with me. It sounds like it was a big sacrifice for you."

"Coming to Jamaica with you and watching your endless parade of sexy bikinis is not a sacrifice. I'm sure they'll be fine."

I felt my cheeks heat. I thought the bikinis were sexy too, but it felt good to hear Auggie had noticed. It didn't matter. That was all Stella had packed for me, so if he didn't like it, he'd have to look away. Right now, he was staring at the strings around my neck as he chewed his food and he looked hungry.

"Um. The food looks delicious."

He turned his attention to the tray and picked up a piece of coco bread and dipped it into a vegetable mixture. I tried it too, but it was too spicy for me. He didn't seem to mind the spice.

"Mmm. What is Russian food like?" I asked him.

"I don't know. Stews and soups. It's often hard to find fresh meat there. There is a restaurant in Atlanta that does a decent job of creating authentic Russian food. I'll take you there sometime."

I liked that he was thinking of seeing me and taking me somewhere after this trip. I wasn't sure where we stood, but maybe we could be friends if we couldn't be more than that. "That would be awesome."

After breakfast, he was loading the rental car, which was actually a small yellow truck, and I decided to give Stella a call.

"Hey, girl. Did you shuck the cockle yet?"

I laughed. "No. I have not."

"Stupid boy still being stupid?"

"I wouldn't say that. Listen, Auggie's worried about his team. Can you check on them for him?"

She was quiet for several seconds. "Does he know you're asking me this?"

"No."

"Let's have a little impromptu orientation meeting to the unwritten laws of alpha-male land. The significant other does not get involved in the details of the ops and never outwardly doubts the team's skills. She also does not make phone calls behind her man's back."

"I'm not doubting them. I just want to reassure Auggie."

"I understand you're coming from a good place, and I will check on them, but you haven't even opened the clam yet and doing something like this has the potential to seal him all up again."

"I didn't think of that."

"Now you know." I could just imagine Stella's face giving me that motherly look and blinking her long eyelashes.

"Okay. I'd better go," I whispered.

"Have fun shucking."

Jeez. There were so many rules to these guys, I didn't think I'd ever learn how to keep up.

I ran out to the truck, and Auggie grinned as we pulled out of the lot. I took a ton of pictures as we cruised along the white sand beaches of Montego Bay. When we stopped at a cove, I spent hours photographing all the wonders of the tidepools.

He bodysurfed and ruthlessly tossed me into the water several times when he thought I was spending too much time staring at the camera screen.

For lunch, Auggie bought us a basket of jerk chicken from a roadside booth, and I took pictures of it as we sat on an old driftwood log.

"Why do you take pictures of your lunch?" he asked me.

"The colors are so pretty together. Red, black, yellow, brown. I like to remember the details and then later I can make up stories about them."

"Do you write?" He looked at his chicken and turned it around like he'd never thought of the colors before. Most people don't see the things I see.

"I write my ideas down in detail, but I've never really written any of them yet."

He took a huge bite and nodded as he chewed. "You should develop these ideas. You'd be a good writer."

"You think so?"

"Yes. I think you've been sort of silenced your entire life. You're always trying to blend in, but you have things to say." He swirled his chicken leg as he talked with his hands. "You have character and soul. You see things others don't. You should share it."

"Well, thank you. Cyrus was always saying my pictures were trash."

"Cyrus is an imbecile. He thinks you're going to marry him."

I rolled my eyes. "I'm not."

"I figured as much."

"He talks like that, but he knows I won't really do it. He only kissed me in front of you to claim me. He rarely does that."

"You kissed him back," Auggie reminded me.

"I didn't want you to follow me."

"I did anyway."

"Yes, you did." And now I was sitting on an old drift-wood log in Jamaica eating jerk chicken with the most fascinating man in the world.

We finished our lunch and watched the waves roll in for a while. He leaned back on the log and smiled up at the sun. Another chance for me to pry the clam open a little more.

"Tell me how you became a Navy SEAL."

He ran his tongue over his teeth. "It's a long story and extremely confidential."

"Then I want to know. I promise I won't tell anyone."

He looked out at the horizon for a long time and finally started talking. "My father was a high-ranking officer in the Russian military. I always wanted to be like him. I joined the service and rose through the ranks and became what most Americans know as Spetsnaz or special forces. It's more involved than that, but I became entrenched in that system and was assigned a specialty as a sharpshooter or an assassin, whatever word you choose to use. They ordered me to kill a woman. I refused. This is unheard of. You do not refuse orders in Russia. It's a death sentence. As expected, they marked me as a traitor," he pointed to the spider tattoo on his shoulder, "and left me to die in an abandoned prison. Vander's SEAL team found me there and rescued me. The US military learned of my background and offered me asylum if I defected, and I accepted." His eyes widened like he couldn't believe the story himself. "I've been a SEAL since then, and the team are my brothers now." He spoke dispassionately, but I could tell by the burn in his eyes this story evoked a lot of pain in him. He'd likely been loyal to Russia for most of his youth, and they'd cast him aside and left him to die just because he refused to kill someone.

"Why did you point to that tattoo?" I ran my fingers over the black and red abdomen of the tarantula-sized spider that wrapped around his shoulder.

He turned his gaze to the sand and sifted it through his fingers. "They gave it to me. It's the symbol of a thief. A criminal. It is crawling upward which means I am heading into a life of crime."

That was not at all what I'd expected to hear. They'd forced him to get a tattoo that labeled him as a criminal? "But that's not true. You should have it changed."

"Isn't it?" He raised his brows and looked at me.

"You think you're a criminal?"

"Murder is a crime, regardless of the reason."

I placed my hand over his in the sand. "And you've murdered people?"

He slid his hand away and looked out over the horizon again. "Lots of people."

"Oh." He was sharing with me but also pulling away.

His mouth turned down into a deep frown. "Now you see why I say I can't love you? Besides, I gave up on the notion of love when my sister was killed."

"You lost a sister?" My heart ached for him. This story was so tragic and sad.

"When I refused to kill the woman, they murdered her to serve as a warning to others."

"Auggie, no. That's awful." I knew the grief of losing a family member. It was a pain that didn't fade with time like they promised. I still missed my mom and my best friend as much as I did when they'd been killed.

"I loved her dearly and haven't loved another woman since they took her from me." When he turned to look at me, his eyes were glossy. This tore him up.

I placed my hand on the back of his strong neck. "Oh my gosh. I'm so sorry. I understand that was painful for you, but I don't think it means you are incapable of love."

"I do, and yet I can't stop myself from wanting it. Especially with you." From this angle, I could see his beautiful Adam's apple move as he swallowed.

"Why don't you let it happen?"

He grimaced. "Love hurts."

I was thrilled that he was sharing his life with me, but he had some messed up ideas about love and pain. "It doesn't have to hurt, Auggie. Many people have beautiful love stories and grow old with their soulmate. You're too focused on the negative. Look at Vander and Misha and Steel and Brandy. They're giving it a go and seem to be very happy."

He turned to me and placed his hand over my hair on my neck and gave it a squeeze. "They're the exception."

"Why can't you be the exception too?"

He shook his head. "I'm the bad guy." He was firmly rooted in his belief that love was for other people but not him.

"I don't think you are." I caressed his hair from the top of his head to his neck. It was still wet from the water and warm from the sun.

"I know you think this. I can see it in your eyes. It makes me feel good, but eventually you'll see the truth. I'm the bad guy and you'll leave me."

Wow. I had no idea this was what Auggie was thinking. "You sure have a lot of rules about what will happen in the future. The truth is you're not a fortune teller, and you're denying yourself all the things you actually want just because there's a chance it might not work out, but what if it does? What if you're missing out on your destiny?"

"Let's not discuss this anymore." He tried to shut me down, but he'd opened a door, and I had to tell him what I thought.

"You're not superhuman. You are human. We all crave love and belonging in a family but especially men like you who see ugly things all the time. You need a safe place to come home to. I'm not sure if I'm strong enough to be that woman, but it feels like we're here in this place for a reason, and we're both fighting it so hard when all we want is to be together."

He stood and grabbed my hand. "Let's go."

His jaw set in a stern line. The door was shut. I'd pushed him too far. At least I'd said what I had to say and he'd heard it. Someone needed to talk to him like that because I had a feeling no one ever had before. Everyone was too afraid of his growly face to force him to admit that he needed love, and he was no less worthy of it because of his past.

***

Despite what he'd said, despite the grumpiness pouring off him, he'd tugged me to his side in the truck and kept one arm over my shoulders throughout the drive back to the bungalow.

We had dinner out on the deck as the sun went down. He drank vodka with his meal and I watched his gorgeous Adam's apple bob up and down as he started to speak with that sexy hint of an accent.

He'd asked me to tell him stories and I'd told him about all the strippers that acted as my surrogate mothers at the strip club when I was a kid. Many of them had much better maternal instincts than my own mom. I'd talked about Cyrus's kids and the games we liked to play together at the community center (air hockey, ping pong, pool, basketball).

I'd told him I liked the tacos at the cantina on the corner, and he said he'd like to try them. He asked about my failed dates and laughed when I'd told him all the awkward details of how I could not get laid no matter how hard I'd tried.

I cried when I talked about Train kidnapping me and the nightmare with Rico in Italy. He held me in his arms and hugged me tight while I wept. He promised me that Train would pay dearly, and he would never hurt me again. I believed him. It helped. It felt comforting to have someone ease the pain I'd carried alone for a long time.

Auggie told me about the young gymnast who was his first sexual experience and how he thought he might've loved her, but she moved away to go to a gymnastics training camp, and he never saw her again.

He talked about his parents and how they'd loved each other, but their marriage was always strained by his father's military obligations. Auggie said that his mom was never happy, and he felt helpless that he couldn't do anything about it. She'd told him she was disappointed in him when he'd joined the military, and I could see how that would hurt him since it was such a big part of who he was.

Pure joy had bloomed in my heart with each word we'd shared. Every time he nodded or grunted that he'd heard me felt like a victory. Every time he started a new sentence, I waited with baited breath to hear the new morsel of his secret life he'd share with me.

I was truly in Heaven and thought it couldn't get any better. And then it did. He looked into my eyes, held my hands in his, and spoke at length and with deep emotion about his fractured sense of loyalty. The ever-present guilt he struggled with over his defection and the unattainable desire to prove himself to Vander and the team. He even shared his disappointment in himself for his lack of a social life and the choices he'd made. At times, it was hard to listen to him berate himself, but mostly it was comforting to hear his voice.

"Thank you for sharing all of this with me. I love to hear your thoughts. The good and the bad. It's an awesome gift because I know how rare it is for you to trust someone with these things."

He squeezed my hands and gazed at me thoughtfully. "I'm surprised how easy it is with you."

We were engrossed in conversation until late into the night. A slight chill replaced the warmth of the day. His arms enveloped me completely, smoothing the goosebumps that had pebbled my skin.

I must've dozed off because the next thing I knew my side was pressed against his chest, and he was carrying me to the bed. Too bad all we'd be doing in there was sleeping because after today and tonight, I wanted Auggie more than ever, but as usual, I didn't get what I wanted.

Chapter 16 Surrender

Auggie

Do not fuck her, Aug. Do not fuck her.

I'd been telling myself this for days, and by some miracle of my own self-control, it'd worked. I'd suffered slow painful torture, but I'd successfully kept enough physical distance between us that she could escape from me unharmed.

My life had not left a stain on hers that she couldn't recover from and move on. She was still a virgin, we weren't in love, and she'd accepted the boundaries that I'd set down. I'd convinced her that a life with me would be miserable for her.

The fact that she'd accepted it only reinforced my conviction. She knew deep in her heart she didn't want to be involved with a man like me. I'd even managed to make it through another night without ramming her from behind. We'd spent all evening talking. She'd pulled stories out of me I'd never told another soul, and she'd listened with a heart full of compassion. Even with all that, I'd kept my dick in my pants and let her sleep.

Her whimpers in the morning were my undoing. The sweet little breaths and the way she spread her legs ever so slightly. It wasn't her fault. She was mostly asleep, but as she woke up, she reached for me. Her hand found my hip. "Mmm," she purred in a way that I felt deep in my balls.

Suddenly, I was bargaining with the devil. If I changed my role at Knight Security, I could wrap my palms over her pert little breasts and squeeze them. If I gave up my vendetta against the Bratva, I could move an inch closer and smash my hard cock into her ass crack. It was illogical as hell, but I'd reached my limit.

Not only was she the sexiest woman I'd ever met, she was the smartest, kindest, funniest, gentlest. Everything I was lacking in my life, she exuded naturally. It bubbled out of her like life juice and I drank it up.

"Mornin'," she drawled, her Southern accent stronger and sweeter in the morning and fuck if that didn't make my cock twitch.

"Mornin', babe." I sunk my lips into her neck and nibbled the soft skin there with my teeth. My dick swelled in celebration of my weakness.

"I surrender," I murmured against her neck.

"Mmm?" She turned to me with her eyes still closed.

I kissed her lips, and she opened for me reflexively. I dove into the sweetest silkiest mouth in the world, but she pulled away.

"Um, Auggie. I thought we weren't because, ya know."

"I'm rethinking things."

Her forehead scrunched in a *W*. "Did something change?"

I took a deep breath and formulated the words out loud. "I surrendered." I shrugged. That was the truth. I'd surrendered to her.

"What does that mean?" She pressed on my chest with firm palms.

"I give in. I give up. I want you that bad, I'll give up everything for you." I leaned in to kiss her, and she arched her neck away.

"I don't want you to give up anything for me."

"I have to. I'll apply to be moved to training and recruitment at KS."

"Do you like training people?"

"I hate it."

"Then no." She rolled off the bed and stood up. "No. You're not giving up your job for me."

"Haven, please. Let me do this."

"Only if you promise you won't change your life for me. I want you, Auggie. Bad. But I know you'll resent me if you give up everything to be with me. You'd take a job you hate after spending so much time telling me how much you love your work? I don't want to be the woman that took Auggie... What's your last name?"

"Provatorova." There was a long story behind the name I hadn't even told her yet, but this was the name I went by now. I'd never give her my birth name because that person was dead.

"I don't want to be the woman who took down Auggie Pro-va-tor-oh-va." She pronounced each syllable slowly and completely incorrectly. "That's like taking down Thor. I am not the girl who takes down Thor. I'm the girl who stands behind him and cheers as he battles the Hulk." She marched to the bathroom and started aggressively brushing her teeth.

"You're killing me again." I'd made this huge decision, and she'd summarily dismissed it. I lay back on the pillow and stared at the ceiling. I noticed a latch up there. Was that a safety hatch in case of flooding? I'd have to check that out later.

She came out of the bathroom and stood before me with her hands on her hips. She'd washed her face and brushed her hair, pulling it up into a neat ponytail. All of it was a challenge to me. She was daring me to mess up her hair, smear her lip gloss, tear off the loose knitted top and shorts that covered her luscious body. She thought she could put herself together? I could ruthlessly tear her apart in seconds and enjoy the fuck out of it.

"It appears we have reached an impasse, Captain." She used a mocking serious tone with a terrible British accent like she was in an old-time World War II movie.

The best part of her stand was the set of her chin, the fierce determination, and the confidence in her eyes. She truly believed she could win this, and that made me hard as a rock. Cute as she was, she was courting trouble. She'd triggered all my competitive instincts, and I'd never back down. I'd also never fight fair. I sat up and watched her pert little ass waltz around the room. "You think you are strong enough to withstand me?"

"Sure. I have a secret weapon." She winked and dipped forward like a dancer giving a bow. Every single move she made brought out more of my wrath and dissolved any chance she had left at mercy.

"Oh really? What's that?"

She raised a small leather pouch from her luggage and held it dangling from her fingertip. "I have rosebud."

"Which is?"

"A vibrator. Stella also stocked me up with every toy I could ever want. I'm set for life. I can withstand you." She crossed her arms under her breasts and nodded.

Oh, now she'd dropped a challenge she'd never win. "Hand me the case."

"No. It's my weapon. I'm not giving it to you."

I stood and stalked toward her. "You have brought a toy to a gunfight." I swiped the bag and carried it with me toward the bed.

Sure enough. Stella had stocked it with a red plastic vibe shaped like a rosebud. It had one lonely double-A battery. "Pft. This thing won't last a few minutes." I tossed it on the bed, and she dove for the bag. I held it up high. "Stay back, Angel. I want to see what I'm up against here."

She huffed and blew out a long frustrated breath.

I dumped the contents of the bag out on the bed. Soft leather wrist cuffs, a silk blindfold, a wide leather crop with a heart cutout. Interesting. There was warming lube, condoms, clothespins, a collar with a hook, a metal dildo, and a few ball-shaped plugs. Oh, nipple clamps. I held them up. "You like your nipples pinched?"

She crossed her arms higher to cover her chest. "I have no idea," she said defensively, and I laughed.

I turned on the rosebud, and it began to spin and hum. "The only thing in this bag you can use alone is this tiny little vibe." I held it against my cock to test the power of the thing. "Does it have a turbo setting? This is anemic."

I took great satisfaction in the wide set of her eyes and the way her mouth dropped open. Did she not think I would play with her little rosebud? I probably wouldn't have if she didn't challenge me so adorably.

I leaned back to show her my bent cock straining against my board shorts. She gasped and licked her lips, eyes riveted to my hand. "Doesn't do anything for me. You really think this cold plastic thing can keep your little bud happier than my big warm cock?"

She scraped her lips with her teeth—hard. "Give that stuff back to me."

I dropped the rosebud inside my shorts. "Come and get it."

She hesitated.

"Oh. It slipped down to my balls. Now there's some potential. Ooh. Nice. I'm starting to see the appeal." I grabbed my balls and pushed the vibe against them. The little rosebud did its best but barely registered on my radar.

Her eyes set in determination as she stalked toward the bed. Perfect. She was playing into my trap. I let her climb up close and hold up her palm. "Give it to me."

I glanced down at my crotch, acting calm and disinterested. She looked too, and I took advantage, grabbing her wrist and pulling it behind her back. I tugged the other one back there and crushed her chest to my torso as I worked the cuffs around her wrists. They closed with Velcro so it was easy to slip them on. She struggled the whole time, which was awesome.

By the time I was done with her, I had her straddling my dick, her core pressed right on top of it. "You feel the rosebud now?"

She growled and tested the strength of the cuffs. Nope. Not coming off. She looked incredibly sexy, and I had full access to her tits, but I wanted her to surrender first. I couldn't force this on her or I'd be a jerk. Okay, more of a jerk than I was already.

"Go ahead and grind on it. I know you want to. Like you did in the cave. Get yourself off on me and my vibrating balls." I wiggled my eyebrows at her.

"No." Her thighs locked in place, but her hips jutted out just the smallest bit, enough that I could see she was struggling with her control.

"Why not?" I asked her, forcing her to talk when we were both panting and horny.

"I can't remember," she whispered, her eyes still focused on my crotch, which was now buzzing very close to her core. It didn't land exactly right, but she still had to feel it.

"Neither can I, so take what you want. I can see it in your eyes. So hungry, so greedy. You want to be my wicked little girl so badly. Remember how good it felt when you came on me? It was glorious. Remember how you ached for me the last few nights, knowing my cock was right behind you in the bed, but you couldn't have it? Did you dream of this? Now, here it is between your legs. Yours to take at whatever speed you like. Don't you want to drive me crazy taking it slow? Or maybe take it so fast I don't even get to enjoy it. Keep it from me, like a selfish little angel who won't share. Won't share her sweet cunt with me even though I'm begging."

She dropped forward, and her head balanced on mine. "Auggie," she pleaded. For what, I didn't know.

I tilted my head back, which brought our mouths together. I pressed my lips into hers, but she didn't yield. Instead, I felt the shuddering exhale of her breath on my lips. She was sending a signal I'd missed before. "You want me to take it. Don't you? You don't want me to beg you. You want me to steal it like a thief in the night who doesn't ask permission."

She nodded and thank fuck because I was about to lose it. Tired of waiting for her to finally grind on me, I was ready to force it out of her. And then, far too roughly, I gripped the back of her head and guided her mouth to the spot where I needed it. I drove her lips apart and chased her silky tongue as I yanked the band out of her hair, which fell down around her shoulders. We tangled in a hot wet mess as my other hand seized her hip and thrust her down on my cock. Her hips jerked in answer, and she moaned into my mouth. I ground up into her, impatient with the clothing I'd forgotten to remove before I'd positioned her.

I wished I had three more hands. I wanted to touch her everywhere now that I finally had access. I settled for one hand on her ass guiding her forward and one hand on her hip steering her up and down in a beautiful undulation that was about to make me come in my shorts. The vibe dropped lower and hit my asshole as she tried to climb up higher on me. We were both so greedy and fighting for it, but we had annoying fabric in the way and a distracting bug in my shorts.

I loosened her wrist cuffs, and she eagerly wrapped her arms over my shoulders and kissed me.

"Shirt off, babe. Raise your arms."

She lifted her arms over her head, and I was able to slip the loose clothing over and off. I moved the bikini top to the side, and when I finally pulled one of her pebbled nipples between my teeth, I nearly went blind with lust. My orgasm gnawed at my spine, and primal instincts took over.

My hands spanned her waist, and I fought the overwhelming urge to ram inside her. I needed to thrust and pump—hard and fast. But, shit, she was a virgin, and I needed to be careful with her.

I kissed her instead and attempted to slow down this out-of-control freight car we were riding. "I want to take you so bad right now, but you're not ready."

She grabbed my cheeks in her palms. "I'm ready." Her voice was deep and passionate. "I'm ready like a turkey after twenty hours in the oven. I'm ready like a pumpkin at Christmas. I'm ready like Ready Whip." Then she pushed my head back and licked my neck in a long swipe. She stopped on my Adam's apple and sucked it between her lips.

I chuckled at her enthusiasm. I'd planned to take it slow with her. I'd wanted to find a way to make it special so she'd remember it for the rest of her life, but nothing with us was going as I'd planned. Haven blew me away at every turn and shot all my plans out of the water.

Chapter 17 Safety Hatch

Then I remembered the latch. The roof probably had some sort of deck that we hadn't explored yet. "I have an idea. It requires us moving."

She wiggled her hips and ground down on my dick. "No."

"C'mon." I climbed out from under her and reached for the latch in the ceiling above the bed. Sure enough, it popped open and revealed a rope ladder. I made sure she was out of the way and pulled the strap causing it to tumble until it hung unfurled next to the bed.

"What is that?" The ladder swung in front of her shocked face.

"I think it's an emergency exit to the roof for flooding, but I'm hoping they have a deck up there. One sec." I pulled the stupid rosebud from my shorts and tossed it. I swiped up the condoms and the throw blanket from the end of the bed and held the ladder for her. "Up you go." A small square of pink morning sky peeked at us through the hatch. Oh yeah, this was a good idea.

She cautiously placed a foot on the bottom rung and it swayed. I leaned over and kissed her. "I want your first time to be special. The sun isn't fully up yet, the view is gonna be awesome up there, and you're gonna feel like you're on top of the world."

"What if we fall off?"

"Then we'll land in the water and have a good laugh, but I promise I won't let you fall."

"Okay."

"Get going. It'll be worth it." I didn't actually know what we'd find up there, but from what I'd seen of similar rooftop access portals, there would at least be a flat surface we could use.

I held the ladder as still as possible, this time stopping the bottom rung from swinging with my foot. She made progress and climbed to the ceiling. I followed close behind her and caged her in. I gave her butt a little push, and she popped out through the hatch.

"Oh my God."

"Is it good?" I was right behind her and had to turn sideways to squeak my shoulders through.

"More than good."

The view was absolutely breathtaking. Totally worth it. A band of crimson sky rose up from the teal water. Thin high clouds had just turned frosty white against an early morning baby blue background. Fantastic.

The roof was a sunning area, complete with a futon, which probably also doubled as a flotation device, and a privacy screen made of glass. It was actually a large patio big enough for a crowd of people.

I dropped the blanket and condoms on the futon and came up behind her. My hands circled her waist and pulled her close. "Rajerio was holding out on us."

She stared at the view with her mouth open. "This is the best part of this place."

I moved her hair to the side and kissed her neck. "You don't have to do anything you don't want to do. We have lots of time."

She turned around and gazed up at me. "I think it's sweet you're being considerate and all, but I really just want you to take charge and rock me like a hurricane right now because I can see in your eyes that's what you want to do, and I know that's who you truly are."

She didn't have to tell me twice. I swung her up and kissed her as I carried her over to the futon. I kept my lips on hers as I pulled the string of her bikini top. We had to separate to get it over her head. I slid her bottoms down and completely off and then she was bare before me. My virgin bride. I tried not to dwell on it being her first time, but it was there between us. I didn't want to hurt her.

She spread her legs and showed me her glistening cunt and all that worry disappeared. I was going to make this woman mine today, and I couldn't wait a second longer. I dove between her legs and swiped my tongue through her folds. "So sweet and slick, babe. Like ambrosia." I found the slippery swollen bud and my cock jumped. I'd never been harder in my life. She moaned and arched her back as her hands came to my head and her fingers scraped through my hair.

"Aug," she gasped.

I devoured my sweet little girl. Once I had a taste of her, I was gone. My tongue feasted, my hands grasped her breasts and teased the nipples between my fingers. She writhed and squirmed, and I held her down with my forearms. When she came, I would've given anything to be inside her right then. As it was, I felt it on my tongue and heard her cries in my ears. I added two fingers in her slick heat to draw it out for her. When her whimpers turned to sighs, I knew the peak had passed for her and she was sated. That meant I was free to be the greedy selfish asshole that I was. I slipped out of my trunks and ripped the condom open. Her eyes were still closed, and I was poised at her entrance. "You feel me?"

I poked her with the tip. So good.

"Yes." Her head tossed from side to side.

She'd told me to rock her like a hurricane, so I didn't hesitate. It had been too long, and we were both primed and desperate for it. I slid inside slowly, using my last bit of coherent thought to keep from ramming into her.

That was it. I needed to thrust, to pump, to nip, to chew.

My hips surged forward, and I surrendered to it, plowing deep into her heat. In her sweet little gasp, we exchanged something. She gave me her trust, and I gave her my adoration. I worshiped her like a deity come to earth to save me. She had me on my knees, weak and at her mercy just by the simple act of trusting me with this.

"Jesus, babe. So tight. So fucking beautiful."

"Yes, Aug. It feels good."

She said that, but I hadn't even moved yet. I hadn't given her what I knew she needed to come. With a tilt of my hips and my hand on the small of her back, I pumped once, dragging my pubic bone over her clit, making sure the tip of my cock caressed her cervix and her G-spot. All her sensitive areas, I made sure to hit.

She sucked in a long deep breath, and her mouth dropped open. "Oh. It's like wow. Just like wow."

"Exactly. When you're with me, you feel that all the time. If you're not feeling it, you let me know, but I want to see you come over and over from my cock pumping into you."

Her breath hitched, and her thighs tightened around my hips. I drew her nipple into my teeth and teased it with a sharp tug. She mewled, squeezing and pulsing around my cock as another orgasm rocked through her. I loved that I did this to her. I made her come undone.

A few more thrusts into her tight cunt, and it stabbed at my balls and twisted up through my hips until I couldn't hold back anymore. She was still coming around my cock, her hips undulating with it. In a huge release of pent up energy, I came hard and exploded into her. As I took her mouth in mine again, we celebrated much more than the physical ecstasy. We'd given ourselves, our souls, our insecurities and uncertainties. We'd laid it all on the table and handed it over in a way that would change our lives. Neither one of us would ever be the same again.

She smiled and panted for air when I finally released her lips. She had a tear at the crease of her eye, and I licked it away. "You good?"

"I am so good," she drawled and her head fell back.

I kissed her neck and sucked her sweet skin between my lips. "My God, that was phenomenal, Angel. You are so incredibly beautiful. I never want to leave this spot."

She smiled and peppered small kisses all over my face. "Me either. Let's lay here all day."

I laughed and relaxed on top of her, giving her my weight without pulling out. "As long as you want. Forever. I could spend forever inside you and still not have enough."

I also did not lie. I couldn't sink inside her without falling in love with her. In fact, I was in love before tonight but too cowardly to admit it. I loved Haven with all my heart. I'd fight anyone who tried to hurt her, I'd give up any-thing to make her happy. I'd be tested on that soon enough when I had to return to the life I'd created for myself, but for now, I basked in the knowledge that I had found love when I'd believed it impossible. Haven had given herself to me as a precious gift, and I'd spend the rest of my life trying to prove myself worthy of her.

"Thank you, Auggie. This was so special. I'll cherish it forever."

"Good." I pressed my lips to hers again. "It's not just this. Now, you are mine and I am yours. Wherever you go, my soul goes too."

Chapter 18 Lesson Four

Haven

Sex with Auggie was ah-may-zing. Holy smokes, I was whipped as hell. Auggie could say anything, touch me anywhere, and I exploded like a live wire in a bathtub.

We hadn't ironed out the details of what he would do about his job, but I had a strong sense it didn't matter. Whatever the future brought us, we'd face it together. It felt like a dream with the blue sky above, the warm air on our skin, the wind humming, the birds waking up. We were floating above the most gorgeous place in the world experiencing the most profound and immersive connection two people could share.

Now I am yours and you are mine.

My spirit did a celebration dance. I'd wanted Auggie so desperately but never imagined he'd give me so much of himself so freely. I didn't know what I'd done to earn it. I was just being myself and he seemed to like that. Whatever the reason he chose to give that to me, I'd never take it for granted.

We'd finally pulled ourselves off the roof (actually he'd practically carried my limp body down the ladder) and spent the morning in the jacuzzi talking. If I'd thought he was an open book the night before, the intimacy we'd shared and the hot water opened him up even further. He didn't go so far as to say he loved me, but he gushed over me and promised he'd always protect me because I was *his* now.

They were words I'd never dreamed I'd hear from Auggie or anybody, and I'd soaked it all up with pleasure. He'd asked

181

more about my biological father and if I'd ever tried to find him using DNA samples.

I'd told him the truth. I'd always wanted to do it but never had the funds or resources, but yes, I would love to find my father. I told him about how I'd made him a hero in my stories. He was a Jack Reacher action-adventure type good guy.

Auggie had talked me into getting dressed and heading out for the day because we only had a week, and there was so much of Jamaica we hadn't seen yet. He talked me into parasailing and I loved it. We snorkeled with the fish and the beautiful coral and returned to the bungalow sun-kissed, happy, and exhausted.

Auggie took a call while I used the restroom. When I came out, Auggie was sitting on the end of the bed. His glow had faded, and he was back to the deadly serious stone statue I had seen so much before this trip. His phone lay face-down next to his hip on the bed.

"Something wrong?"

"I just received a call from Vander."

"Oh?" I raised my eyebrows trying to act cool. "How is everything going?"

"Did you call Stella to ask about the status of the mission?"

Shoot. Darn. Okay. He already knew so I wasn't going to lie to him. "Yes."

"Why?" He sounded impatient and frustrated.

"You seemed worried and I thought it would reassure you." I shrugged.

"You thought that, did you?" His voice was measured like he was trying to control his temper.

"Did it reassure you?" I smiled, trying hard to turn the path of this situation around. We were having such a great day, and now it was going south fast.

"Yes, I am reassured that my team is fine. However, I knew they would be. I am not assured that you went behind my back to call Stella and created a string of contacts that could potentially reveal their location and ours." His dark eyes were as cold as his words as he glared up at me.

"I didn't think of that."

"And you didn't think to ask me first?"

"No. It was just a spur of the moment thing. I had the new phone. I wanted to talk to Stella anyway, and I just mentioned it while I spoke with her. You said it was secure."

He took a deep breath and pinched the bridge of his nose. "In the future, if you wish to make contact with someone, run it by me first. While we're here, don't use your phone at all. Nothing is completely secure. I should've explained it more clearly to you, but I thought it was obvious."

"It wasn't to me. I'm sorry. I'm not well versed on this stuff."

"That's okay. I'm about to educate you."

"What?"

He stood and scooped me up behind my legs. The room spun, and I was over his shoulder watching his feet walk out of the bedroom, through the living area, to the kitchen. The room flipped again, and I landed on my butt on the counter with my legs dangling off the edge.

"Stay." He touched my nose. "I'll be right back."

He left and came back with the leather bag of sex toys and condoms gripped in his fist.

My stomach dropped. "Are you angry?"

He stood between my legs and worked his hand under my hair to grip my neck. "I'm not angry." He gave me a reassuring squeeze, and his voice softened. "I'm going to teach you a few things to help you trust me enough to ask me first before going to someone else."

"Oh boy."

"Are you ready?"

Was I? Fear was coiling deep in my gut. Stronger than the fear was my hunger for him, the excitement, and the trust I had in him from the way he'd handled my first time. He was considerate, and he'd made it good for me. I knew he would do that again if I was brave enough to put myself in his hands right now.

I nodded slowly.

"That's my girl. If at anytime you feel uncomfortable just tell me. Say slow down or stop, and I will do exactly as you wish. There's no pressure at all on you to do anything you're not comfortable with."

"Oh my."

"Hands and knees."

"What?" I squeaked.

"On your hands and knees, my angel."

Okay. That was sweet and gave me the enticement I needed to find out what he planned to do to me once he had me on my hands and knees.

His hand caressed my back and on an upward slide, he worked my shirt over my head and arms. On the downward slide, he pulled my shorts to my knees. "Lift." I lifted my right leg and then my left, and he removed my shorts.

I was wearing a skimpy red bikini bottom that was almost like a thong, and his hand went immediately to it, his fingers exploring the crack.

"Lesson one." He dug into the bag with his other hand. "Wrist cuffs also work on ankles."

I gulped.

He tugged my feet together and worked the cuffs around my ankles. His hands pushed my knees out so I was more open to him.

"Lesson Two." He took the crop from the bag and dragged the soft leather over the swells of my butt. "The heart in the middle marks the places I will suck you."

"Oh God." That sounded wonderful.

"Lesson three." I felt a silk strip cover my eyes. "You'll feel more if you can't see." He fastened the blindfold around my head.

Then he was done talking and he started moving. I felt him curl his front over my back, and the heat and friction felt amazing. He peppered gentle kisses that tickled my neck and spine. At the same time, he moved both hands, one with the crop, over my arms, breasts, stomach, and inner thighs. Wow. He was right. I could feel everything magnified like crazy with the blindfold blocking my vision. The scruff from his chin scratched down my back followed by his warm breath. Where the string of the bikini bottoms crossed my hip he stopped, nipped it with his teeth, and growled.

That sent a current of electricity rocketing through my body. I was already primed and ready. "Auggie, please."

"You can beg me to hurry, but I will take my time with you. But go ahead and beg. I love it."

"Ugh. Auggie." My frustrated cry was interrupted by a sharp smack near the crease of my right butt cheek. "Ow." My feet jerked up and tugged against the cuffs.

His warm mouth sucked the spot and soothed the burn. "Too hard?"

The area tingled and cooled, and my feet settled back on the counter. "No. I was just surprised."

Another smack hit the curve on the other side. I growled as he licked and kissed the ache away gently. Yes, Auggie knew exactly what to do. I didn't want to think about how he'd learned it, but I was happy to be the recipient of his knowledge.

"Are you enjoying the lesson?" His voice rumbled through my body like the deep bass of a cello.

"Yes. I love it. More." I panted through the breaths I was struggling to take to calm myself.

"As you wish, my queen." I could hear the smile in his voice.

He brought the crop down again in a different spot and sucked it before moving higher. It was like he was a painter placing his brush strokes exactly where he wanted them.

My skin responded by heating and tingling like an inferno.

"You look incredible like this. Your skin reddens so nicely, and the hearts taste warm and hot on my tongue like candy."

I wiggled my hips and the crop came down again in a rapid sequence followed by another round of sensuous sucking.

I felt a tug on my bottoms that jerked my hips to the side and a scrape against my skin and then the air hit my sex. Auggie had torn my bottoms off. Oh well. At least it wasn't the loincloth one that I loved. His fingers worked on my back and tickled under my hair and the top was gone. Okay. He didn't rip it.

"Fucking beautiful." His hands caressed all the areas he'd just exposed. He ran a finger through the wetness between my legs. "Delicious."

Oh God. He was going to eat me and I couldn't see it. "I want to see you."

"At my leisure." He landed a smack between my legs that hit my sex. It didn't hurt, but I held my breath anticipating the suck. He did not make me wait and came down to gorge eagerly from me. I felt his head squeeze between my thighs, his hands pulled my hips to tilt them back, and then his tongue landed on my clit. Oh my Lord. That felt freaking incredible. An orgasm was already beating down the door, but it felt like it was too soon. "Oh."

"You taste fucking incredible. Come now for me." He wiggled the tip of his tongue in a magical way that instantly had me coming.

I pulsed and writhed, and he didn't lose contact as I bucked around. He rode the whole wonderful ride out with me. When it passed, I closed my knees and sat back on my calves. "Okay. Okay. Okay." I could barely speak because that was the most powerful thing I'd ever felt in my life. I'd been missing out on this for all these years.

I felt his fingers loosening the cuffs around my ankles, and he tugged away my blindfold. It didn't matter at that point. I had my eyes closed. He curled his warm body over my back again and spoke in my ear. "Lesson four."

"Oh no."

"You'll like this one." He wrapped me in his arms, lifted, and carried me like a baby to the bed. I lay on my side and stretched out next to him. He was still fully dressed, but it was too late for me to feel embarrassed. I loved it all. He removed his shirt, and I moaned. His shorts came off next and Auggie in all his magnificent glory was before me sliding a condom onto his massive cock. I reached for his arm, and he crawled on top of me. His weight pressed me to the bed, and his dick settled between my legs. "Lesson four is there's nothing better than just you and me naked in a bed."

He kissed me and teased my clit by sliding his thick shaft up and down over it. He was right. Nothing could be better than that. He angled the tip of his cock and kissed me again as he forged in. I gasped as he stretched me, but his kisses swallowed it.

I wrapped my legs around his hips, my hands around his back, and he started to move. Yes. Nothing better than the way he filled me. I loved it. He moaned and picked up speed. I tilted my hips to get him closer, deeper, harder. He pumped in and out in a smooth motion that had another orgasm brewing and threatening to explode.

He rose up, sat back on his calves, reached out and pulled my hips up his muscular thighs. He held me in place and drove into me. I couldn't move, only lay there and take in all that Auggie was offering me. His eyes were on mine, his head tilted down, jaw set, raw hunger on his face.

His palm landed on my mound and ground against my clit in a tiny pumping motion, and I was gone again.

"That's it. You got it. Go ahead," his deep voice rasped.

I saw stars and my ears rang as my shoulders arched back. My whole body was absorbed in riding out this orgasm that was consuming me.

His body shook, and he rooted his cock as deep as it would go as he grunted through his orgasm. I felt all his energy and strength barreling down on me, and I loved it. I wanted to take it, be a part of it, share it with him, watch him experience it.

And it was beautiful.

He fell forward and kissed me hard and wet. "Jesus, babe."

"I know."

I didn't have much to compare it to, but his comment made me think he'd felt something earth shattering like I had. Neither one of us would ever forget the lessons he'd taught me today. What we'd shared transcended all the material worries and imagined barriers between us. He didn't say it in words, but it was loud and clear to me. We were in love.

Chapter 19 Mile-High Club

Auggie

Haven was sucking my cock on the flight back. She'd begged to do it. Said she wanted to create a new picture in her head. I'd been putting her in situations where she had no choice but to take what I wanted to give, and I'd intentionally avoided giving her the chance to go after me with her mouth.

But once we reached altitude, her eyes lit with thirst, her bottom lip pushed out, and I decided it was time to quench her desire. So she was between my legs, on the floor of the cabin, giving it her all, and I was fighting coming in her mouth.

She pumped and sucked with her soft and pliable lips. Tentative at first, then awkward trying to get the whole thing in there. She finally accepted it wouldn't fit and was using a combo of handjob and vacuum cleaner to get me off. Everything Haven did was juiced with pure, unguarded enthusiasm for the experience. She wanted to soak it all in and glow in the wonder of it all.

I didn't guide her or push on her head. I didn't want her to gag on it. Not yet. While I loved the feel of her hot, wet tongue licking up my shaft, I still felt consumed by guilt for the shit I'd pulled with Crystal before I'd known about Train.

I pulled her off by lifting her under her arms, and she stared longingly at my hard dick as I maneuvered her up and placed her with her knees outside my hips.

"Is something wrong?"

I kissed her and worked her skirt up. "No, baby. I just want your face right here." I kissed her again and groaned when I found her soaking wet from sucking me off. "I want to watch you moan as you squeeze my cock in that ironclad grip you have down here." I massaged her clit, and her head fell back. I couldn't get the condom on fast enough before I was lifting her up and plunging her down on my cock.

We'd done it countless times since the first time. Lots of locations and positions. We still had more to discover, but one thing I'd learned about Haven. Each time she came apart, I came together a little bit more.

Puzzles I'd struggled with my entire life, she'd untangled with her grace and tolerance of me that I didn't earn or comprehend.

For the first time in my life, I'd allowed a woman to unlock my withering heart and plant herself inside.

"Aug?" She stared down at me, and her brows pulled together.

"Yeah?"

"Where'd you go?"

I didn't realize I'd stopped moving and was staring at her tits.

It would've been the ideal time to tell her my feelings, but instead I said, "Just thinking about how much I love fucking you." I should've said *I fucking love you*, but I didn't.

She braced her hands on my shoulders and bounced impatiently, her breath panting as she urged me to take control. My cock twitched inside her.

I could easily stay buried in this woman for the rest of my life and never have a thought of another woman.

My hands stopped her on an upward slide and held her poised at the tip. "You in a hurry?"

"So hard to go slow," she whined.

I pressed her hips down, slid back inside, and held her in place. "You're joining the mile-high club right now. Slow down."

"But we don't have time. Our seatbelts."

She was worried the short flight would end, and we'd be caught with our pants down. The pilot knew better than to interrupt something like this happening in a private cabin. "Don't worry. I've got the timing down."

She leaned forward and pressed her tits under my chin as she hugged me. "You take us there when you're ready? Yeah?"

"Yeah, Angel." I loved that she trusted me, let go like that, enjoyed it like she did. I kissed her for a long time and just savored being hard inside her, devouring her hot mouth, and denying myself the urge to fuck her senseless.

Finally it was time. I rammed her down on my cock, and we both groaned. She rose up, and I let her take some control because I was losing my fucking mind trying to stave it off knowing she had to come first.

Luckily she didn't make me wait and her high-pitched keen filled the cabin.

"Oh my God, Auggie."

I knew what she wanted. She felt lost in that moment like she might come untethered. "I have you." I dug my fingers into her hips and pounded her through the end of her orgasm and the beginning of mine. I lost track of her for a minute as the earth tilted, and I suddenly felt like I was sitting on the wing of the plane, thousand mile an hour winds blowing in my face.

My hands never left her hips, driving the whole thing from there. In a rare moment of clarity, I loosened my grip, worried I'd cause bruising, but she didn't look like she was in pain. All her moans were pure pleasure.

I knew when her climax ebbed because she turned to jelly in my hands. I loved her this way. Pliable. Unworried. Simply sublime. She'd had that look a lot this week, and I wasn't looking forward to returning home and facing the bullshit, but it needed to be done.

The stakes were much higher now that I was fully invested in her and cared about her more than I had ever cared for anyone before. Now that I *loved* her. I was getting used to the word in my head but hadn't yet placed it on my tongue.

I rearranged her so her head was in the crook of my arm, her body turned toward me, her hand on my abs as she looked up at me.

It reminded me of the time we flew back from Italy and Steel and Brandy were sharing a similar position. Within a few minutes, though, Steel had said something wrong and they were sitting apart on the seat, destined to separate.

I stopped thinking about that because I didn't want that for me and Haven. I wanted to keep her close as long as possible without screwing things up. For the first time in my life, I was planning a way to make room for a woman. Thinking of ways to make changes so she could feel safe with me and hoping on fate that we could make it through the minefield we were wandering into, both emotionally and physically.

"I don't want to go back," she murmured.

I brushed her hair from her forehead. Her bruises were fading and the swelling was gone. She looked healthy, tan, and sated. "Are you afraid of Train?"

"No."

I was a little surprised at her answer but also happy to hear it. "And this is because?"

"I trust you to protect me." She shrugged like it was simple, but I knew how much it took for her to get to that point. She'd been running from Train for a long time. I also knew she was relaxed right now, but we were heading back into the fire.

"That easy, huh?"

"Not that easy. Still difficult, but I'm getting there."

"My brave girl." I gave her a soft, gentle kiss and she smiled. "The team'll be back tomorrow. We have a meeting with the feds."

"What's my part in this?"

"I negotiated you out of this one, so if Cutlass keeps his word, you'll hang out at a safe house until the coast is clear. We'll use the Bravo location this time." The Bravo location was also my house. It was the closest thing to bringing her home that I could give her.

"How many safe houses do you guys have?

I'd given her some information on the workings of Knight Security. She'd seen much of it in action already, but I'd wanted to give her an idea of how successful the company had become. The Knight brothers had built a reputation for being the most elite security firm in the U.S., and I'd wanted her to know she was in good hands.

"It depends on the logistics of the location. I believe there are five near Atlanta because it's a big hub for international travel and thus criminals. Other cities may only have one near the airport. Sometimes a lot of travel is required to get to remote safe houses."

"So I'm going to hide out again?" Her voice sounded disappointed.

"You were hiding out when I found you at the compound."

She flinched. "Looking back at it now, I'm embarrassed that I used Duke and Cyrus like that. I should've gone to the police. I shouldn't have run away from you when you offered me help." She looked away. "I'm sorry."

I turned her back to face me. "We've been over this. I understand why you did it. I forgive you. You were running scared and doing what you thought you needed to do to survive."

"I'm tired of hiding. I'm not afraid of him anymore."

Good. I was proud of her and excited to see what she'd do when she was out from under his shadow. After we knew she was safe, she'd be free to roam and soar. "I don't usually support the idea of hiding out in a safe house either. I like to be out there letting my presence be known. But with you, I didn't want to take chances in the beginning. It was too hot with Train having the tracking device on you."

"But since he doesn't have me tracked anymore, things have probably cooled down. Right?"

I squinted down at her. "What are you saying?"

"It's probably safe enough for us to go out on a date."

"You want to go on a date?"

"I want our vacation to continue. I don't want to go back to the real world just yet. And I'm hungry. Let's go for dinner. What about the Russian place you were telling me about?"

"Not a good idea." My team was away. We didn't have intel on Train's location. But her hopeful eyes were pleading with me to extend her break from the stress, and I was tempted to give in. I did owe her a proper date if I truly wanted to call her mine.

"There's no way he knows where we are. We'll just grab a bite before we go back on lockdown. Show me your favorite food. After that, I promise I'll cooperate and stay quiet in the safe house while you go fight the bad guys, but let me have one more evening with you. Please." She slipped her hand under my shirt and ran her delicate fingers through the hairs on my chest.

"It's very difficult to say no to you."

"Then say yes. We'll keep a low-profile. It'll be fine. Just one dinner. You can tell me more active combat secrets."

I grinned down at her. She had pulled a lot of info out of me over the past week. I'd never talked about my military experiences with anyone but the team before, but I found that sharing it with her, even if it was a watered down version without identifiable details, helped me to see it through her eyes. She saw me as a hero. She liked hearing about the enemies we'd defeated, and she absorbed all the details with her special brand of youthful wonder.

"Only if you promise to tell me more of your stories." When we weren't fucking or watching TV, I'd asked her more about her ideas. She truly had a brilliant imagination and a gift for weaving a tale, but mostly I enjoyed watching her light up and laugh at herself as she conjured up grandiose situations.

"Yay!" She sat up and kissed me.

"One dinner for you, my love, and then we return to kicking ass."

"Hmm. Okay. Thank you." I'd let the love part slip. She didn't miss it and closed her eyes with a full grin gracing her beautiful lips.

Chapter 20 My Hero

Haven

The Russian restaurant he'd mentioned was not at all what I'd expected. I was imagining more of a mom-and-pop sidewalk cafe. As we walked into a leather-boothed, linen table-clothed dining facility on the thirtieth floor of the Continental Hotel, the view of downtown Atlanta took my breath away.

"I feel underdressed." I'd worn a golden slip dress I'd found in my luggage and spiky-heeled sandals that I didn't think I would ever need but ended up being grateful for when Auggie said we'd have to dress up for our date.

He'd changed into an all-black outfit of slacks, a shirt without a collar that looked like a tuxedo shirt, the top buttons open, and a jacket, buttons also open. He looked fabulous and had no problem producing a dressy outfit from his luggage. I looked like I was wearing a beach cover to a restaurant, which I totally was. At least it wasn't transparent like most of the dresses Stella had packed for me.

As we waited for a hostess to seat us, he leaned in close to my ear. "You look good enough to eat with that alluring tan on your flawless skin. Every man in this room wishes he was me right now." I blushed as his palm, which had been at the small of my back, slid down an inch and intimately touched the crack of my ass. No one could see it as we were standing against the wall, but I felt like everyone knew he'd just pressed the trigger on my hormones.

I did feel eyes on us as we walked to a booth by the window, but I was pretty sure everyone was looking at him, even the men. He commanded the entire room as he pulled out my chair and tucked me in. "Such a gentleman."

He smirked. He'd been a pretty vulgar sex fiend for the past week, but he'd cleaned up nice and shifted gears with ease. I was still thinking of our futon on the roof and the things he did to me on the kitchen counter.

I was perusing the menu when I noticed his eyes scanning the place. "Are you worried about something?"

"Always good to be alert." Auggie had shifted back to protector mode, and I felt him pulling away from me again. I understood that we were back home, and we had to be careful, but I was hoping to enjoy one last meal with him before we returned to the real world.

"I doubt Train or any of his men have ever heard of this restaurant."

"I won't let my guard down around you."

The waiter approached the table. I ordered schnitzel, and Auggie ordered beef stroganoff.

"No vodka?" I asked him.

"Not tonight."

"Mmm. I miss Jamaica already. Relaxed Auggie was incredibly sexy."

"You will be safe again soon. Right now, you are not."

"I know that. Thank you for keeping your guard up for me."

He nodded and looked down.

"I'm very lucky to have you, Aug. I'd be lost without you. I'd have no hope of being free of Train. I'd still be scared and hiding at the compound."

He cleared his throat but didn't look up.

"Thank you for looking out for me. No one has ever treated me as good as you do. You're my real-life hero."

He shook his head and slowly looked up at me. "You should've been protected your entire life. Your mom did her best, but you two shouldn't have been alone in the hood like that. She should've gotten you out of there and done whatever she could to get you a father figure. Instead, she dug in deeper and all you had was Eugene while she ran around stirring up shit that eventually caused her death."

"I don't blame her. It was the life she knew. She made money stripping. I could've left too and I stayed. What's familiar is easier even when it's harder." This was something Auggie and I had touched on in Jamaica and I was coming to see more clearly the more I talked about my mother.

"Are you ready to leave Lamar Gardens now?"

"I think so. Yes."

"Good." He held his hand out on the table, and I reached out to slip my fingers into his. It felt warm and strong, and I shivered thinking of the magic his fingers had done all over my body.

He grinned and leaned in deep to plant a kiss on my lips. It wasn't a small peck either. It was a full-on tongue-in-mouth extravaganza. The waiter walked up and Auggie froze. I sensed his attention leaving me and shifting toward the waiter.

I turned and wiped my lips as my cheeks heated. Kissing Auggie in public was my new favorite guilty pleasure.

"Dimitri."

This was a female voice which I turned to see was coming from a very tall woman standing at our table. She wore a tight black dress with ruching up the sides and between her very round, very high breasts. She towered over us with perfectly shiny straight blonde hair and blue eyes with dark, arched brows.

"Tatiana," he said.

I was shocked for many reasons. Firstly, he knew this woman's name. Secondly, he'd said it with a Russian accent he'd never used around me before, and thirdly, because he smiled up at her as he reached for her hand.

Chapter 21 Moonlighting

The woman he'd called Tatiana snapped her hand back and stepped away from Auggie as she glared at me with her eyebrow all crooked.

"Is this the reason you do not return my calls?" She spoke with a thick accent that I assumed was Russian based on her statuesque frame and fair complexion.

Auggie sat back in his seat slowly. "I was out of town for a while." I couldn't read him at all. He was guarded but acting so nonchalant about this woman who was clearly furious about seeing him with me.

"Konstantin is dead," she spat out and braced her hands on her hips, which caused her breasts to push forward. She was everything I wasn't. Composed, confident, voluptuous, dripping in makeup and jewels. I was wearing a bathing suit cover and a tan. That was it. "The family suspects an insider betrayed him."

Auggie glanced quickly over his shoulder then up at her. "Watch yourself."

"Why were you not at the funeral?" she asked him.

"Again. Out of town."

"I don't believe you. How do I know you didn't kill Konstantin?"

He stood abruptly, and I stared in shock as he gripped her arm by the wrist and pulled her side into his chest. "Shut up."

Her demeanor changed when he touched her. Her shoulders softened, her eyes fell half-way closed like she was smelling him and he had her under a trance. She turned to me and smirked. "He's fucking me. If he told you you're the only one, he lied."

He snapped at her in blunt Russian, and I felt like I was in a movie. A horrible replay of the movie I'd seen of Auggie with Crystal but much more intimate. These two had history, and I knew nothing about it. He'd rarely mentioned other women at all, and I suddenly felt very stupid for not asking him more questions. I knew he'd probably slept with a lot of women. I just didn't think to ask him if he was actively seeing anyone. As Tatiana just told me flat-out, he was fucking her.

My stomach roiled and bile rose in my throat. I swallowed it down. I couldn't throw up here in front of them and the whole restaurant. I started looking for an exit. I had to escape this place and vomit in the bushes somewhere. He ushered her away toward the bathrooms, and the other customers pretended they weren't watching, but they were.

I left my seat and tried to hold it together as I stumbled through the front door. I braced my arms on a potted plant next to the elevator.

Just like that, my relationship with Auggie was over. We couldn't recover from this. He was seeing someone else and didn't tell me or her.

She'd called him Dimitri. Who was this dead Konstantin person? Did he have a secret second life? Why didn't he tell me? Because he knew I wouldn't have been with him if I had known.

I thought he was a loner. He made it seem like the team and his work were his life. God, how stupid was I? Of course he needed sex. He was a virile man. I should've assumed he had someone he regularly dated. I should've asked him about it directly, but would he have told me the truth?

The elevator door opened, and I stepped in. I didn't know where I was going, but I had to get far away from the lovers' quarrel unfolding in the restaurant. I knew from the second we'd arrived there that I didn't belong.

Auggie lived in a world of sexy Russian lovers and multiple identities. I was just a girl from the hood trying to stay alive.

The more I jabbed the button for the lobby, the longer the door stayed open. What was wrong with this fancy elevator? It couldn't close fast? It had to be one of the slow elevators that waited patiently for all the rich people to meander inside? I was used to the metro. Hop in during the split second the doors opened and make sure the tail of your jacket cleared before it closed.

This was another reason I didn't belong with Auggie. We weren't from the same world.

Finally, the doors began to slide closed. I'd done it. I'd made my escape. Where would I go? I couldn't go back to the reservoir.

Maybe Duke or Cyrus would take me in again, but I doubted it after the way they reacted to the news that Train was involved.

A large hand slipped between the closing elevator doors. The knuckles turned white as he gripped it and forced it open.

Auggie stood there looking red-faced and furious.

He huffed and puffed as he walked in and stood in front of me like an angry dragon. The doors closed behind him.

He stalked forward until my back hit the wall. "I'm sorry you saw that."

I turned my head to the side. I couldn't look at him the same way ever again.

"It's not what it seemed."

"Are you fucking her?"

"I was. Yes. Not since I met you."

"That's not the way she described it at all."

"She was confused."

My weight shifted as the elevator slowly moved down, and the queasiness flared in my stomach. "Why did you touch her like that? She melted into you."

"It's complicated."

"You just had an entire week with plenty of chances to explain your complicated life to me, and you didn't. You gave me inconsequential nougats and left out the fact you had a girlfriend."

"She's not my girlfriend."

"She thinks she is. What did you do that made her think that she was? Did you pull that *dominate you in the bedroom and now you are mine* routine with her too?"

"No." He sounded offended by my question, but how was I supposed to know what had passed between them? It was only logical that he'd done the same things with her that he'd done with me.

"I feel like such an idiot right now. I guess it's my fault really. I should've asked you explicitly if you were seeing someone else. I just assumed that because I was yours you were mine that there could only be one of those for each of us, but clearly she is yours too."

"She is not mine. You need to listen to me right now." He gripped my upper arms, and I looked down at his hands. He wouldn't hypnotize me with his touch anymore.

"Whether she is or she isn't, she still called you Dimitri and rattled off a bunch of details about a life you told me nothing about."

"I told you. You didn't hear me."

"When? When did you tell me you're pretending to be Dimitri and fucking Tatiana?"

"I told you about the moonlighting."

I stuttered and stopped cold. "She's part of your moonlighting gig?"

"Yes. Let's go somewhere private, and I'll explain it to you, but now is not a good place or time."

The elevator opened in the parking structure, and he took my hand to walk me out. I didn't fight it and allowed him to tow me to the car.

"I don't have anywhere else to go otherwise I'd be saying no to you."

"You can't say no to me."

I didn't know what he meant by that. Did he mean he wouldn't allow me to say no to him? If so, that was crap. I could say no to him, and he'd have to honor it.

Or did he mean that I simply couldn't resist him and everything about him? If so, he was absolutely right. It was impossible to deny him anything, but now that I'd seen him with Tatiana, I'd have to find my strength.

He opened my door and waited for me to buckle my seatbelt before he walked behind the car and climbed into the driver's seat.

"I was undercover." He looked straight forward as he spoke. His voice dripped with frustration and a touch of regret. "Tatiana was my contact. I slept with her, and she got me in touch with Konstantin. Now he's dead."

"Who is Konstantin?" I asked, trying to keep up.

"He was the leader of the Bratva."

I nearly choked as I gasped for air. I knew about the Bratva. I'd read stories and seen movies. "The Russian Mafia? Did you kill him?" I whispered.

"Please don't say that out loud." He glared at me with a side-eye.

"You did. Didn't you? You slept with her and killed Konstantin. Why? Why go through all that trouble?"

He pressed his lips together and looked away from me. He seemed like he was struggling with the decision to hide behind the brick wall he'd used to keep people out for many years or let me in.

"They took from me so I take from them."

Now we were getting somewhere. The truth had come out. "Are these the people who killed your sister?" It was a challenge to him. Let me in, Auggie or I'm out.

"No. They are their children."

At least he'd chosen to let me in, but what he was sharing didn't make sense. "So, what? Your vendetta is that strong that you're eliminating the children of the people who killed your sister? I grew up with gangs all around me. I know about this shit. It's not good. Vengeance killing just leads to more suffering. It never ends. We talked about this."

Finally, he turned to me fully and looked me in the eye. "I know. I heard you. This was all before I met you. I'm getting out."

"Sure. I've heard that a million times too. You can't get out of gangs. They grow on you like tentacles. The Russian Bratva is notoriously brutal. Worse than any Atlanta street gang. You'll never get out."

"I'm not a member. Dimitri is only a recruit. I'm free to go."

"If they find out you killed Konstantin, you are toast."

"I know this. I have a contingency plan for that."

He reached behind my seat and pulled out a black case. He opened it and unearthed a large gun, which he quickly loaded and placed in his lap with the barrel pointing at the driver's side door. His head was constantly moving, checking all the windows.

"Let me guess. Kill them before they kill you. I hate this. I don't want this in my life. I just want out. I thought you were different, but you're just like Cyrus and Train."

The muscles in his neck twitched, and he slammed his fist against the steering wheel. "I'm nothing like them," he growled. He took a deep breath. "Let's get out of here and go talk somewhere safe."

"Where is it safe, Auggie? Everywhere I go, danger follows."

"You are safe with me."

He pulled out of the spot, and we exited the parking structure. Once we hit the road, his eyes locked on the rearview mirror. "Shit."

"What's wrong?"

He made a sharp turn into an alley. The car behind us followed. "We got a tail."

"A tail? How did they find you so fast?"

"Tatiana must've called them and revealed my location. Stay calm. They have no proof it was me." He pressed some buttons on his phone, which was installed in a rack on his dashboard.

"Aug Dog. Is that you? How was Jamaica, mon?" Stella mimicked a Jamaican accent and sounded like she was laughing.

"I need backup at Atlantic Station. Who is closest to me?"

Stella stuttered. "Uh, what's up? Are you in trouble?"

"I got a tail and need some backup. Who is closest to me?"

"Me."

"Besides you, Stella. Did the team make it back?"

"They're delayed."

"Shit."

"Anyone stay behind?"

"Helix, but he's nowhere near Atlantic Station."

"Tell Helix to meet me at the Delta location ASAP."

"Will do, Aug. Be careful."

He ended the call and hit the gas. We weaved through traffic, and I held my breath.

"Why are you leading them to the safe house? Just keep driving. Eventually they'll run out of gas."

"Fuck that. I don't fucking run from these fuckers."

Okay then. Apparently the Russian Bratva brought all the fucks out of Auggie. I decided to sit quietly and let him handle the situation in his own way because I had no idea what to do. I slouched down in my seat and tried not to hyperventilate. Oh my God, we were going so fast and nearly crashing into every car. I was definitely going to pass out from lack of oxygen.

Tatiana was such a bitch. I couldn't believe Auggie would be with a woman like that, even if he was undercover.

I felt confused again. I needed time to think about all that he'd said. He was sleeping with her as part of some covert operation. She thought they were still together. We got together on the trip so there's no way he could've told her yet. I wanted to ask him about it, but he was driving fast and furious through downtown Atlanta. We'd have to talk it out later.

Chapter 22 Panic Room

Auggie

Until Helix arrived, I was on my own with these assholes. I was still in shock that Tatiana had shown up and caused a scene. Couldn't keep her bitter mouth shut to save her own life.

I'd brushed her off too early. Should've kept her around until the dust settled, but I knew even then I didn't want anyone but Haven. I couldn't sleep with Tatiana again, no matter how useful she was to my plan. I was faithful to Haven before she was mine, and I would be faithful forever if I didn't lose her over this.

When I broke it off with her, Tatiana had played it off like she didn't care. Said she knew it was just sex. She'd lied. The second she saw me with another woman, the claws came out and she struck fast and hard. She confronted Haven and called up Konstantin's henchmen within a few minutes of walking into the restaurant.

Tatiana had made her moves. Now I had to make mine.

The alpha plan was to lead whoever was following me to the Delta safe house, get Haven in the panic room, and then take them out one-by-one on my own. I could use Helix at my back right now, but I was always comfortable flying solo.

We pulled into the garage of Delta, and I cut the engine. "Let's move quick." By the time I made it to her side, she was already out of the car and waiting for me. I ushered her through the inner door, down the hallway, and into the panic room at the back of the house. "You stay here. You'll be locked in. Either Helix or me will let you out when it's safe."

She stood frozen as she took in her new surroundings. This room was nothing like the other rooms in the house. It had high-tech screens covering all the walls, a closet full of weapons and gear, and a metal door as thick as a vault. "You're not coming in here? Those guys are still out there."

"I hope so." I flipped on the dormant monitors and checked for signs of the car that had been following us. They hadn't approached yet. Good. I quickly swiped and loaded a rifle, another nine millimeter, and a knife. I threw on a vest, and that was all the time I had before Konstantin's guys approached the driveway.

Haven sat down in the chair by the main monitor. "Oh my God. There's people outside. Is that them?"

"Yes."

"Holy shit. This is scary." She had that terrified look in her eye again that I hated.

My selfish choices caused it. As much as I'd bagged on Cyrus and Duke for not protecting her, I was the one who brought her into the crosshairs this time. We shouldn't have attempted a public outing so soon after the Konstantin hit. Dumb move on my part. Now I had to go deal with it.

"I'm locking you in now. Just sit tight. It'll be fine."

"Okay." Her voice was timid and her eyes big and round. Being locked in a room alone would be stressful for her, but it was better than being outside the panic room if shots were fired. I fully expected shots to be fired.

As soon as the door clicked, I shifted gears. She was safe, and I could focus on the task at hand. Time to kick some ass. The monitors showed two men in the driveway, none at the rear of the house, so I took a position adjacent to the front door. I reached out and unlocked it. I wanted them inside like sitting ducks. It didn't take long. Within a minute, they knocked, which I thought was odd, and then opened the door. These Bratva thugs were too easy. After they entered, I kicked the door shut and trained my weapon on the lead guy's head. He turned, and I recognized him.

It wasn't Konstantin's man at all. Ignacio Herrera stood in front of me. One of the top men in a Mexican drug cartel that Konstantin was attempting to form ties with. I'd met him twice before when I acted as a middle man. Their deals had gone sour, and Herrera was extorting Konstantin for millions.

"Ignacio," I said, and he turned and aimed his weapon at me. "Why are you following me?"

"I need to speak with you."

"You need to speak with me, you pick up a phone. You don't track me from a restaurant to my home."

"It's a sensitive issue."

"Drop your weapon and we'll talk."

He glanced at the other guy, who I didn't recognize.

"All your weapons on the floor now, and then maybe I'll hear what you have to say."

They hesitated at first then Ignacio nodded, and they placed their weapons on the floor. I moved them behind me with my foot.

"Anything else?"

"No. Can we talk now? You can lower yours."

I took a step back and slowly lowered my weapon but held it ready. I didn't trust Ignacio Herrera at all. "Talk."

"Yulia thinks I killed Konstantin."

Yulia was Konstantin's wife. She wasn't on my list of revenge targets because she wasn't involved in his business dealings, and I didn't kill women. "*Did* you kill Konstantin?" I asked him, knowing full-well that I had done it myself.

"I did not, yet I'm paying the price as if I did."

My brain quickly jumped through the logic on this. If Konstantin's wife suspected Ignacio, that meant she didn't suspect me. This was good news. They weren't pegging me for his death. Perhaps Tatiana hadn't ratted me out at all.

Maybe she was trying to *give* me an out.

I could blame the murder on Ignacio and walk away clean.

Jesus. She was smarter than I gave her credit for. I knew that jealousy shit was an act. The woman didn't care about me in that way, but she cared enough to cause a scene at the restaurant, get me on the run, and send Ignacio to me. She'd sent Ignacio as a sacrificial lamb.

"What do you want from me?" I asked him.

He walked away from his man, and I tensed as he moved closer to me. "I want you to remove Yulia from the equation," he said in hushed tones.

He wanted me to kill her. I took a step back. Being asked to kill a woman struck a deep, bitter chord in me. I'd never do it. The last time I'd refused to assassinate a woman I'd been immediately marked for death myself. I didn't respond to Ignacio for a long time while I processed this.

He was handing me a lot of cards here. I had to play it smart. "Why do you think I would be the person to ask this of? I am part of his family, and his death hurt me too."

"You have access to her, and you're not yet a made man. The loyalty oath has not been sworn. Every man has a price. Name yours."

It was true. I had access to Yulia. In fact, I'd be considered tardy for not appearing earlier to comfort the mourning widow. I thought I'd test him out.

"A million."

He scoffed. "That's insane."

"Two million to betray the memory of my dear friend Konstantin."

He scuffed his feet on the carpet. He had no cards to play. He had no choice. If Yulia decided to place a target on his back, he was already dead. "Fine. Two million if you do it clean. Nothing leading back to me."

"Of course." I shook his hand. We had a deal. I stepped back again to offer him passage through the door.

He nodded and turned to leave. "I'll be in touch."

I closed the door and stared at the empty room. This was true irony. A hit on a woman had begun my career and a hit on a woman would also end it.

But I had no intention of killing Yulia, but I had to kill Ignacio to clear my name of suspicion.

Then I'd take out Train and get Haven to forgive me for all I'd put her through to get to that point.

Then we could be together.

It was a fucked up twisted way to start a relationship, but I'd screwed up my life up until now. It would take some time to unfuck it, and it would be extremely risky, but I'd do it for her. If there was a chance we could come out clean together at the end of this, I'd risk anything for her.

Chapter 23 Stay

Haven

I held my breath as I watched Auggie approach the front of the house with a rifle. He moved with stealth confidence while my heart pounded out of my chest.

Auggie let the intruders in, and they pointed a gun at him. I gasped for air and fought back tears. How did Auggie face these men so bravely?

They lowered their weapons and talked, but there was no sound in this room, so I couldn't hear them. Finally, he shook hands with one of the men and watched him leave.

When I knew he was coming back to me, I could finally take in some oxygen. Watching him like that put everything in perspective. I had overreacted at the restaurant. Auggie's work was extremely dangerous, and I shouldn't freak out in jealousy over Tatiana or get angry at him for what he did. It came with the job, and I'd told him I didn't want him to give it up. If I loved him unconditionally, I had to be brave through moments like this and trust in him. I would give anything to just have him back in my arms again.

After an eternity of waiting, Auggie stood in the light of the doorway like it was a portal to another world.

I rushed him and jumped into his arms. "I was so scared."

He caught my legs by my butt and brought me through the door. "It's okay now. All clear."

"What happened? Are you okay?" I ran my hands frantically over his head, ears, neck, and shoulders. He didn't appear to be injured, but he may still have been hurt.

"I'm fine." He chuckled and placed me on my feet. "I thought you were angry about Tatiana."

"I was, but then you almost died, and I realized I was overreacting. You were undercover and doing the thing you do. I'm sorry I freaked out. It was so not cool." I was rambling fast and still kinda freaking out. I needed to calm down. I took a deep breath. "We just got together a week ago. There's no way you could've told her yet. I mean you are going to tell her about me. Right? It's over? The op is over because Konstantin is dead?"

He shook his head as I spoke and reached out to hold my hand. "Listen to me."

"Okay."

"I already told her about you even before Konstantin died." He held my face in his palms and looked me in the eyes. "As soon as I met you in Italy, I called it off with her. She told you we were still fucking, but that was a lie to cause a scene."

He'd called it off before our trip? "What do you mean Italy? We weren't even in contact after Italy."

"Exactly. Even though you'd left me for Cyrus, even though you'd bailed on Stella, despite all of that, I was changed by you. I didn't know what it was—anger, lust, bitterness, love—but I couldn't sleep with Tatiana again even once after I'd met you in Rome."

It was hard to believe, but I also understood him deep in my bones because I'd also felt that connection and longing after we'd first met. I ran my hands over his head and smiled up at him. "You changed me too. I thought of you all the time. I dreamt about you. I regretted not having a picture of you. That's why I had my camera. I just wanted a picture of you if I could have nothing else. I'm sorry I got angry in the elevator. I'm sorry about what I said in the car."

I kissed his cheek, and he turned to press his lips to mine.

"It's okay. You didn't know."

"So, tell me now. Who was at the door?"

He sighed. "It wasn't Konstantin's men. Tatiana caused that scene tonight on purpose. She wanted me to leave the restaurant quickly, and she sent someone after us."

"Why would she do that?"

"I think she was helping me in her own twisted way."

"Okay?" I was trying to follow along, but it kept getting more complicated.

"Tatiana sent them to talk to me. Don't ask me who they are. It doesn't matter. They are my path to freedom."

"Freedom from what?"

"From the Bratva and the mistakes I've made. I have to go take care of something now, but this is the last time. I promise you that." He stepped back through the doorway.

I reached for him, but he didn't take my hand. "The last time for what?"

"The last time I fail you."

"Auggie, what's going on?"

He stepped further away and looked toward the front door.

"Are you leaving?"

"I'll be back. I just have to walk through fire before I can swim in the ocean."

He wasn't making any sense. "We just swam in the ocean less than twelve hours ago." I stepped closer to him, but when

I reached up, he leaned back. I felt that like a dagger in my heart. "Please, don't leave."

"Helix will stay with you while I'm gone."

The warm cloak of our trip disappeared, and I felt the loss of it as a chill on my skin. "Please don't leave. I missed you so much while I was alone in here, and it was only a short time." My voice broke and pain rippled through his eyes. He felt it too. We needed to be together in this moment. Tearing us apart would physically hurt us both. "Walk through fire tomorrow. Stay with me tonight."

His muscles were tense, and his chin jutted out in stubborn defiance. I reached for him again, but this time he let my fingers trace down his cheek, and I sensed a subtle cracking of the ice. "One more night without the real world. Let's pretend like we're still on vacation. Please. I don't want to be without you. Stay with me. Tomorrow we'll talk again, and if you still need to go, I'll understand."

His shoulders fell, and he exhaled. He'd let go of whatever was holding him back. "I will need to go. The sooner I get it done, the quicker we can be together."

"I understand, but tonight, stay." I popped up on my toes and pressed a kiss to his hard lips. "I love you, Auggie. Dangerous life, whatever women you've slept with, however locked up your heart is," I pounded his chest over his left pec, "I see it now. This is who you are. I don't want you to change for me."

He slipped a hand under my hair and cupped my neck. His eyes grew soft, and he leaned down close to my lips. "I want to change this for you. I want you to feel safe always."

"If you want me to feel safe, all you need to do is stay close to me."

That must've been the right thing to say because his mouth finally relaxed, one side curled up, he squeezed my neck and dropped in for a kiss. A deep, wet, desperate kiss that melted my bones and made my legs feel wobbly. Luckily he caught me around my waist as he leaned in deeper and bent my torso back.

A soft moan escaped from my throat. How could he be so overwhelmingly sexy? Suddenly I didn't care about Tatiana or the strangers at all. My only concern was getting my naked body next to his.

Then I was off my feet with my side pressed to his chest. He carried me to the bedroom and laid me down on the bed. There were no toys, no spankings, nothing but us peeling off our clothes, his eager cock reaching for me, and my open legs gleefully receiving him. Lesson number four. Nothing was better than us naked together in a bed.

He grunted as he filled me, and I cried out. We were connecting on a visceral level in a way I'd only heard of but never thought would happen to me. I wasn't lying. I did love him as he was. Whatever came with this man, I would accept it because I couldn't imagine anyone else in this world who could make me feel so loved, wanted, and cherished or anyone I could admire and connect with more as a human.

We both flew high as he thrust inside me, our breath jagged, skin growing slick, moans coming unbidden as I arched my hips to get closer to him. I scratched down his back. I would crawl inside him if I could. And the moment we came, it was virtually impossible to tell where he ended and I began. We were one being bound together in love.

After a long leisurely glide down, he rested his head next to mine. "Thank you for asking me to stay," he whispered in my ear.

"I never want you to leave."

He propped himself up on his elbows and brushed my hair away from my face with his palms. "Anytime I will have to leave you will be a void that can't be filled until I return to your side."

"Wow, Auggie. That's so romantic."

"You extract many words from my mouth I never thought I'd say."

"Aww."

"For example, I love you." He closed his eyes and pressed his soft lips to mine like a prayer.

I was lost to him and his sweet words. My chest ached with the need to kiss him, but I had to reply first.

"I love you too, Auggie." My voice shook with the effort to hold back tears. Finally, he kissed me fully, deeply, longingly, eternally.

I didn't know the details of our future, but no matter what happened, Auggie would always be my first love. I hoped that we could be together and tell our kids about these days when we fell in love despite all the danger, but even if something awful happened and we couldn't be together, I'd be forever changed for having known him.

Chapter 24 Bravo House

Our afterglow was cut short by a rapping on the door. "Aug? You cool?" I assumed the deep voice on the other side of the door came from Helix.

"We're good." Auggie groaned. He'd called in his friend for backup not too long ago. I didn't know why he was surprised when he showed up.

"What's the plan?" Helix asked through the door.

"We're moving her to Bravo." Auggie ran his hand through his hair as he pulled away from me.

"Now?" Helix asked impatiently.

Auggie kissed me once more and flopped to his back as he stared at the ceiling. "In the morning."

He seemed to be unhappy about moving to Bravo, which I assumed was a different safe house. Why didn't he like the Bravo safe house? Was this the nicest one they had? This one kinda had a deserted motel vibe to it, but considering these guys flew around the world on private jets, they probably had places nicer than this.

"You don't like the Bravo house?"

"I don't like what it means."

"What does it mean?"

He didn't answer but kissed me softly. And as was his way, he was telling me something with his actions. Bravo house meant he had to leave me.

***

227

Helix arrived early in the morning. He turned out to be the one with tattoos all the way up his neck that extended into his shaved head. They looked like gears and deep dark spaces you could see into. It was fascinating, and I wanted to take pictures, but he and Auggie were in Ocean's Eleven mode, so I stayed quiet. Helix drove Auggie's car as a decoy, and we loaded our stuff into a big black Suburban that was already in the garage.

We drove in a random pattern for a while like we did last time and finally left downtown on the highway. We took an exit I'd never heard of and proceeded up into the hills via a narrow, winding road. When we reached what looked like the peak of the mountain we'd been climbing, he pulled off onto an unmarked road. Dense trees lined it on both sides and created a shade canopy over the top. A sprawling house came into view, and I gasped. Auggie seemed steady and calm as he parked in front of one of the many barn-like garage doors.

"This is so beautiful."

He nodded because it was obviously a stunning house.

"This is a safe house?"

"It's my house. We use it as a safe house because I'm rarely here."

What? My mouth dropped open as I stared at the windows and balconies of what looked like a mansion. He hadn't told me he had a house or that he lived in Atlanta. "This is your house?"

"One of them," he threw out casually.

"How many do you have?" My voice came out high-pitched and squeaked at the end.

"I buy property in most of the cities we base ops out of."

He bought property? He just bought it? Most people saved their entire lives to buy a house. "Wow. I don't even own a bicycle."

"There's bikes here. You can have any of them that you like."

"Oh. I didn't mean you needed to give me a bike. I just mean I've never owned anything valuable. I feel so inadequate compared to you."

He gripped the keys in his fist and turned toward me. "Nothing about you is inadequate. Please don't feel that way. You are one of the kindest people I've ever met, you're beautiful, you care about people—especially me—and you see little things others take for granted. These are traits of value that make you more than adequate. They make you exceptional."

"Wow." I was blown away by his outpouring of adoring words.

"Apart from that, owning property doesn't make me better. It means I've been lucky enough to find a career that paid well. Houses here aren't that expensive compared to other parts of the country. It looks impressive, but it's not."

"I'm totally impressed, and I haven't even seen the inside yet."

"You ready?"

"Yes."

"Then let's go."

We climbed out of the vehicle and walked through the garage to an inner door that led to a staircase to the main floor. Windows on all sides allowed the light to shine through the dappled leaves of the trees. Everything was pristine and white. The floors were bleached wood. The first thing I noticed was the lack of plants. The second was the lack of pictures on the walls. There were a few, but they were just scenescapes that matched the trees outside. It looked like a model home that had been made up for sale. Impersonal and perfect.

The kitchen shined with quartz countertops and a stainless steel hood over the stove. There was even a fresh bowl of fruit on the counter. I squeezed a banana to see if it was real. Yep, someone had been here recently and kept it nice and clean like this.

I followed him down a long hallway to a master bedroom that was surrounded by even more windows than the other rooms. He set our stuff down next to a big fluffy white bed and looked at me expectantly for my reaction.

"Who brought the bananas?" I asked him.

"I'm sorry?"

"The bananas in the bowl. They're perfectly yellow. They couldn't have been here more than a few days, and we've been in Jamaica, so who brought them while we were gone?"

He stared at me blankly. "I don't know."

"How could you not know? It's your house."

"I believe that Stella maintains the safe houses or has someone who does it for her."

I slapped my knee and laughed. "Oh no, if Stella pimped this place out with her own special style, we're in for some surprises."

He raised his eyebrows and walked back out to the kitchen. "Let's see how adept she is at stocking the cupboards." He turned and opened the pantry, grunted his approval, grabbed a few things, went to the fridge and pulled out something green and what looked like chicken and carried it all over to the counter next to the sink. "Hungry?" He grinned.

"Actually, I am." We hadn't eaten anything for awhile except a few snacks for breakfast. "You cook?"

"When I'm here and I have time, I cook."

"You made me PB and J and cracked open a coconut. That's all I've seen you do."

He chuckled, and he looked handsome as the wrinkles around his eyes relaxed. "But I crack open a coconut like a master chef."

"More like a gorilla."

His grin remained on his face as he sifted through several cupboards full of cooking equipment and finally decided on a large, flat, round skillet. I had my relaxed Auggie back and I loved it.

I watched in fascination as he peeled a clove of garlic and smashed it with the flat side of a cleaver before adding it to a pan with olive oil which he'd poured with a skilled twist.

"What're you making?"

"Chicken chasseur," he said with a funny accent.

"Why'd you say it like that?"

"It's French. Hunter's chicken. Nice and hearty."

"Don't tell me you speak French too."

"Oui, mon ange." He tore off a sheet of plastic wrap and placed it over the chicken on a cutting board. I flinched when he unearthed a mallet and began pounding the hell out of it. The intensity and the rhythm of it combined with the look of concentration on his face reminded me of his other pounding talent. My core heated, and I was suddenly very turned on by Auggie's cooking.

"What does that mean?"

He stopped for a second and gave me a breath-taking smile. "Yes, my angel," he said softly before resuming his hammering of the meat.

The sweetness in his voice knocked me back. I felt wholly out of place in this big gorgeous house with a man who spoke several languages and was skilled at everything under the sun. I had no skills at all. I took pictures sometimes. That was it. And here he was calling me an angel?

"How did my luck change so quickly that I find myself here with you instead of running for my life in the projects?"

He finished beating the chicken breast into submission and slipped it into the pan of oil and garlic. It sizzled as he sauntered over to me and pinned me with his long arms braced on the counter behind me. "You won't believe me, but among us, I'm the one lucky enough that you're sticking around."

He kissed me quickly as I blushed. He turned back to his chicken which was now simmering quite angrily. Auggie seemed like the kind of guy who would never let his food burn. I had burned my fair share of everything. Even eggs. My mom didn't cook for me, and I never caught the hang of it.

I began to study Auggie more closely. The way he worked around the kitchen. The way he tended that stove like it was a campfire he'd built for himself but also knew the right times to walk away and get more ingredients.

"Can I help?" I asked. I wanted to be a part of his scene. I wanted to be the woman who could cook dinner with a man and actually be helpful.

"Sure. Chop some mushrooms for the sauce."

I found the mushrooms on the counter. "Do I wash them first?"

"You don't know how to clean mushrooms?"

"No."

"Well, you could wash them, but they get soggy. Best to wipe them with a paper towel like this." He wrapped his arms around me and gently rubbed the mushroom top in a way that had my lady parts jealous of fungi.

I leaned back on his chest and he kissed the top of my head before he was back to his skillet again. "We'll add those and some tomatoes, and then it's done."

"That easy?"

He'd picked up a bottle of something from a shelf and poured it over the chicken. Blue and orange flames flared up into Auggie's face. I jumped back and dropped a mushroom on the floor.

"That's the cool part," he said like a science teacher who liked exploding things.

"I thought it was hot."

He winked at me and started adding a bunch of stuff to his pan. I finished my mushrooms and added my measly contribution, dropping a few off the side which he quickly tossed in too.

"Excellent job on the mushrooms, Angel." He patted my hip and I laughed. I liked his use of the nickname. Not sure

I was much of an angel or if I'd done a good job, but if he thought of me that way, I wasn't going to disavow him of it.

Chapter 25 When It's Done

Auggie's food tasted delectable, as I knew it would. We sat out on the deck and watched the sunlight shift through the treetops as we scarfed down his hunter's chicken with rice that he'd also whipped up out of nowhere.

Auggie's phone buzzed, and he checked it quickly. "Stella and Brandy are here." He didn't sound happy about it, but I was excited to see my new friends.

He carried the empty plates back to the kitchen and slowly rinsed them under the sink. I was about to ask him if I should get the door, but a burst of voices and the sound of clicking heels answered my question.

"Haven? Girlfriend, where are you? This house is so damn big, I swear. How can two people even find each other in here?"

Stella was entering with her signature flare. I laughed and looked at Auggie, but he didn't look up from his chore.

I left the kitchen and met them as they reached the top of the stairs from the entry. Stella embraced me in a huge warm hug. She smelled good and looked fantastic in red leather pants and a black leather jacket. The jumbo braids in her hair started at her hairline on her right side and curved around her head, ending in long braids tied with red beads over her left shoulder.

Brandy waited patiently behind her. Helix dropped some bags next to the closet and slid past us all to go find Auggie, who still had not come out to greet our guests for some reason. Hopefully, Stella and Brandy knew Auggie could be moody like that, and they wouldn't take it personally.

Stella wrapped an arm over my shoulder and guided me to the living room. We all sat together on the couch. She was bubbling with anticipation. "So, tell me the goods. Is his package all that it promises?"

I pressed my lips together, unsure how to answer her very direct question. I decided honesty was the best choice with Stella. "Yes." I grinned. "All that and more."

She squealed and clapped her hands. "I told you so, I told you so, I told ya."

"You were right."

"And the resort was fabulous." She looked at her nails like she needed to have them done, which she didn't, and she didn't ask it in the form of a question, but I answered it anyway.

"Oh my gosh, yes. An overwater bungalow and Auggie in board shorts for a week? I was in Heaven."

"What else did you do besides bow-chicka-wow-wow?" She made a pumping motion with her fist and stared at me expectantly.

Brandy giggled and waited for me to answer Stella's question.

"We went cliff diving. We ordered food in. We soaked in the jacuzzi. We talked." My gaze slid to Brandy. She'd been skeptical that Auggie would open up to me.

Her eyebrows perked. "Talking is good. He told you about his life?"

I nodded. "I feel like I know him infinitely better now. He's so much more than what you see on the outside. He's complex and romantic and thoughtful." I sighed. "It was like a dream come true. I wish it didn't have to end, but we have serious issues here we need to take care of."

"Going after Train?" Brandy asked.

"Yes, and Auggie mentioned some, uh, other stuff on his to-do list." I was pretty sure Auggie hadn't told his team about his Bratva moonlighting gig, so I shut my mouth and held that part inside.

"How about you guys? How is Steel?" I asked her.

"I missed him like crazy while he was in Syria."

"Oh my God. They went to Syria?"

Stella pursed her lips and gave Brandy a motherly glare.

Brandy looked down and blushed. "I wasn't supposed to let that slip."

"It's okay. I won't tell anyone. And did they all make it home safe?"

"Based on what he told me, it was a successful mission. No injuries except for some stomach issues from the food."

"So that's what these guys do? They go away for a week and come back unharmed?" This was starting to sound like something I could handle. I'd miss Auggie terribly while he was gone, but when he came back, it would be awesome. "Did you have reunion sex?"

Brandy squinted and smirked. "Reunion sex after missing someone and worrying about them so hard is freaking mind-blowing. When he comes home, he smells all dirty and rugged."

That did not sound bad at all, and I'd just had my first taste of reunion sex. It was awesome. "I might be able to handle this life."

"It doesn't always go according to plan like this," Stella warned me.

Auggie emerged from the back room carrying two huge bags, and my stomach dropped. Helix followed behind him with more stuff. He was leaving like he said he would.

"What kinds of things go wrong?" I asked Stella.

"Anything can happen. They come back early, or someone is injured and we all spend time at the hospital. There have been some really dangerous situations and sometimes one of them doesn't make it back alive. Then there's a dark period while we bury a brother and all the guys face their own mortality first hand."

"Oh no." That sounded so awful. I could just imagine the pain they felt when they lost one of their own. Probably guilt too even if it wasn't their fault.

"It's not all happy commandos and roses. I've been Helix's best friend for many years. It wears on you, to be honest. Never knowing if he's coming back, how long he'll be gone. You're happy when he comes home, but then it's like he's been through hell, and he can't tell you about it, but the ghosts haunt him and then your little life problems seem very inconsequential compared to the potential for him to develop PTSD or pull away emotionally. This is a seasoned team, but they're also human. Some things you see out there leave a permanent mark on your soul."

Brandy nodded, and her face grew darker the whole time that Stella was talking. "Steel struggles with PTSD. He's been better lately, and he took this mission because he'd committed to it a long time ago, but this was his last overseas assignment. He says he wants to stay close to me." She grinned, but I sensed some tension underneath it.

"Do you feel bad sometimes that he gave up the big commando ops to be with you?" With any other woman, I'd be worried I'd overstepped my bounds, but Brandy was so open and nice, she didn't even think about my question. She just answered me honestly from the heart.

"No. I don't. He was running himself into the ground with the stress. It's good for him to come home to me. I soothe some of his crazy. He's still doing whatever he wants with the danger. It's just a shorter plane ride home now."

Auggie walked in and stood in the doorway to the kitchen. "Angel, can I see you for a second?"

I gave one last look to Stella and Brandy, and they tilted their heads for me to go. Why did I feel like I was walking toward the firing line with each step I took through the living room?

"Auggie, I—"

He tugged me deeper into the kitchen and silenced me with a kiss. Not just any kiss. It was a deep, hot, bonanza kiss with arguably more fervor than Auggie had ever exhibited before, but the sharp edge of it stung my tongue.

One of his hands twisted and pulled my hair. The other pressed my hips up against his as he moaned out a mournful cry. I didn't feel his hard cock there like I usually did. All I could feel was despair, loss, longing, and regret.

It felt like goodbye.

My gut wrenched, and I dug my nails into his biceps, as if I could somehow hold onto the sand slipping through my fingers.

"Mmm. No." I broke the kiss and peered up at him. "Stay." I repeated my plea that had worked last night.

I could tell from his lack of response that it wouldn't work a second time. He wasn't staying.

"I'll be back when it's done."

I wanted to ask what "it" was, but I knew it was probably following through on what he'd talked about last night. He'd said that Tatiana had offered him a way out of the situation he was in with the Bratva. Hopefully she wasn't setting him up for a fall. Did "it" also include bringing down Train with the FBI? That could take a long time. Train was extremely powerful and lucky. No one had ever caught up to him.

Tears and worry bubbled up in my throat, but I swallowed it down. I wanted to be strong for him. I'd said that I loved him and accepted him as he was. That meant he would have to leave and do dangerous things, and I'd have to believe in us until he returned.

I bit my upper lip and memorized his face. If I had my camera, I could snap a picture and hold it with me while he was gone. "Wait. One second." I held up a finger.

"I have to get going."

My new camera was sitting at the top of my bag and easy to pull out. I ran back to him at full speed, and he laughed as I tucked myself under his arm and smiled. I needed proof this had happened.

I had a ton of pictures of us together in Jamaica, but this would be the first picture of us in his house. If something terrible happened, it could end up being the last picture of us together before his death. My smile faltered, and I felt him turning his focus from the camera to me. I kept snapping shots. My camera captured us as we dropped the facade. I was worried for him, and he was concerned for me. It meant we loved each other, so that was good. This was the closest thing to a healthy relationship I'd ever had, and I didn't want to blow it. I had to keep the faith that he'd return to me soon, safe and sound.

When I had taken more pictures than I could ever need, he reached up and slowly lowered my camera.

"Why so worried?" He trailed a finger across my creased forehead.

"Is it that obvious? I was trying to hide it."

"I can read you like a book, Angel. I'll be safe. You don't need to worry. Is something else bothering you?"

He was asking me to be honest with him, so I told him my true thoughts. "It's just that this is all so new and precious, and I'm worried it could fade while you're gone."

"It won't."

"If things could change so much for the good in a few weeks, they could just as easily go bad."

"It's not going to go bad. Let me give you something to keep you warm at night when I'm gone."

I whimpered. I didn't like the idea of him being gone at all.

He curled his abs and bent my torso tight against his. He made eye contact with me and the intensity of it knocked me off my feet. He caught me and tightened his grip around my waist. "I have tasted the heavenly nectar of your sweet cunt."

I gasped and covered his mouth with my fingers. "Auggie."

"The memory of that will not fade. It'll only grow stronger, and it's all the motivation I need to complete these pointless tasks quickly, so I can return to my place between your legs and drink you in again."

A zip of tingles ran down my spine, stopped between my legs, and made a trek up to my nipples that were pressed hard to his chest. "Okay," I squeaked out lamely.

"More than that."

"Auggie, if you've got more, I think we should take this to the bedroom because I'm about to drop my drawers and spread my legs for you right here in the kitchen, and I don't think you'd want Helix to see it. Now, Stella would get a kick out of it."

His arm behind my back gave me a little shake. "More than that. I've never wanted to give something like this to anyone. I've been selfish my entire life. I feel like if I don't clear my name and make a safe way for us, I have no purpose. Everything I've ever done has led to this moment, so I can clean the slate and start fresh with you."

"Wow. No pressure."

"No pressure on you. Just stay here. Stay safe. One of the guys will be on you always until I'm back. When it's done, we can be together free and clear."

"No Train?"

"No Train. No Konstantin. Just you and me, and God help the next person who tries to come between us."

I laughed and he kissed me again. This time I felt his erection pressing against my belly. That memory would also keep me warm at night while he was gone. The promise of things to come.

Too soon, he pulled away, helped straighten me on my feet, and stepped back. He wiped his lower lip with his thumb, and his eyes glowed with hunger.

We didn't say anything else. There was nothing more to say. He walked away from me, and I felt his demeanor change from sweet, loving boyfriend to badass commander in charge.

On wobbly legs, I made my way over to Stella and Brandy on the couch. Helix and Auggie were still loading the car with bags from one of the rooms.

"Oh, girl. That was hot." Stella smacked her lips. "Auggie is totally smitten by you. You got him by the ballsack."

"Stella. I do not. How did you even hear any of that?"

"I'm a professional eavesdropper. If I'm here and it's happening, I'm going to hear it."

"Well, then you know he's leaving."

"Yes. Don't worry. We'll take care of you. Shopping every day, charcuterie with lots of wine every night. You won't be alone."

"You don't have to do all that for me."

"We want to." Brandy took my hand. "The first time's the hardest. Well, they're all hard, but the first time stings differently because you don't have that positive experience of him coming home yet, but you will."

"Hopefully soon," I said. At least I wasn't alone in this. I had my own little team supporting me.

Stella took my other hand. "Auggie's very efficient. It should go quickly."

Chapter 26 The Black Widow

Auggie

Ignacio Herrera didn't see the nine-millimeter round before it landed between his eyeballs. He didn't hear the discharge from my rifle because I'd calculated the exact distance required to mute the sound, but he felt it when it penetrated his brain cavity and ended his life.

His men didn't trace my footsteps because I'd slipped into the storm drain and skipped the scene before any of them could even take inventory on what had happened.

I'd wanted to go back to Haven, but I'd hid out in a different safe house for the night. I'd requested an audience with Yulia the following day, and my request had been granted. So far everything was going according to plan.

When I arrived at Yulia's mansion, a man led me to a sitting chamber where she was having tea with Tatiana, of all people.

While I was surprised to see her, it wasn't completely out of the realm of possibilities. Yulia would've had many visitors during her mourning period, and Tatiana was the daughter of Konstantin's brigadier. However, I had a feeling it wasn't a coincidence. Tatiana was likely taking advantage of the situation to see me again.

I nodded to her, and she rolled her eyes with a petulant shake of her head. She was attempting to rub in the fact that she didn't have to answer to me at all anymore.

"Tachi," I greeted her more aggressively because I knew underneath her act, she had done a kind deed for me. She'd given me Ignacio's head on a platter, and I was grateful to her. "Good to see you."

The edges of her lips turned down. "Dimi," she said nonchalantly, but I knew with that, we were good. She was not angry with me anymore. She'd accepted the relationship was over. We were friends like I'd told her I'd wanted.

"You're late to pay tribute to your pakhan." Yulia's raspy voice pulled my attention from Tatiana's little display.

"I was delayed by an unexpected trip. I apologize." I knelt at her feet and bowed my head. She was officially the new pakhan, or Boss, unless the family did something to shift the power away from her, which could also happen, but likely wouldn't occur during her bereavement.

"You're here now, so that is appreciated."

"My condolences for your loss."

She patted my shoulder, and I rose to my feet. "Thank you, Dimitri. Konstantin is now watching from Heaven, and I'd bet he's frustrated and ranting about how he's not in charge anymore."

I didn't respond with what I wanted to say, which was that he'd likely passed through the Gates of Hell and was serving eternal penance for the grief he'd caused while he was on Earth.

"Have a seat. Some tea. A biscuit." She motioned with her hand toward the empty chair across from her, which would sit me next to Tatiana.

I didn't enjoy tea at all, but tea in Russian culture was considered a cure for everything, especially grief. It would be extremely rude to refuse her offering. Drinking tea with the widow of a friend was part of the grieving process, and since I'd killed the dude, I needed to play along.

She poured me a cup and placed a biscuit on the saucer. I dutifully took a sip and offered her a wan smile.

Tatiana didn't take advantage of my compromised position and had turned her attention to her own tea. Yes, I definitely felt on stable ground with her, and sensed I had not lost my ally after all despite the risk I'd taken.

"Did you hear that Ignacio Herrera was found dead last night?" I looked down at my tea as I spoke to Yulia as to make my confession seem more casual when it was anything but.

She paused, slowly lowering her cup. "No?"

"He's gone. The word was that he was involved in Konstantin's death, and he did not survive the night."

She nodded. "Many people loved Konstantin and would be eager to seek retribution for him."

"I'd like to ask you for a favor, if I may."

It was understood that my request was a favor in return for killing Ignacio.

"Ask away, Dimitri."

"I'd like to cancel my candidacy." I took a bite of my biscuit to show her I was accepting her hospitality while also asking to be free of it.

"Oh really?"

"Konstantin's death has helped me to see a new path."

"Do you repudiate the Bratva?"

"No, ma'am. It is a good family. The kind I thought I wanted. Now I see I want something different."

"With a woman?"

"Yes."

"I see." She made eye contact with Tatiana, and I was happy to see Tatiana nod graciously. "You were Konstantin's favorite recruit. I thought you might join the Vor-life and rise up the ranks, perhaps marry his brigadier's daughter?" Her suggestion that I marry Tatiana hung awkwardly in the air. If Yulia declared it then it would be law. I'd have to break it, and I'd spend my life fighting against the Bratva instead of living in peace with Haven.

"It's okay, Yulia. Dimitri and I have talked. He doesn't feel for me in that way, and I want someone who loves me to the depth of his being." Tatiana spoke with a disarming naivete, as if she could ever have what she'd described. Her life would be surrounded by violence. Anyone who loved her would be subject to the whims of her father and the family. Tatiana would most likely never get the chance to make the move I was making right now.

"So you agree that I should grant his request?"

"Yes."

Yulia picked up her cell and punched out a message. She sighed and placed it back on the table. "It is done."

Excellent. With Yulia's word behind it, no one from the Bratva would seek me out. This op had gone well. I'd infiltrated just enough to kill him but not too far in to leave clean.

I stood from the table and pushed in my chair. "Thank you, Yulia. I wish you all the best."

"You too, Dimitri. I hope she is worth all that you're giving up here."

"She is. Goodbye, Tachi. I'm sure it'll all work out for you too."

She nodded shyly. She was a sweet girl stuck in this toxic situation.

As I walked away from the room, a sinking dread filled my bones. This went too well. Too easy. You didn't just walk away from the Bratva unscathed. The only way out was a casket.

If Yulia had more in store for me, I didn't care. Whatever she dished out, I'd take it for Haven.

A tall bruiser of a dude appeared near the front door and blocked my path. I knew he was one of the men who protected Yulia. "This way." He guided me into a dark garage. I couldn't see them, but I felt them around me. Four, maybe five men, amped up on adrenaline, ready to pounce.

I braced for it, but the first few blows hit me hard in the chin as my eyes hadn't adjusted, and I had no sight at all. The second I caught a feeling for where he was, I threw out a blind left hook. I misjudged his height and hit his chest. Shit. He was huge.

A kick to my lower back knocked me to the ground. The resulting blows came fast and furious.

I was still fighting back until a blunt object collided with the back of my head. I saw stars and kissed the pavement. I had enough awareness to cover my head and bend my knees to protect my vital organs, but I was outnumbered and outgunned. In order to prove to Yulia I intended to leave peacefully, I hadn't even brought a weapon.

Now I knew what Yulia had ordered on her phone.

The Bratva was jumping me out.

I had to take every painful hit and suck it up.

They seemed to enjoy it and worked each other up into a frenzy. I tasted blood and heard my bones crack.

It was probably one of the worst beatings I'd ever suffered, and I'd been through a lot of brawls. I closed my eyes and savored the pain.

If I survived, I'd be one step closer to Haven. Each blow made me clean, every crush of my flesh purified me. Their aggression exorcised demons buried deep in my psyche that I'd harbored for far too long.

Just when I thought I was going to die, a lone fluorescent light flickered on. I risked peeking out of one eye and saw Tatiana opening a side door to the garage.

She allowed a line of tall men to pass through. I knew that line.

Vander was the point of the spear. Steel at his six. Magnum behind him. They marched in with fists tight, arms bent, fury on their faces.

I had barely grasped the concept that my own team had come through the garage door of a Bratva pakhan, when I heard the first smack of a fist fight. A melee broke out, and I felt myself being lifted.

"Come on. We got you."

"I can fight with you." Blood poured from my mouth as I stumbled on weak legs.

I heard Mag chuckle. "We got this."

How in the fuck did they find me?

Were they tailing me?

Of course they were. Prying motherfuckers couldn't mind their own goddamn business.

I wasn't complaining. I was happy as hell to see them. They'd just returned from an overseas deployment, and they had a meeting with the FBI in a few hours, but they took the time to track me to this location and step in when trouble found me.

"Alright."

I allowed them to help me out of the side door to the garage. As they loaded my battered body into the van, from the corner of my one eye that wasn't totally jacked up, I saw Tatiana turn and walk slowly up a set of back stairs.

"Who's the babe who let us in?" Magnum asked me as he watched her ass shimmy up the stairs. "We coulda broke it down. She didn't need to open it, but since she did, we got to you faster."

"She's a friend." I garbled out the words through a few loose teeth.

"She's hot." Magnum sounded like a horny teenager as the other guys hoped in the van.

"Move!" Vander gave the command that meant everyone was safely in the vehicle or prepared to leave.

"Haven?" If they were all here, who was guarding her?

"She's secure."

"Thanks."

"No problem, Aug. We got you."

They certainly did. Even when I didn't ask for help, and I tried to go solo, they had me. Most solid group of men I'd ever met in my life.

"I'll check you out, and then we'll bring you to her," London offered.

"No. I don't want to see her. Not till it's over."

"From the looks of you, it's over." Vander chuckled, and I heard his back hit the wall of the van.

"No. Train. When Train goes down, I'll see her."

"Listen, bud." Vander put a hand on my shoulder. "You're beat up. You need downtime and someone to tend to you. London patches you up. Haven does the bedside manner."

"No." He was my boss and technically my commander. I was being insubordinate and pigheaded, but I refused to return to her unless it was done. "She doesn't want me." She shouldn't want me if I hadn't kept my word and cleared her of all threats.

"If she's like Misha, she won't mind the cuts and bruises. She'll be happy you're home safe with her."

"She's not like Misha. No one is." The rock and sway of the van made me nauseous.

He chuckled again. "True."

"Take me back to Delta." I held my hand over my bruised ribs and tried to fight off the dark cloud of unconsciousness that was threatening.

"Nope. We're taking you to Bravo. We all have to unpack then we have a meeting with Cutlass."

"I'm going to the meeting." I coughed up some blood that was clogging my throat.

"No, you're not. You're confined to sick bay, which is in Haven's bed in Bravo House."

Haven's bed was the last thing I heard him say before we hit a bump, and the pain knocked me out.

Chapter 27 Sick Bay

Haven

I'd worked all day on my Auggie-inspired story. I'd somehow incorporated the jerk chicken guy and the red plastic cups, and it was all coming together. I'd even stopped worrying about him for a split second as I'd become absorbed in weaving my plots together. It wasn't a full story yet, just a brainstorm of ideas, but I felt like it was good enough to be a real story someday.

The garage door at the bottom of the stairs burst open, and my heart leapt into my throat. Train. Could he have found me? Who was here watching me? These guys were so secretive, I didn't know who was on guard most of the time. Train couldn't get past them. Could he?

The hairs on my arm prickled, and I looked around for a weapon. The panic room. I need to get there fast. I jumped out of bed and ran down the hallway. Locked! Of course it was locked. I forgot to ask Auggie how to get in the room when I was here by myself.

I stood in front of the door and shivered. I felt vulnerable in my sleep clothes, short boy shorts and a spaghetti strap crop top. I had no shoes. If I had to run outside, I'd be stuck in my underwear with bare feet.

A commotion of footsteps and movement clomped down the hallway. I squinted to see who was coming to get me.

Oh my gosh. It was Auggie's team. They were dressed in various shades of black, and they were carrying a body. Auggie's body! Vander had his shoulders, Steel and London had his legs. He dangled from their arms like a load of bricks.

Not thinking about anything except him, I ran full-speed toward them and grabbed his face. His mouth hung open in a grimace, and blood stained his teeth. Huge bumps on his face sealed his eyelids shut. Oh my God.

"Auggie!" I sucked in a huge breath that came out as a sob.

Someone pulled my upper arms so they could pass. "He's fine."

I whirled on whoever was holding me. Helix. I glared up at him. "He doesn't look fine!"

"He will be fine. He needs some rest." He rolled his eyes like I was overreacting to the fact that they had just carried my man in the house, and he was unconscious.

"Which room?" The guys holding him stopped and stared at me, and I suddenly became aware of all the skin I was showing.

I crossed my arms over my chest and watched their eyes look my body up and down. One of them smiled, Magnum, I think was his name. The others were assessing but kept their reaction hidden. Whatever. It didn't matter what I was wearing. I needed to help Auggie.

"That one." I pointed to the bedroom Auggie and I were using.

The men hauled his carcass into the room. They unceremoniously plopped him on the bed and walked away like they'd just dropped a load they'd been carrying for weeks. "Heavy-ass motherfucker," Magnum grumbled.

They filed down the hallway and back down the stairs. "Where are you guys going?"

"We have to go. He'll be okay." Vander gave me a brief glance before he took the stairs quickly and quietly. For such big guys, they sure were light footed sometimes.

He was almost out the door before I got my question out. "What do I do?"

He paused like he was thinking about it. "Let him sleep."

"Okay."

"Also, he's on orders to stay here. He can't leave."

Why was he telling me this? Did he think I'd be able to enforce orders? "I can't make him do anything."

"If he wakes up and tries to leave, call me. We'll be back tomorrow after our meeting."

Auggie had programmed all the guys into my phone, so I had Vander's number if I needed it. "What time?"

The closed door didn't answer me, so I ran back to the room to check on Auggie. His black slacks and boots had dirt and blood smeared on them. A wide cloth bandage wrapped around his chest. Scratches and cuts marred his beautiful face, and his nose looked painfully bent out of shape. Someone had beaten him up.

What should I do for him? I slipped on a T-shirt and some sweatpants in case the men barged in again. I blew my hair out of my face and stared at the sleeping giant in my bed.

"Well, I guess I'll take off those boots."

This was no easy task. The thick laces were tied in a complex knot, they snagged on the hooks as I worked them open, and his limp ankle twisted awkwardly when I tried to wedge it off. I didn't want to hurt him, but I felt like it was important to get those boots off so he could sleep. In the end, I straddled his shin, squeezed his massive calf between my legs, and pulled the boot up in the air. After repeating the process on boot two, I lay down next to him and panted. The yanking and jerking hadn't stirred him at all.

"Oh, Aug. What happened to you?"

The swelling on his face was turning bright red and blue. The bandage on his pecs showed the beginning blooms of bruising at the edges. Someone had beat the shit out of my man and real anger roiled in my gut. I wanted to hurt them out of justice for him. Although, knowing Auggie and his team, the other guys probably looked worse.

I covered him with the sheet and went to the kitchen to pour him some water. When I came back, he was still out, so I set the glass on the nightstand next to him. At least I had him back early. I wasn't sure how long he would've been gone with all his talk of waiting until "it" was done.

The bed creaked as I lowered the lights and crawled in next to him. I didn't know where I could touch him without causing him pain, so I gently placed a hand close to his side.

"I love you so much. It hurts to see you in pain like this."

In my mind, I envisioned the Auggie I knew standing tall, diving off cliffs, driving scary fast through the streets of Atlanta. The man who'd carried me down from the roof of the overwater bungalow without a bump on my skin. The man who'd spanked me and held me down with just the right amount of force, never making me feel uncomfortable. He was so in tune with me. So alert. So in love.

"Was it worth it?" I asked him. He didn't answer of course, so I closed my eyes and tried to sleep. "Whatever this is, Aug, we'll get through it. You're going to wake up and re-cover, and we're going to be strong together. Okay? We have a future waiting for us. Hopefully we're closer now because you sacrificed yourself like this. I love you, and I'm here for you. If you wake up, I'm here."

Chapter 28 Live Carriers

"Haven?" A deep male voice called my name. Auggie was still passed out next to me, but the sun was up. The clock said eleven in the morning. His eye had grown more blue and swollen, but oddly, he looked like he was in less pain than before. The blood was gone from his teeth, and his mouth was more relaxed instead of turned down in a grimace.

"Haven?" A soft knock at the door followed the voice, which I now recognized as Vander's. "Can we talk to you?" It was the nicest tone I'd ever heard from him.

"Uh, I'll be right there."

I didn't want to leave Auggie, but maybe it was important that they talked to me now, and who knew how long Auggie would be passed out? I did my business in the bathroom and walked out to find a kitchen full of very serious commandos. Jade and Misha were also there, so it wasn't all men, but I noticed that Stella and Brandy had not been invited to this pow-wow.

These guys had amazing stamina and drive. They'd just arrived home from Syria a few days ago, went to wherever Auggie was and brought him home yesterday, then today they'd attended an important meeting, and now they were all assembled in Auggie's kitchen.

"How is he?" Vander asked me.

"He hasn't woken up yet. What happened to him?"

"That's up to him to tell you. Right now we need to talk. This is Special Agent Lachlan Cutlass." He tilted his head to another really attractive man, tall with perfectly mussed hair, wedding ring, and a very solemn look on his face.

"Nice to meet you. Have a seat." He pointed to a chair at the dining table and took a seat himself. Vander and Steel sat with us while the other guys lingered in the kitchen. Lachlan Cutlass had very pretty brown eyes. He wasn't as buff as Auggie but more broad shouldered like a swimmer. "I know what Ocampo put you through."

"I think of him more as Train, but I hear you."

"Okay. Let's call him Train." He leaned forward and lowered his voice so the guys in the kitchen couldn't hear. "I know he kidnapped you, you escaped, and he stalked you."

"Yes." It was hard to hear someone summarize it like that, but it was the truth.

"I know that's gotta be upsetting, and you probably don't want anything to do with him, but I need something from you that no one else can give right now." His gaze slid to the hallway and then back to me.

"What do you need?" I asked him.

"I need you to go to a human auction and let us sell you to Train." He sat back in his chair and shared a look with Vander and Steel. They didn't react to his statement, so they already knew he was going to ask me this.

My hands trembled, and my stomach felt queasy. "You want to sell me to him?"

"Not exactly. We're posing as traffickers, but Train doesn't trust us because someone," he glanced over at Steel, "spooked him. He thinks the feds are onto him, which we are, so we need to earn his trust, and we need to get into an auction. We want to tell him we have you, we bought you from someone else, and we want to sell you. Since he's clearly obsessed with you, we think he'll jump at the chance to get close to you again."

"Oh." This sounded really dangerous and challenging. I'd have to face Train again. "Auggie said I wouldn't be involved."

"Auggie needs to be updated," Lachlan said in a stern voice.

"No, I don't. I heard everything you said." Auggie slipped on a T-shirt and limped slightly as he walked toward the table. He'd also put on jeans in the short time since I'd left him sleeping in the room. Seeing his eyes open again, his face fierce, made me smile. He came straight to me, sat down next to me, and took my hand. "Hey, babe." He quirked his swollen lips.

I blushed and looked down. "Hey."

"She's correct," he spoke to Lachlan. "She won't be involved in any op to take down Train."

"We need her to gain access." Lachlan's brow creased.

"Gain access some other way," Auggie said harshly.

"She won't be in danger," Lachlan replied even more firmly.

"Because she'll be here." Auggie squeezed my hand.

Lachlan took a long slow breath and looked to the ceiling. When his gaze came back down to focus on Auggie, his lips were tight like he was forcing himself to speak gently again. "Listen. There's one thing Train wants more than anything, and it's her. He's irrational about her. He might not trust us, but he'll take his chances if he can get her."

Auggie shook his head. "No. We can't use her like that. After what he's put her through, it's too much."

"We only need her to get in the door. After the first sale, we take the whole operation down, and it's done. My undercover guys get to go home to their families, Train finally sees the inside of a prison cell, Haven and all the other women are free of his terror and can start healing."

Lachlan brought up a lot of valid points. He had men working on this who were away from their families, Train needed to be stopped at whatever cost, and most importantly, the other women. We had to do anything we could to save them. Auggie had to understand that. He'd done it for me. Why not them?

"The other women, Auggie. We have to do this for the others. Imagine how scared they are. They're about to be sold into slavery."

"They aren't about to be sold. Their organs are," Lachlan said.

I felt a new stiffness in the air, and all the movement from the people in the kitchen stopped. "What do you mean?" I asked him.

"It's an organ auction. The women are the live carriers."

Grumbles and growls came from the kitchen as the men unfroze and started to move.

"Those guys are scum. There's a special place in Hell for someone who would do that. It makes me want to round up everyone I know and take these guys down in one blow." This was Magnum in the kitchen. Apparently the words *organ auction* had triggered his protector instincts. I understood how he felt. It was shocking to even contemplate.

I took Auggie's hand in both of mine and squeezed. "This is horrible. It's so much worse than I ever thought. I want to do this. I can face Train. I want to be part of this."

Auggie looked from me to the men in the kitchen, to Vander and Steel, who were also dead serious as they listened to the stakes of what we were facing. "I don't want her near him," he finally said.

Yes! Progress. He was stating his terms.

"She'll be safe. She'll never be in danger. We'll keep him from being alone with her. Look. I know how it feels to put your woman out there like that, but it's also part of the deal sometimes in order to protect them. You have to trust us."

Auggie looked down. I didn't know how much he trusted the FBI. I knew he liked to act alone and take matters into his own hands. This would require extreme cooperation on his part, especially if I was going to be involved.

Lachlan looked at me. "You ready for this?"

I was nervous and uncomfortable with the idea, but I still said, "Yes." I would do anything I could to keep those women from getting sold and murdered. If I had to face Train, I could do it.

"When?" Auggie asked Lachlan. In other words, *Yes, but get it done quick*.

"Three weeks."

Auggie blew out a long slow breath, and his stiff shoulders finally became unshrugged. "I don't like it."

"Noted."

"If she's going to be there, I'm with her. She doesn't leave my side. We never turn over possession of her to him."

Lachlan looked at Vander. Vander shook his head curtly.

"You're out. Steel's out."

"What? Why?"

"You were compromised in Italy. Some of the same people could be there."

"I'll wear a disguise." Auggie's voice grew loud and agitated.

"Not risking it."

He let go of my hand to lean forward over the table. "I'm by her side or you don't get her. I'll change my appearance. No one will recognize me from the five minutes I was with Rico in Italy."

Lachlan wasn't budging. "It's going to be a very tense situation. They'll be treating her like property. You'll have to play along. You won't be able to control your shit."

"You don't know me very well then." Auggie stood up and hovered over Lachlan. "This ain't my first rodeo. I've been playing assholes like this since you were in diapers. She's not going in without me." He turned and walked back to the bedroom, limping a little less this time. He also looked incredibly growly and sexy.

Lachlan looked at Vander first then turned his attention to Steel. "Alright. Auggie and Steel can be there as long as they're not identifiable."

Vander and Steel nodded.

"We'll have several more prep meetings, but if Auggie doesn't kill him, this could work."

Auggie came back out. "If he aims a weapon at me, her, or any of my team, he's dead. Why are you so eager to see him in prison? Guys like him run their ops from inside. He can't sell women from Hell."

Lachlan rolled his eyes. "I would like to solve a case without one of your men killing the suspect before the trial."

Vander chuckled. "They do stupid shit around us, they die. Not our fault."

"Alright, fine. Even if Train eats a bullet, we'll still get the rest of the ring. Try not to kill them all, please."

Auggie grunted and walked back to the bedroom.

"Is it okay if I follow him?"

"You sure you're okay with all of this?" Vander asked. "It's a lot to handle."

"If this team is there, I'll be fine. Thank you for considering my feelings about this, but I'm not scared. I know Train won't be able to pull anything over on you." Vander took that in and grinned. "Now, if you'll excuse me, I haven't spoken to Auggie yet, and I want to see how he's doing."

"Sure."

***

I found Auggie lying flat on his back in the bed. He was holding his ribs with one hand, his head with the other.

"Here's some water, some ibuprofen, and pain killers that London left if you need them." I handed him the cup of water that had been sitting on the nightstand for hours.

He waved it off. "Not right now."

I curled up next to him, and his hand slid onto my back. "What happened to you? Who did this to you?"

He took a piece of my hair and twirled it in his fingers. "My gig with the Bratva is over. I'm free. No repercussions."

He didn't directly answer my question, but I figured he was telling me all that he could. "Well, that's good. Did you really have to go through so much pain to get free?"

His hand caressed my hair from the top of my head to my neck. "Yes. I wanted it cut and dry. No chance for misunderstandings. They won't come after me."

"I was worried Tatiana had set you up."

"Nope. She came through for me."

"That's good."

He didn't sit up and kiss me, probably because of his bruises, but I was happy with him stroking my hair. I needed to go get him some ice or something else that would make him more comfortable.

"I didn't want to come back here." His voice had a ragged edge.

"Why?"

"I told you I'd be back when it's done. It's not done."

He was beating himself up again, but he didn't need to. "You mean Train? Yes, but that's going to take weeks. I'm glad you're back. I'm glad I get to help out in a small way."

He growled. "I'm not."

"It'll be fine and then it'll be really done."

"Yes."

Then we could get on with our future and loving each other without all this hanging over our heads. It would be amazing, but mostly I wanted to help those women who were still under Train's control. Only then could the nightmare truly be over.

Chapter 29 Midnight Train

After three tense weeks of high-anxiety and preparation, everything was ready. The team had gone through every scenario with me, and I knew what to do. Basically, I had to stay calm and trust them to take care of any risks that popped up. Trusting them was the easy part. Facing Train was the hard part.

The auction was going to be held at a private banquet hall outside of downtown Atlanta. I was surprised when Lachlan told me it would be a formal event, but he'd said they do it to get higher dollar amounts.

I decided to wear a simple little black dress that covered my breasts and thighs. I curled my hair and applied light makeup. When I walked out into the living room, I nearly fell off my feet. The guys were all wearing tuxedos. Gorgeous, shiny, elegant, deadly tuxedos with weapons expertly concealed.

Everything suddenly became very real. These guys were hardcore, armed, and dangerous. I was way out of my league.

My eyes immediately scanned the room for Auggie and found him walking toward me. He looked like a rock star in a tuxedo. Big broad shoulders, narrow waist, the fabric of his lapel and tie glinting off the lights. His bruises had mostly healed, and he'd recovered from his beating. He hadn't shaved or cut his hair in three weeks and it grew faster than I ever thought possible.

He'd colored his now-longish hair and beard dark black and styled them into slick angles. He wore dark brown contacts, and it almost seemed like he'd painted his lashes, they were so thick. He offered me a lopsided smile and took my hands. "You look exquisite."

I looked down and closed my eyes. Everything about him was severe, excessive, and lethal, and I felt humbled standing next to him. "Thank you. This sorta feels like a date in a very bizarre way."

"It's definitely not. This is a high-risk op, and we are all on alert. The place will be crawling with feds, but the bad guys will be armed, and Train is jumpy. It's a recipe for chaos. Just stay calm and stay close to me."

"Got it." We'd gone over the same instructions several times, but I needed to hear it again now that it was really happening and fear was deafening me.

"I know you're scared. You gotta learn to operate through the fear."

"Is that what you do?"

"Yes. You feel your heart thumping, your stomach sinks, just take note and stay smart. It's your body's reaction, but what's in your head is the most important part."

My cheek scratched on the lapel of his tuxedo when I hugged him. He caressed my back gently. I peered up at him. "That must be what bravery is. Feeling scared and doing it anyway. You really are a hero."

I'd never seen Auggie blush before, but the uncomfortable look on his face and the slight change in color was the closest he'd ever gotten to it. "And you," he tugged my hips tight up against his body and tucked me in close, "are the epitome of tempting, but it's go-time." He bent down and pressed a quick kiss to my lips.

After a brief recap of the plan from Lachlan, we filed into our respective vehicles and headed toward the auction location.

My heart felt like an out of control metronome, but I remembered what Auggie had told me. Thinking about the rewards if we pulled this off would give me the courage to see it through.

***

We pulled up to the banquet hall and split into our groups. The second Auggie stepped out of the vehicle, he was a different man. His posture became more hunched forward. He didn't look at me, and I felt completely invisible. We stood outside in the cold for twenty minutes and not once did he turn to check on me, look at me, or reach for me.

He'd told me he was planning to treat me like property, but I didn't realize how much it would hurt to get that treatment from him. It reminded me of the time when Train had kidnapped me, and I was dependent on him for everything. He was just as rude and dismissive, so I guessed Auggie was playing his role accurately.

Once we were inside, a weird calmness came over me. It was like this was too important to be nervous. I had to be on my game, and there was no room for fear.

Auggie's cold shoulder turned more glacial once we were inside. He walked in front of me and strutted around like he owned the joint, one shoulder low like he was some kinda pimp. There weren't a lot of women in the room, but he made a point of looking down at them and checking them out.

He'd better never act this way in real life, or I'd leave his ass so fast his head would spin.

All the men were wearing tuxedos or really nice suits. The women wore short evening dresses like me, and they all seemed meek and shy like me.

"Eyes down," he barked at me and I looked to the floor.

What a horrible situation to be stuck in. I instantly felt empathy for the women here, and the urgency to get them out grew to a fever pitch. I felt eyes on me as we walked through the crowd.

A short man approached us and talked to Auggie. "Train wants to meet with you."

Of course he did. The second Train saw me, he probably flipped out. His favorite object to prey on had just walked into an auction house wearing a little black dress. It was like dangling raw meat in front of a hungry tiger.

Auggie nodded, and we followed the man to a room off a narrow hallway.

This was it. I was going to see Train for the first time since he'd beat me up and left me for dead at the reservoir. My stomach dropped when I saw him. He looked the same as always. Shaved head, tall and thin, tattoos everywhere, trimmed mustache and goatee, loads of jewelry.

His dark eyes locked on me. I expected Auggie to tense or growl or something. He did nothing. He was all about saying hello to Train, being friendly with Train. Gah, I hated this. I knew it was an act, but I hated it. I couldn't pretend to be nice to that man under any circumstances. Luckily, tonight I didn't have to pretend to like him.

"Where you been, Haven? You fucking disappeared." His voice hit me like a fist, and I took a step back.

"She's been with me," Auggie said casually.

Train ignored Auggie, and kept talking directly to me. "I didn't believe it. Didn't think you'd show, and yet here you are." He swiped his hand up and down and gave me that gummy smile I hated so much.

"Here I am," I said. I didn't smile back. I crossed my arms over my chest and prepared for battle.

"She's mine," Train said to Auggie without looking at him. "Leave her with me."

Auggie shifted his weight. "Where she ends up will be decided in the auction."

Finally, Train moved his attention to Auggie. "Where the fuck did you come from? You know Raphael?"

"I know lots of people." Raphael was the code name of one of the FBI undercover agents who had penetrated the ring.

Train reached for me, and fear shot through my spine as I cowered. Auggie moved slightly to block it. "You want to touch her, you gotta pay."

I saw the black anger swarm in Train's eyes. I knew that look too well. It was the face he made before he hauled off and slapped me. My heart was beating fast, and seeing Train this close was a lot harder than I thought it would be. "Haven won't be in the auction," Train said to Auggie. "She's already mine, and she's not for sale."

Auggie had been doing a good job of controlling his anger, but Train attempting to claim me as his made his jaw tick. "She is not yours. She's mine because I paid for her, and if you want her, you'll pay more than what I did. A lot more." Auggie's tone left no room for discussion. It wasn't the same anger I was used to seeing from him. It was more greedy and slimy and less protective. Auggie was really good at this.

"This is jacked up, man." Train threw up his hands when Auggie didn't give him what he wanted. "She's mine. She ran away. Raphael sell her to you? He ain't got no rights to her."

Auggie lowered his voice and spoke directly into Train's ear. "You got papers proving any of this?"

Train's nose wrinkled, and his upper lip pulled up. He really did have big gums. "Fuck no. There's no papers."

Auggie pushed my back roughly, and I stumbled forward before I caught my weight. "Then it's your word against mine, and I'm telling you she's mine. She's up for auction tonight, so if you wanna buy her, better get your bids up."

Not getting anywhere with Auggie, Train turned all his fury on me. "You cause me so much headache, Haven. Every time I think I'm rid of you, you come back like a shit stain."

I had to force myself to breathe through the instant fear and memories of being kidnapped that were all rushing back now. Why didn't I fight back then? I was too afraid. Well, I was done letting Train silence me. "Fuck off, Train." Oh my gosh. That felt great. "I don't want anything to do with you. I'm not here because I want to be. You're acting like I have some kinda choice. If it were my choice, I'd never see you again. You're the one following me around, chasing me down, beating me up, throwing me off a cliff." My ears were ringing, and my voice felt like it was floating outside of my body, but I was doing it. I was standing up to him. Of course,

Auggie's big frame in front of me bolstered my courage, but I'd spoken up for the first time, and I felt proud of that.

"I didn't do that shit." His gaze shifted to Auggie then back to me. "You lie. Always lying about everything. Always bitching and moaning."

"Sorry to interrupt your little lover's spat here." Auggie was still doing a great job of pretending not to care about me, but I had to admit it hurt that he didn't defend me when Train started throwing out the insults. "But it's time to start, and she needs to be where she needs to be in order to participate."

"Fine. Take her backstage. Give Raphael her stats."

Auggie turned to leave, and I followed him out of the hallway with my head down. Phew. That was so stressful, but it seemed like Train was falling for Auggie's cover. He didn't seem suspicious at all. The fact that these kinds of conversations really happened in back hallways at human auctions made my stomach sick. Human beings were not property to be sold. I was a woman with free will and rights, and I felt like everything had been taken away from me tonight. I totally understood how the other women must feel who were really in a bad situation right now.

I was eager to get to the auction and get the first sale done, so we could shut all these assholes down. I couldn't wait to see Auggie drop his act and kick some ass.

We walked behind a curtain, and I was taken aback at the group of frightened women standing there. Lots of women. Not a handful, but like a whole herd of women. All of them stuck back here waiting to find out their fate.

Auggie pointed where he wanted me to stand, and he went to talk to a guy who I assumed was Raphael.

The lights dimmed, and a voice mumbled from a speaker somewhere. I couldn't make out anything he said, but he droned on like he was explaining how it would work.

Auggie sauntered back over to me with his shoulder dipped low. "Make me proud, babe," he threw out as he smacked my butt.

Oh my gosh, I actually hated Auggie the pimp. Hated him with a passion.

He turned his back on me and strutted away. He'd promised he wouldn't leave my side, and he'd just abandoned me in a corral full of women about to be sold on the black market for their organs.

The next ten minutes went by in a blur. Women scuttled around in the dark, speaking quietly but urgently. The air filled with tension. Someone started to cry, and a man told her to shut up.

Okay. I'd had enough pretending. I couldn't do this. I'd changed my mind. This was too agonizing. I felt like cattle lined up for the slaughter, and Auggie had left me here to fend for myself.

No. I had to trust in the team and the feds that they knew what they were doing.

A murmur of anxious whispering erupted in a corner and grew louder like a wave. Heads were turning to look around.

"What's going on? What is it?"

No one answered me.

I grabbed someone's arm. "What is it?"

"People are saying there's cops."

I gasped. "Cops?" This was not good. The team had been found out. Their cover was blown. I needed to warn Auggie. I tried to run, but Train was standing by the exit. He jutted out and grabbed me by the waist. "No, you don't."

"Let me go. I have to go." I squirmed, but he tightened his grip until I could barely breathe.

Something popped loudly in the other room, and chaos broke out. People started screaming and running.

"We're just gonna go for a little ride." He tugged me out the door.

"No. I need to go that way." I struggled to break free, but he smacked my face.

"Shut the fuck up, Haven. I swear I thought you were dead, but you come back like a bad horror flick."

"You almost killed me."

"Let's see if I can do a better job tonight."

I looked back and tried to see Auggie, but all I saw was smoke and people running. "Help! Aug—"

He covered my mouth and dragged us through a back door that led to the parking lot full of cars. Oh no. I couldn't get in a car with him. Auggie would never find me again. I knew I had to fight like hell, so I swung my arm back and dug my nails into Train's face. "Let me go." I tried to get my fingers in his eyes, but he was too strong.

He pushed me up on the front of a car and pressed between my shoulder blades. "Listen, bitch. Stop fighting me, or I'll blow your brains out right here." I felt something hard and metal against my neck. A gun. Shit. My whole body shook with fear. He would kill me. I had no doubt.

"Get in." I had to do what he said. I had no choice. I got into an old sedan and tried not to hyperventilate. If Auggie or someone else didn't find me here, I was dead. This was how my short life would end. Killed in a sedan by an O.G. from Lamar Gardens. In the end, the hood killed me. I never made it out.

Train climbed into the driver's seat, and he was messing with his keys when a huge shadow darkened his window.

Auggie yanked his door open and pulled Train out by the neck.

They went down, and I heard them fighting on the other side of the car. I jumped out and ran around the back.

Auggie had Train pinned to the ground in the space between Train's car and the car next to it. He held a gun aimed at his head and punched him hard on the side of his face.

Train groaned in pain. "Get off me, fucker."

Auggie jammed his knee into Train's lower back and punched him again. "Shut the fuck up and I won't kill your ass." His eyes were wild. He looked like he really wanted to kill Train. As much as I hated Train, I didn't want to watch his brain get blown out in front of my eyes.

"It's over, asshole. As much as I want to, I'm not gonna kill you because I'm gonna enjoy watching your ass go to prison more than watching you bleed out right now. I want you to pay for the pain you caused Haven and all these other women."

"You out here, Aug?" A male voice approached from the direction of the building.

"Here." Auggie spit on the ground next to Train's face.

Several guys came over and took over restraining Train. Auggie came straight to me. "You alright?"

"I'm a little unsteady, but yeah, I'm fine."

He pulled me to his chest and wrapped his arms behind my back. "You did so well. Jesus. Good job."

"You too. I thought for sure you were secretly an asshole pimp on the side."

He caressed my hair. "No, babe. No. Walking away from you in there was the hardest thing I've ever had to do."

"I thought you'd left me."

"Nope. I had eyes on you the whole time, but I couldn't do shit about it."

"Is it over?"

"It will be soon. Gotta clear this place. Let's go." He walked me over to the vehicle we'd arrived in. He clicked open the back door and climbed in with me.

My hands were shaking. I couldn't breathe. "Oh my God. Did that just happen?"

"It did." He took my hands and squeezed them. He looked fine. No injuries.

"Is everyone okay? I heard gunshots."

"We'll find all that out later. Are you okay?"

"Yes." I fell into his arms and let him hold me. "He was going to kill me."

"Not on my watch."

"Thank you. I'm so glad you came. I seriously thought I was going to die."

"I'll never let that happen. You're safe. You're good."

He pulled me onto his lap, and I snuggled in. His body was a hard pillow, but I needed something solid right now, and Auggie was my rock.

Chapter 30 Unimaginable

Auggie

She shivered and whimpered in my arms while I held her and rubbed her back as gently as I could manage with all the adrenaline spiking through my system.

So close. Too close. Train had put his hands on her, and I was stuck impotently watching as some asshole opened fire on the room.

When Train dragged her to the door, I went for it and caught her just in time. He'd almost driven away with my everything. God, I'd wanted to kill him, but with her standing there watching, I couldn't do it. I didn't want her to see me kill someone. Before her, I wouldn't have thought twice, but now that she was in my life, I wanted to be the man that held his fire, took down the bad guy, and walked away without taking another life.

I did it for her. If I'd shot him and she'd watched the life drain from his eyes, she'd never look at me like I was her hero again. She'd always see me as a killer. So I was glad I'd made that decision. Despite my inner turmoil, I was no longer a killer. I'd taken one step closer to being the man she thought I was.

Haven nuzzling my neck and burrowing deeper between my legs quickly drew my attention from what had happened. Her warm body clung to me like a lifeline. I couldn't stop thinking about the way she'd played my slave so well tonight. It was wrong of me to find it attractive, but my mind was twisted in weird ways.

By the time we reached Bravo house, my cock was aching to get inside her. I carried her to the bedroom, and we crashed into the bed in an urgent swarm of kisses.

I yanked the strap of her dress impatiently and growled when it didn't break. I could barely get my fingers to work the zipper down and tug that thing off of her. She sensed my need and stripped off her bra and underwear before I could ruin them.

I didn't take my boots or pants off, just lowered my fly and climbed on top of her. Every second we weren't joined felt like agony. She'd been taking birth control, so we didn't need a condom anymore.

Surging inside her, I groaned with the overwhelming affirmation that she was alive and well in my bed. We were connected, we were perfect. I couldn't get enough of her skin, her scent. I had to kiss every swell, nip every curve.

Then the urgency overtook me, and carnal lust drove my every move. I flipped her to her stomach, and she easily complied. I took both her hands and held them high up on her back.

She moaned and pushed back against me, urging me to resume the fucking, but I stopped and took a breath. I leaned over her, and gripped her breast in my palm. "No one else will ever own you. No one will fill this sweet pussy except me. No one will make you come except me. I own you."

Fuck. I didn't know what I was saying. It wasn't good. It was rude, horrible animalistic impulses that I couldn't hold back. The stress of pretending to be her master and having to walk away messed with my head. She would hate me after this. She'd angrily tell me no one owned her, and she should.

I was a bad, bad man for talking to her like this, but I couldn't stop.

"I own this sweet tight cunt, and it's fucking mine to rip apart and put back together again." I slammed into her.

She whimpered and I let go of her wrists. "Keep 'em there. Keep your hands on your back."

She did as I said, and it made this all so much hotter. I loved the way she submitted, the way she trusted me. I didn't have the patience for lube, so I gripped her where we were joined and let her wetness coat my fingers as I caressed her clit. She was bucking like a bronco, but she kept her hands on her back like I'd told her to.

I hadn't done this before, but the haze was making me push her limits. I probed the tip of my finger inside her back hole and waited for her reaction. She stilled and gasped but didn't drop her hands or pull away. We hadn't talked about her ass or how open she was to being penetrated there. I slid down to one knuckle, and she moaned.

That was not a no, so I gave into the urge and fucked her cunt with my dick and her ass with my finger. The whole time she kept her hands on her back, her head turned to the side, her mouth open. "I own every part of your gorgeous body. Anything I want to do, you'll let me because you're my fucking slave, and you love the way my giant cock works you from the inside. You love my finger up your ass, and when you're ready you'll take my cock here too if I say it's time. Whatever I want to give you, I'll give you full throttle, and you'll take it without objection."

"I love it, Auggie. Whatever you do to me. I love it."

"That's my girl. Now beg me to make you come."

She felt so good, so wet, so tight. I almost came too early, but I held back. Her first. Always her first at least once.

"Beg me, Angel."

"Auggie, please make me come." She dragged out the words.

"How do you want me to make you come? Is my finger in your ass enough? My dick pounding your cunt isn't enough?"

"No, please."

"Please what?"

"Please touch my clit. Please. Please make me come."

"You beg so nicely. I could listen to it all night."

"No, please. Touch me now. I need it so bad."

"As you wish." The truth was that I couldn't hold back any longer. She'd destroyed me. I was seeing stars and ready to blow.

I cupped her mound and pressed with the palm of my hand, mashing it in circles. "Like this?"

"Yes!"

I removed my finger from her ass and gripped her shoulder so I could drive her down on my dick. I slid my hand up and targeted her clit with my fingertips. After a few tiny but accurate revolutions, she seized up, her breath stuttering, her tight cunt gripping my cock and pulsing like a strobe light. She cried out my name as it engulfed her.

"Hands over your head, now." She stretched out like a cat and arched her back as I kept gliding in and out of her slick heaven. "You're fucking beautiful, Haven. Most incredible sight in the world right now." I wrapped an arm under her chest and pulled her up next to me. "I want to see your face when I come inside you. Spin around."

She worked with me to turn her around and straddle my hips. "Open your eyes. Watch me claim you."

Her eyes opened and I saw nothing but pure hunger there. I was free to ram up into her. She sucked in a quick breath. "You feel that? You feel me inside you, hitting you just right."

I leaned her back and adjusted my hips so I was rubbing her clit each time I hit her G-spot on the inside. Her tits bounced, and she bit her lip as she watched me with the sexiest look I'd ever seen.

"Again, baby. Come again."

"I can't."

I reached down between us and grazed her clit. "You can. Come again. Let me see it."

She didn't disappoint. Her lips fell slack, eyes closed, head back, riding me like a pony, clenching around my cock.

"I love you, Haven. I want to marry you. Put a fucking ring on your finger that tells the whole world that I've claimed you."

She was too gone and lost in her climax to respond, and I couldn't hold back a second longer.

It rended up in my hips, through my spine, and exploded from my balls like a goddamn missile. With it came all the angst, the longing, the regret, the love, the joy, the total fulfillment I felt with her. I gave it all to her in the pumping of my cock, my lips on her neck, my hands holding her up.

Finally, I released her, and she fell back on the bed, her arms flailing out, her head rocking side to side. God, I loved watching her come undone.

I kissed her cheek, her chin, her neck. "Good job, my queen. You are so exquisite."

She panted and gasped for air. "How can you talk so much? I can barely think."

I chuckled and broke our connection as I moved to her side. "I wasn't thinking about what I was saying, and if I offended you, I'm sorry. I barely remember what I said."

"You said some heavy shit, Aug."

I laughed and kissed her. "I meant it. Well, maybe not all of it exactly but that last part I meant whole heartedly. I love you, and I want to marry you."

She turned and looked at me. "Are you serious?"

"Oh yeah." I climbed out of the bed and pulled the ring box from the nightstand. I got down on one knee and opened it for her. She looked at me like I'd lost my damn mind. I had. I was lost for her. I didn't plan to do this tonight. I'd thought I'd take her back to Jamaica and propose there, but I was flying on instinct and letting it all flow. "I want nothing more than to see this ring on your finger right now."

She turned to the side and stared at the ring. "Oh my gosh."

It was a good-sized round solitaire surrounded by a thick band of rectangular baguettes. I took it out, grabbed her left hand, and slipped it on over her knuckle. A little tight, but it fit.

"When did you buy this?"

"I bought it after our night on the roof in Jamaica."

"You knew then?"

"I knew the first time I laid eyes on you. Just thought I didn't have a chance. The second I saw that I did, I bought the ring. You taking it?"

"Yes, yes. Of course. I love it. It's so soon and a little sudden, but I love it."

"We'll work out the details later, but right now I need to know that you're mine forever. I feel like this will make it permanent. It makes it real and right now. Not the past, but the future. A future I never thought I saw for myself."

She wrapped her arms around my neck. "You've made me so happy, Auggie. I love you so much."

I fell into the bed next to her. We kissed and laughed and made love again, this time slowly and purposefully. When things calmed down, she turned and rested her cheek on my abs, her hair falling over my chest.

"Do you want kids?" she asked me.

My spine tingled as I caressed her upper arm. "Hmm? Kids?"

"We're going to get married? Right? You'll be my husband. I'll be your wife. Do we want kids?"

"I have not considered this option before," I answered honestly.

She stopped and looked up at me. "You haven't?"

How stupid of me. Of course she'd want kids. She was young and beautiful. I'd spent my life being careful not to get anyone pregnant, so this threw me. "My lifestyle. I'd never bring a child into that." If I caused the death of a child, I'd never recover from the guilt.

"Not now, but someday, when your commando life slows down and you're ready to make a change." We hadn't talked about it in detail again, but I planned to switch to training and recruitment as soon as things settled around here. She'd told me she didn't want me to give up the active ops, but it was time. I needed what she gave me more than I needed the rush of adventure.

"Do you want kids?" I asked her.

"I love kids."

"Do you want to have kids with me?" She'd have to be crazy to start a family with a man like me. I fully expected her to say no, but then I looked into her eyes, and her face softened.

"Auggie. Of course. You'd be such a great dad. They'd have something I'd never had. A father. And you're a badass hero Navy SEAL private military contractor. They will brag about you to their friends. You're protective and open and honest. And you can cook them breakfast in any language. They'll have the best father in the world."

I had to look away. My heart ached. Did she really see me that way? I wanted to be that man so badly. I just didn't know if I had that kind of fortitude in me. "My life has always been unstable."

"When we were in Jamaica, you said you wanted stability and a family like when you were a child. The love you had for your sister, the love Vander and Steel have found. You said you wanted it."

I had said that late at night once when we were in the jacuzzi sharing our deepest secrets. Of course she remembered it word for word. "I don't want to disappoint you."

"You won't, Auggie. You haven't yet, and I believe in us. I believe we could make it through anything because this love is so strong. If we have children together, it will only grow stronger. We'll be forever tied together, and your beautiful genes will live on."

I laughed. "I don't care about my genes."

"Your legacy will live on too. Your kids will know that you were a brave hero and that you rescued mommy from the projects where she grew up and could never escape. They'll know that you kept your word to me and risked your life for me. Children need father figures like that. My whole life could've been different if I'd had a father like you to guide me."

I threw her to her back and buried my head in her chest. "You must stop."

"No. You must accept that you're a good man. If you set your mind to being there for me and our kids, I know you'll do it. I know we'll be lucky and happy for the rest of our lives, and I'll just have to do what I can to be worthy of you."

I kissed across her chest. "I am the unworthy one."

"You're gonna look so hot with a baby in those muscular arms. I'm gonna take a ton of pictures." She squeezed my biceps.

I laughed and kissed her. I loved this woman beyond words.

Epilogue Rooftop Surprise

Haven

I couldn't control the butterflies. Auggie was waiting for me under an arbor covered in tropical flowers. After a year of planning, waiting, and falling deeper in love, we were back in Jamaica on the roof of an overwater bungalow, but this time the whole team and all our friends were with us.

I'd been willing to have a simple ceremony in the backyard at Auggie's house, which was now our house, in Atlanta, but Stella and Auggie both thought it would be fun to go back to Montego Bay.

Stella wanted to see the place herself, and Auggie wanted to replicate the laid-back atmosphere that we'd shared when we fell in love. All the guys needed a break, and it turned out to be a great time for a group vacation.

The roof over the bungalow we'd stayed in was too small for our wedding party, so we'd chosen the roof over a banquet-sized bungalow where the resort held large events. This turned out to be a wise choice because Rajerio had warned me that walking in sand in heels was squishy business. Auggie wanted the privacy that the roof provided, so here I was waiting at one end of a roof just like the one where I'd given myself to Auggie for the first time only bigger.

Rajerio acted as our wedding butler, but he felt more like a friend. He'd done a fantastic job seeing to all the details and working with Stella. I was waiting behind a privacy screen with my bridesmaids; Stella, Brandy, Misha, and Jade. They wore silky slip dresses in a rose-blush ombre fabric that sparkled like diamonds in the sun.

The guys and our other close friends were sitting in linen-covered chairs on either side of the aisle, which was a beautiful white runner, also decorated in lush flowers. The blue sky and turquoise water provided views from every angle. The whole thing was like a picture postcard, and luckily we had a photographer collecting the images because I would cherish them forever.

I peeked outside the privacy screen, and my heart exploded when I saw Auggie looking gorgeous in a black linen suit with a black tie. I was wearing a flowing mermaid dress made of cream lace and silk charmeuse that Stella had helped me pick out. It was light and airy with beaded spaghetti straps, sexy with a low-cut front, but also sweet with a dainty silk bow at the waist. Hopefully, I'd captured the beachy yet romantic look that matched with this beautiful setting.

I didn't want our wedding to be a formal event with tuxedos, not after the last event involving tuxedos ended in gunfire. Magnum had been shot that night, and none of us wanted any memories of that tainting the wedding. Luckily, he'd recovered and was able to join us at the resort for the ceremony.

"What's taking so long?" I asked Stella.

She checked her watch. "It's time to start."

We were waiting for Rajerio to give us the signal, but nothing was happening.

"I'm so nervous. He's not changing his mind. Is he?"

Brandy gave me a warm hug. "Shh. No. It's going to be wonderful. It's just a little stagefright. Breathe through it, and you'll make it to the other side."

I took a deep breath, and my heart still pounded against my chest, but it did help.

Throughout the engagement, I'd worried this would never happen. It was too good to be true. Something would come up to get in our way.

But it didn't. Auggie started working at headquarters hiring and training new Knight Security recruits. I thought he wouldn't be satisfied with a day job, but he grew to love it. He found he had more patience for teaching than he thought he would, and it still gave him enough of an adrenaline rush when he made the practices extra challenging.

He came home to me each night, and we made love before we fell asleep. He'd set his alarm early, so we could do it again in the morning before he left for work. This also seemed to satisfy the unmet needs he was chasing before he met me. He said it grounded him. It settled his bloodlust. I didn't know how giving me orgasms did all that for him, but I was happy to oblige, and I was on board with anything that made him happy.

I'd enrolled at the college and was taking writing and English classes. My fiction ideas were coming at me faster than I could keep up with. Auggie had said I should publish them, but I wasn't ready for that yet. I wanted to just keep writing as they came to me and worry about sharing them later.

We all gasped when Auggie poked his head around the divider.

"Auggie!"

His eyes devoured my wedding dress and turned to pure hunger. His smile was lit with pride and love. "You look incredible, babe."

He'd caught glimpses of me and the dress as we were traveling and getting ready. There was only so much privacy on a plane or a bungalow with no walls.

"What're you doing here?"

He stepped fully behind the divider and wrapped his arms behind my back. "I have a present for you." He grinned like a maniac. Was he losing his mind? It was time to start, and he wanted to exchange presents?

Stella and the girls quietly walked away. What the heck was going on? "Before the ceremony? We can do those later."

"You need this one before the ceremony because you might want him to walk you down the aisle." He winked like this was some cute joke.

Oh my heaven of all heavens... "What?" I spat it at him in a not very ladylike way, but he'd shocked the hell out of me. I lowered my chin and squinted at him with fierce Bridezilla eyes. "I'm walking myself. We already decided." It wasn't like him to interrupt a plan in action. In fact, I'd never seen him go off-task. Something was very wrong here. Who did he think was important enough to delay the ceremony so he could walk me down the aisle?

He lost his smirk, and his face grew serious. He peered into my eyes like he could see my soul. "Only because you didn't have your father here."

My stomach twisted and dropped. I knew what he was hinting at.

"My father?" The words came out as a tortured breath with no sound.

"I sent your hair sample to the feds to check the DNA database. It came up with a few matches, and I followed through. One of the names was a guy Vander knows from Special Ops Command. We called him up and asked him if he'd had sex with a stripper in Lamar Gardens exactly twenty-five years ago."

I was frozen to the spot. I heard his words, but they were blowing past me in the wind. Hair. Database. Stripper. Twenty-five years. I'd just turned twenty-six. Did he find him? My chest heaved. Did he find my dad? My eyes filled with tears, and Auggie got very blurry. "No." Another word that was just a gasp.

Auggie tugged my hand and walked me out from behind the partition. He pointed to the top of the stairs that led up to the roof from the banquet hall below.

Light brown hair appeared first, then a black suit, a tall man with long legs. Deep-set eyes and wrinkles but still very much an attractive man. For a second I thought this was a trick because he looked so much like Tommy Lee Jones from Men in Black, it had to be a prank.

I couldn't breathe. I felt something. I felt connected to a stranger who'd appeared out of nowhere. I knew it. I knew it was my dad.

His lips pursed, and he looked both cautious and insecure but also excited. His face mirrored everything I was feeling inside.

We were walking toward each other, but I couldn't wait. I was pulled to this man like I'd been pulled to Auggie in the beginning. I ran up and hugged him. And then I knew for sure. When I felt my arms around him and his hands on my back. I knew it was him.

He looked exactly like I'd imagined all these years. Tall, easy-going, and friendly.

"Are you really my dad?"

"Yes." He hugged me around my shoulders, and I could hear the emotion ripping through his voice too.

Tears burst from my eyes and streamed down my cheeks. I didn't care about my makeup or anything else. I'd dreamed of this moment my entire life.

"How did they find you? Where were you?"

"Everywhere. I was in North Carolina the last few years. I'm in the Army. The government had my DNA in a database, and it turned up a match."

"You're in the Army? You're a hero too?"

His lips pulled back into a smile that was half-grimace. "I was once. Now, I pretty much ride a desk."

"I always thought you'd be a hero."

We had to get back to the wedding, but I had one more burning question that would not be ignored.

"Did you know about me?" I asked him.

He shook his head. "I wish I had known. I would've been there for you. I had no idea until Auggie called me up."

I looked back at Auggie who was watching all this unfold with eager eyes. His lips were pressed in a tight grin, and he looked quite pleased with himself. He knew me so well, I imagined he was feeling everything with me. "Did Auggie ask you to come to Jamaica?"

"No, Haven. I asked if I could come. I didn't want to miss your wedding. I've missed so much already."

I couldn't stop smiling. I had a million questions, but emotion had clogged my throat. Later we'd sit down with my dad and find out everything about him.

"You have a beautiful smile," he said.

"It's like yours."

He smirked. "It is, in fact, like mine."

"Oh my gosh. We have so much to talk about, but we're supposed to start. Everyone is waiting. I'm going to marry Auggie." That was a stupidly obvious thing to say, but my brain was mush.

"I know."

Auggie was grinning up a storm. I ran to him and crashed into his chest. "You kept this from me?"

"It all happened in the last few days. Didn't know if he'd make it to Jamaica. You gonna let him walk you down the aisle?"

"Oh yes. I forgot." I spun around, grabbed my bouquet from Stella, and ran back to my dad. "What's your name?"

"Grady Morrison."

"Nice to meet you, Grady. Will you walk me down the aisle?"

"It would be my pleasure." He held out his arm, and I took it.

"Auggie, go back now." I waved my arms like a mad woman. This show needed to get on the road.

He laughed and walked down the aisle back to his spot under the decorated arbor.

Rajerio started the music.

My legs shook as Stella, Brandy, Misha, and Jade walked ahead of us.

When Rajerio gave the signal and the wedding march started to play, my dad helped us get started walking. The wind dried the tears from my cheeks, but new ones were coming. I just knew it.

I leaned on his arm, and he stiffened to support me. "I've got you."

Oh my gosh. My dad was as dreamy as I'd always imagined. No wonder my mom fell for him. I just wished she hadn't kept him a secret from me, but she'd said she didn't really know who the father was. Now we had DNA proof, and it was obvious from looking at him that he was my dad.

When we arrived in front of Auggie, Grady gave me a hug and pressed his lips to my cheek. "Good luck."

"Thank you for being here."

Then I took my final steps toward the man I love. He took my hand, our eyes locked, and I was gone. The man was too beautiful, and he was all mine. He looked down and when his eyes came back to mine, I saw it all there. His soul and mine were connected as one. We were soulmates.

The ceremony went by in a blur, but I knew it was romantic because I kept crying. Auggie's vows were about how he'd move mountains for me. The only thing I was sure I heard was, "In rough seas, you're my safe harbor."

I barely remembered mine and blubbered on about how I just loved him so much. "You're my safe harbor too."

When Auggie kissed me as his new bride, everyone cheered and I was fulfilled. For the first time in my life, I had a family and friends who loved me and a man I could trust by my side. I was enjoying life and even more joy was in store for us as we traveled this road together.

***

After some pictures and hugs all around, we celebrated with our friends and had a grand party. Auggie didn't dance more than stand on the dance floor, so I danced around him, and he watched me with silent but deadly hungry eyes. Only a few other couples danced. The rest mingled around the bar. Steel and Brandy danced and err my gawd, Vander and Misha knew how to mambo. Misha especially had some Latin in her because the woman was born to samba. Vander was more bending around her, but they made an amazingly hot couple.

The big surprise on the dance floor was Helix. Never thought I'd see him out there, but one of the songs moved him. "Drops of Jupiter" by Train of all people. He strutted out there like a freaking rock star, dragging Stella behind him with the funniest look of shock on her face.

They fell in sync like magic. They were absolutely beautiful together. Stella's dark skin in the sunset, Helix's tattoos creating mysterious shadows on his skin, her butt looking fantastic in that dress. I knew then it was on like Donkey Kong. They were going to do it again. Helix would not be deterred.

They were sharing an overwater bungalow too. No way to walk away from one of those without getting thoroughly fucked. This made me very happy to see my friend who was always looking out for my sex life finally getting some. I made a mental note to have some champagne and strawberries sent to their cabana tonight.

We sat with my dad for a little bit and I found out I had three half-brothers. He was married and lived near Fort Bragg. He told me to go have fun and we made plans to meet for lunch the next day.

After everyone had left for their respective bungalows and I had hugged my dad goodbye, Auggie and I thanked Rajerio and returned to our bungalow, the same one we had rented the first time. We crawled up onto the roof through the hatch in the bedroom.

"We know where the stairs are now." I teased him because we totally didn't have to climb through the hatch. It was fun but unnecessary. All the bungalows had a set of stairs to the roof.

"I know, but I like the view from here." He climbed up behind me, and his face was right on my ass.

"I see how you are."

He gave my tush a little bite that stung.

"Ow."

Up on the roof, he placed a blanket down on the futon, and we cuddled together.

"It's so pretty out here." We gazed up at the stars, and I wondered what it was about the Drops of Jupiter song that had motivated Helix to make his move.

"I wanted to tell you something, Mrs. Provatorova." Auggie broke me from my musings.

I laughed. "I'm still getting used to that."

"Yes," he said, inexplicably.

"Hmm?" I was tired and a little spaced out from the day, but I was pretty sure we hadn't been talking about anything before this. "Yes, what?"

"Yes, I want kids."

"Oh." I gasped and stared at him. Auggie had shocked me again. We hadn't talked about it much since that first night. I'd noticed he was showing some interest in kids when he saw them in public, and he'd asked his friends if they'd planned on kids. Vander and Misha, not yet. Steel and Brandy, not trying but not preventing, so probably soon. Mostly we'd been enjoying being together and getting to know each other.

"I'm happy with the life we have now. I don't need kids."

He moved on top of me and kissed me. "I want to see your tummy swell with my child."

"That's really sweet in a caveman kind of way." I was just teasing him. Inside I was reeling with joy, but I shouldn't have joked with him. This was a sensitive topic for him.

"I want to see you as a mother. I want you to make me a father. If you want that too."

He was tearing my heart apart with the vulnerability in his voice. As if I would ever say no to him. "Yes, yes. I want that too."

His mouth turned up into a sexy smile. "Good."

"Should we start now?" I asked him as my hands drifted down to his tight butt cheeks and gave them a squeeze.

"Yes, right now is a good time, Angel." He slipped his tongue into my mouth as his hips pressed me down into the futon with the perfect amount of force. Auggie always knew exactly what I needed.

###

Playlist

"Drops of Jupiter" by Train

"Female" by Keith Urban

"Fingers Crossed" by Lauren Spencer-Smith

"Foolish Games" by Jewel

"Hanging By Your Knees" by The Rolling Egg Rolls

"Hey Sexy Lady" by Shaggy feat. Brian and Tony Gold

"Jealousy" by Will Young

"Midnight Train to Georgia" by Gladys Knight & The Pips

"Mr. Brightside" by The Killers

"Stay" by Lisa Loeb

"Stay With Me" by Sam Smith

"Stupid Boy" by Keith Urban

"Three Little Birds" by Bob Marley and the Wailers

"When I Was Your Man" by Bruno Mars

"Unsteady" by the X Ambassadors

Other Books by Bex Dane

Men of Siege Series
  Violet (0.5) Free at bexdane.com
  Rogan (1)
  Tessa (1.4) Free at bexdane.com
  Lachlan (1.5)
  Zook (2)
  Torrez (3)
  Falcon (4)
  Men of Siege Box Set (Books 1-4)
  Twist Brothers Series
  Fighting for Foster (0.5)
  Captivated by Cutter (1)
  Memorizing Mace (2)
  Twist Brother Box Set (Books 0.5 - 2)
  Knight Security Series
  Blue Honor (1)
  Steel Valor (2)
  Safe Harbor (3) This book
  Knight Security Box Set (Books 1-3)

Sign up to Bex Dane's mailing list to receive free books, exclusive bonus content, and updates on all Bex's new releases.